Crossword Traitor

Steve Schach & Sharon Stein

with a Preface by David Astle ("DA")

Wandering in the Words Press

PUBLISHED BY WANDERING IN THE WORDS PRESS

WANDERING
IN THE WORDS
PRESS

ISBN: 978-0-9991129-1-5

First Edition

To Jackson and Mikaela

Also by Steve Schach

Old Bach Is Come
Highly Satisfactory
A Matter of Trust

Also by Steve Schach and Sharon Stein

Coopers Island
Bakerloo Line
Double Two
The Book Buyer

PREFACE

by David Astle ("DA")

When Clues Know More Than You Do

As a long-time crossword compiler, I'm here to warn you: there is a thing called clue voodoo. Every now and then an answer, or the clue's surface story that aims to camouflage the answer, becomes relevant in unsettling ways.

One eerie example related to Steve Irwin, back in 2004. As you may recall, the naturalist was gored to death by a stingray one September afternoon. A Monday in fact, September 4. The date is etched in my mind for reasons of panic. During that same week, for reasons I still can't fathom, my Friday crossword was due to include this clue: **Steve Irwin's property career cut short (3)**.

Alarm bells rang. I lunged for the phone. Back at the drafting stage, the clue had meant no harm, of course, a simple deletion formula where the verb **ZOOM** (or **career**) is **cut short** to spell **ZOO**, as in the Beerwah **property** owned by the **Irwin** family. But then a stingray intervened, and I had to call Lynne

Cairncross, Fairfax's crossword editor. In a journalistic first, I urged her to halt the presses! Stop the trucks! Block the website! My 25-down was in desperate need of fixing.

Despite all the drama, clue voodoo is more common than you might imagine. Only last week, while reading the galleys of *Crossword Traitor* on a Serbian holiday, I felt a chill enter my bloodstream. This time the culprit was a puzzle in the London *Times*, published in a 1998 collection. To paint the full picture, my wife and I were trekking the muddy outskirts of Subotica, a winterscape of corn stubble near the Hungarian border. The landscape was lake marsh, furrowed loam and intermittent mongrels surging out of farmyard gateways with drool flying and all fangs bared.

The beasts were terrifying. We needed sticks and stones—or thunderous voices—to make any progress. By late morning, taking a spell in rare sun, I tackled an old *Times* crossword to calm the nerves, only to confront this clue: **Quail we caught tucking into cut crop (5)**.

This time the answer was **COWER**, a terrified cousin of the verb **quail**, and the upshot of **WE**, in this case Tracy and I, entering (**caught tucking into**) a fright-fest of the **CORN**, a **crop** that is **cut** to **COR**, yielding **CO-WE-R**.

Flukes. Coincidences. Nothing too remarkable, you might think, but imagine if a crossword murmured far more than a pack of Serbian mutts or a snorkelling calamity. Imagine if a series of puzzles went far beyond chance, entering the realm of insidious. Or devious. Or downright treasonous.

That was the accusation levelled at Leonard Dawe, a Classics teacher at the exclusive Strand School in 1944. Stretching the bounds of plausibility, Dawe was responsible for airing several hush-hush terms relating to the looming D-Day strike of June 6. Any one codename—such as the landing beaches of **OMAHA** or **JUNO**—might be easy to dismiss, but Dawe's *Telegraph* puzzles continued to peddle secrets as the operation loomed, compelling MI5 agents to come knocking. If their fears were right, England's favourite pastime seemed one Englishman's greatest betrayal.

Or was it an alphabetical accident? A random act of vocab? That same what-if is the engine of *Crossword Traitor*, where authors Steve Schach and Sharon Stein treat the infamous Dawe episode as their own imaginary door, a portal into a darker retelling of this dramatic wartime chapter. Instead of Leonard, we meet a bumptious git called Hector Longstreet. Instead of a harmless fluke, the teacher's black-and-white squares adopt a dozen murky shades of grey, the deeper the novel unfolds.

Add to this scenario a genius astronomer (who's criminally insane), a clue-cracking prisoner-of-war, a double agent, false maps, red herrings, double bluffs, dead-body drops, and a flock of hand-picked pigeons, and you'll soon appreciate how *Crossword Traitor* is a smart and sweeping race against catastrophe. Chances are you may **COWER** as it **ZOOMS**.

David Astle is a pre-eminent composer of cryptic crosswords. Based in Melbourne, Australia, his puzzles appear each week in The Age and The Sydney Morning Herald under the pseudonym "DA." His clues and contorted themes have garnered a worldwide audience of fans, including the avid solvers on datrippers.com who share the pleasure (and pain) in a chatroom devoted to DA crosswords. On top of crafting clues and writing a weekly language column for Fairfax's Spectrum, David is the author of several wordplay books and is a regular presenter on television.

In wartime, truth is so precious that she should always be attended by a bodyguard of lies.

—Winston Churchill to Joseph Stalin, Tehran Conference, November 1943.

Cuiusvis hominis est errare, nullius nisi insipientis in errore perseverare.
(Anyone can make a mistake, but only a fool persists in his folly).

—Cicero, *Philippics* XII, 5.

FOREWORD

On August 17th, 1942, at the height of the Second World War, the word **DIEPPE** was the answer to a clue in a crossword puzzle published in the London *Daily Telegraph*. The solution was published in the newspaper the following day, and the Dieppe Raid took place on August 19th. The military intelligence officer sent to investigate the apparent security leak, Lord Buchan, reported that it was all "just a remarkable coincidence—a complete fluke."

Nearly two years later, in the weeks leading up to D-Day (June 6th, 1944), words appeared in crossword puzzles published in *The Daily Telegraph* that once again caused alarm bells to go off in Allied military intelligence circles. The words included **JUNO**, **GOLD**, **UTAH**, **SWORD**, and **OMAHA**—the code names of all five of the landing beaches in Normandy; **OVERLORD**, the code name of the overall D-Day operation; **MULBERRY**, the code name for the floating harbors to be used in the landings; and **NEPTUNE**, the code name assigned to the naval assault phase. Officers from MI5 interviewed Leonard Dawe, the man who had created the various puzzles. Like Lord Buchan, they concluded that it was all just another coincidence. No one seemed to notice a third coincidence: Lord Buchan was the son of the author John Buchan, the author of World War One spy thrillers, including *The Thirty-Nine Steps*.

Had the military authorities looked a little deeper, however, they would have found that truth is indeed stranger than fiction.

CHAPTER ONE

Saint-Auban-sûr-Lot, France
Saturday, June 21st, 1941

François was breathing heavily as he joined the others. It was dark at the side of the main road; the light from the moon had to fight its way through the luxuriant trees. Nevertheless, they could see that his blue workman's shirt was wet with sweat. Perspiration ran down his florid face, which was punctuated with a three-day growth of patchy stubble.

"Jean-Michel, I'm really sorry to be late," François said. "but two German soldiers are patrolling the woods tonight. I know you told us that we all had to be here by half past one, but it was just impossible. I had to be sure that I didn't lead them to this place, and that's why I went all the way round past the shrine on the edge of the forest."

"Don't worry, everything's under control," Jean-Michel replied.

"But why have you fastened that wire across the road between those trees? And why is Henri painting it black? And where did you steal that wire, anyway?"

"François, keep your voice down to a whisper!" Jean-Michel ordered. Speaking in an undertone, he continued. "Better still, just shut up and listen. The Free French in London have learned that the German occupiers are sending motorcycle dispatch riders all over the country. Our people in Britain have transmitted radio messages to every Resistance group here in France, ordering us to waylay a dispatch rider to get our hands on a copy of whatever it is that they're distributing. As you know, those Nazi bastards have built one of their military bases about fifteen miles from here at the T-junction at the end of this road, and we're waiting for a dispatch rider to turn up so we can knock him off his motorcycle. Henri is painting the wire black; that way it won't shine in the headlights of the vehicle."

"But what if a cyclist comes by? Or a car?"

"François, that's enough questions. You know very well that the military regime has imposed a curfew, and that means that only the Germans should be on the road tonight. If a car or a truck comes by before we kill a dispatch rider, so be it—we won't be able to take down the wire before the vehicle smashes into it. Also, the only cyclists we might encounter would be members of our group, and everyone's here."

But François persisted. "What if a family has summoned Father Patrice to give someone the last rites? If he rides into the wire, it'll probably kill him. After all, he's nearly seventy, and a fall like that could be fatal."

"Relax, François. We can see him coming because the road is straight for about twenty-five yards on both sides of the trap. We've chosen a spot where huge leafy trees on each side touch. That means that almost no moonlight is falling on the wire; it's unlikely that the dispatch rider will notice it in time. But enough light is filtering through for us to observe Father Patrice pedaling ever so slowly toward us on his old bike. If we see him coming along the road in either direction, I'll jump out and warn him in good time.

"As you can see, Henri has just finished applying the black matte paint. Get down behind that bush, don't say a word, and point your rifle in the direction of that large oak over there, the one that was struck by lightning two months ago—that's where the dispatch rider will land after he slams into the wire at about thirty miles an hour and the impact tosses him onto the road."

"Won't the impact slice him in half?" François asked.

"No. He won't be traveling at high speed when he reaches the wire, because has to slow down for the S-bend. And that's enough questions, François," Jean-Michel continued. "Three of us will take cover here, and the other three will hide on the other side of the road. Get behind the bush."

François obeyed with obvious reluctance. He waited in silence together with the other five members of the Resistance group. Finally, nearly an hour later, they heard the faint roar of a motorcycle penetrating the humid summer night air. The volume of the sound grew steadily, like an approaching swarm of killer bees, and soon they saw a motorcycle with a sidecar slowing down as it traversed the S-bend. As the vehicle neared the wire, they all observed the MG34 machine gun mounted on the front of the sidecar.

Jean-Michel froze. He had not anticipated a sidecar, let alone a guard armed with a powerful weapon. His men had carefully adjusted the height of the wire to try to ensure that it would strike the driver in the upper chest. But the soldier in the sidecar was seated more than a foot lower than the driver. If the guard's helmet passed under the wire and the motorcycle came safely to a halt, he might well be in a position to use his MG34 to kill all six of them.

The wire caught the driver in the middle of his chest, throwing him off the motorcycle as the machine lunged onward. At that moment, his left hand was gripping the handlebars considerably more tightly than the right. Consequently, at the instant of the impact with the wire, the driver involuntarily swung the handlebars firmly to the left. The motorcycle swerved sharply and smashed into a hundred-year-old tree. Momentum propelled the guard forward—his head, which had slipped harmlessly under the wire, now slammed into the huge trunk with a neck-breaking thud. The driver landed heavily on the road and lay still; it was obvious that he, too, was dead.

"Quick," Jean-Michel ordered. "Get the dispatch case before the motorcycle bursts into flames." He rushed towards the fallen vehicle.

"No, no, it's here on the side of the road. It must have fallen out when the motorcycle hit the tree," François shouted. For once Jean-Michel did not have to tell him to keep his voice down; the noise of the crash would undoubtedly have attracted the attention of the two German soldiers on patrol in the area.

"Well spotted, François!" Jean-Michel stooped down and picked up the leather case with a large black swastika embossed on the front.

"Everyone listen to me," he continued. "When they find the bodies, the Germans will do a house-to-house search of the village. Go to your hiding places and stay there for at least two days. Armand, come with me."

The two men rushed off together. Jean-Michel headed south, in the direction of the shrine on the edge of the forest.

"Why are we going this way?" Armand muttered softly. "The radio is in the other direction."

"I know that and you know that, but the others don't, and I want to keep it that way. We'll talk later."

They hiked swiftly through the woods, turning slightly to the left every hundred yards or so. As a result, their route traced out a wide curve. After about half an hour of fast walking, they crossed the main road along which the dispatch rider and his guard had sped toward the site of the ambush. Fifteen more minutes brought them to a wooden barn on a farm at the edge of the woods. They entered through the back door and climbed up a flight of stairs. Armand struck a match and lit an oil lamp. The light revealed a platform festooned with empty crates and pieces of old furniture, most of them broken. They moved a tall rickety bookcase aside, revealing an ancient desk. On the desk lay a suitcase. Armand opened it. Inside was a Marconi radio transceiver. He switched it on. A green light began to glow.

"Excellent! The farm has electricity tonight," Jean-Michel said. "Let's see what's in the dispatch case while we wait for the valves to warm up."

They broke the lock open with a handy screwdriver and took out a thick sheaf of paper. Neither man understood German, but one glance at the maps made it unambiguously clear that the Germans were planning to invade Russia in twenty-four hours' time.

"*Sacrebleu!*" Armand said. "What do we do now? The British need to see this. But how can we get it to them?"

"We can send a radio message to London to tell them that Hitler is invading Russia at dawn on June 22nd. Draft the message, please. Keep it brief, but they have to know that we followed their orders and killed a dispatch rider and guard to obtain the plans for Operation … Operation … what did they call it? Oh, I see it here, they've named it Operation BARBAROSSA. Then encode the message and send it to London."

"And after that?" Armand asked, his fingers caressing his Morse code tapper in anticipation of the message he would shortly transmit.

"My bicycle is downstairs. I'll ride to the coast and try to get a boat to cross the Channel."

"Jean-Michel, you're crazy. It'll take you two hours to get to Port-Vincent, and then you'll have to find someone to take you to England without the Germans arresting you. *Gestapo* officers obsessively observe the comings and the goings in every harbor. If they see you approaching a fisherman, they'll interrogate you, search you, and find the plan. And how can you trust a boatman? He may turn you in. And the fishermen aren't allowed more than a certain distance offshore. Even assuming you do find someone crazy enough to attempt a Channel crossing, a German E-boat will blow you out of the water. No, a trip to Britain is out of the question."

Jean-Michel thought for a minute.

"Reluctantly, I have to agree with you. But do you have a better idea?"

"Well, after sending the message, we can study the plan and then transmit a series of reports to London telling them as much as we can understand."

"Can we get someone to translate it for us?" Jean-Michel asked. "The only person I know who speaks any German at all is François, and he knows only a few words."

"So go and fetch François."

"Under no circumstances," Jean-Michel said.

"Why not?"

"Because I think he's a traitor. That's why we went south when we left the other four, even though this farm lies to the northeast of where we ambushed the dispatch rider."

Armand looked at him with wide eyes. "François? A traitor? What have you discovered?"

"Nothing beyond suspicions yet."

"But if he's betrayed us to the Germans, why don't we just kill him?"

"Armand, unlike the Nazis, we don't murder people without hard evidence. Also, if he really is a traitor, François might be more useful to us alive than dead. Now let's get to work on that message."

Composing, encrypting, and sending the message took them nearly an hour. A few seconds after Armand finished transmitting, London sent an acknowledgement of receipt. The two men looked at one another and smiled.

"That's step one," Armand said. "Now let's take another look and see what we can make of these plans. Let's begin by—"

But before he could finish his sentence, heavy blows from rifle butts smashed down the back door of the barn.

CHAPTER TWO

Lower Stragham, Buckinghamshire, England
Monday, December 13th, 1943

The four men burst into the office of the headmaster's secretary.

"We're from the Special Branch. We understand that Hector Longstreet is the head of the Classics department here at Stragham College. Where can we find him?"

The elderly woman seated behind the desk became flustered. She fiddled with the plethora of long hairpins that were intended to keep her overabundance of grey hair neatly in place on top of her head—but instead looked like twigs forming part of a badly constructed bird's nest.

"The headmaster is out at the moment, but he should be back later this afternoon or early this evening. As soon as he—"

"No, we want to see Hector Longstreet. Where is he?"

"Well, um, I think Mr. Longstreet is in his classroom."

"Which is where?"

"Go down the corridor—it's the third door on the right. Or is it the second? Well, you'll find him."

The four men rushed down the hallway. The first three classrooms on the right were empty. In the fourth room, they found a tall, skinny, elderly man seated at a table in front of rows of vacant desks. His suit had seen better days. A long black academic gown hung over the back of his chair and trailed onto the wooden floor, which was coated with chalk dust. To his right were two piles of exercise books. A book was open in front of him, and the officers could see copious red ink scrawled across a page written in a schoolboy hand.

"Hector Longstreet?"

"Yes? What is it?"

"This is yesterday's *Sunday Intelligencer*. Did you compose the crossword puzzle?"

The tall man slowly rose from the chair, towering over the four policemen. A long, thin nose dominated his white wrinkled face. He peered through his thick glasses at the newspaper that one of the policemen pushed in front of him.

"Yes. I'm the crossword compiler for *The Sunday Intelligencer*."

"This is your puzzle?"

"Yes. Why do you ask?"

"Hector Longstreet, I arrest you under the Treachery Act 1940. I warn you that anything you say will be taken down and may be used in evidence against you."

"What's this nonsense? I'm a schoolmaster. I teach Latin and Greek. And, yes, I certainly compose crossword puzzles in my spare time. Treachery? What on earth are you morons babbling about?"

"You need to come with us."

Longstreet reluctantly complied. Seated behind her desk, the headmaster's secretary gasped at the sight of the four men leading the handcuffed schoolmaster out of the building. The Special Branch policemen walked him to their black, unmarked car and carefully levered the tall, thin man into the back seat. They drove in silence for nearly an hour, the elderly teacher's anger building up inside him by the minute. As a result, he did not realize that their destination, a large country estate, was actually quite close to the school; the driver had deliberately taken them on a roundabout route.

The guard at the gate waved the car through. At the end of the long gravel drive, Longstreet saw a Queen Anne manor with rows of white sash windows set flush with the brickwork. The driver applied the brakes more violently than strictly necessary, and the car skidded to a halt between two identical staircases leading up to the carved stone door-case. Longstreet looked up and observed a central triangular pediment mounted against a hipped roof with dormers. *Christopher Wren,* he thought, unable to suppress his pedantry even when in handcuffs and boiling with rage.

Two of the men helped Longstreet out of the car, taking care to ensure that he did not hit his head against the top of the doorframe. They then took his arms and assisted him up the left-hand flight of stairs and through the front door of the mansion. A hand-knotted antique Axminster carpet covered the floor of the entrance hall. On a paneled wall, he saw a full-length portrait that he was sure was the work of Joshua Reynolds. The one next to it he identified as a painting by Thomas Gainsborough. But his escorts did not allow him to stop and admire the eighteenth-century art; they hustled him up the double cantilevered staircase and into a large room that was so different from the rest of the house that it took his breath away.

A fresco depicting gods and goddesses on a vast white cloud sumptuously decorated the ceiling of the room. But the original furniture and the paintings had been removed. In the center of the room, a battered wooden desk now stood, with two chairs on the far side and a third on the side facing the doorway where he had entered. Other than that, the perfectly proportioned room was empty of furniture. Longstreet had no idea that the desk contained a hidden microphone; listeners downstairs could hear every word, and they recorded all conversations on tape.

As the schoolmaster entered, the two men seated behind the desk rose to their feet. Both were in their mid-twenties and wore well-cut three-piece suits and discreetly patterned ties. But the resemblance began and ended at the sartorial level. One man was tall, with fair hair parted on the left, an elongated face with a pointed chin, and brown eyes with long fair lashes. The other was fully a head shorter, stockily built, with slicked-back black hair. The snub nose seemed too large for his round face. When he wanted to, he could charm people with his ready smile and crinkly brown eyes.

His escorts removed the handcuffs and led Hector Longstreet to the empty chair. Then they left, locking the door loudly behind them.

"Mr. Longstreet," the taller man said, "please be seated. I'm Johnson, and this is Carlyle."

"What in the name of Beelzebub is going on here? Those imbeciles said they arrested me for treason. What unadulterated rubbish!"

Both Carlyle and Johnson immediately realized that any attempt they might make to calm the furious teacher would be futile and quite possibly counterproductive. Instead, Carlyle decided that the best way to continue the interview would be to ignore Longstreet's anger and speak quietly and politely.

"Mr. Longstreet," he said, "we're here to help you clear the whole matter up. We'd like to ask you a few questions, if we may. You were the composer of the cryptic crossword puzzle in yesterday's *Sunday Intelligencer*?"

"Yes, that's what I told those blockheads. But nothing whatsoever could possibly be wrong with composing a crossword puzzle. It's perfectly legal to do so. And it's certainly not treasonous. Bringing me here on a trumped-up charge is an absolute disgrace."

"Perhaps we should start with this clue here, 17-across. It reads: **Lecher attached to north French city (5).**"

"Well? What about it?"

"What's the answer?" Carlyle asked.

13

"It's obvious." Longstreet replied. "A lecher is a ROUÉ, and the abbreviation for north is N. When you've attached the one to the other you get ROUEN, a French city. And it's five letters long, as indicated in parentheses."

"And 17-down? What's Arid attack (4)?"

"Equally obvious. The word attack tells you to rearrange the letters of arid, giving the four-letter word RAID. And an attack is a synonym for a raid. It's really rather an ingenious clue, don't you think? As I'm sure you know, a cryptic crossword clue consists of two parts: the definition and the wordplay. In the case of ROUEN, the definition is French city and the wordplay is ROUÉ attached to the letter N. But 17-down is particularly brilliant, because the word attack is not only the definition of RAID—it's also part of the wordplay, instructing you to rearrange the letters in the word arid."

Boasting about his own cleverness had somewhat diffused Longstreet's white-hot rage. But he was still indignant, and this was reflected in the way he demanded to know, "But what's all this nonsense about?"

Carlyle ignored the schoolmaster's question. "And finally, Mr. Longstreet, what about 4-down? It reads, Largest flower for classical lady warrior (6)."

"That clue is just as straightforward as the other two. The answer is AMAZON. The definition is classical lady warrior; in the Greek myths, the Amazons were a nation of female warriors. And the wordplay is largest flower. You can pronounce the word flower in two different ways. One way is to rhyme with 'tower.' An example of a **flower** that rhymes with tower is a rose. But **flower** can also be pronounced to rhyme with 'lower'—something that flows is a **flower**. And the **largest flower** that rhymes with 'lower' is the Amazon—it's the largest river in the world.

"And for the last time, why am I here in this room? The solution to the crossword will appear in next Sunday's paper. Couldn't you two have waited until then?"

"Hector Longstreet," Johnson said, "17-across is **ROUEN**, 17-down is **RAID**. As you obviously know, on Friday, the seventeenth day of this month, we're going to carry out an air raid on Rouen. And the code name for the attack is Operation AMAZON. In fact, we're obviously going to have to cancel the air raid, now that you've informed your Nazi chums that our planes are going to bomb the railway marshalling yards and the fuel depot. They'll make quite sure that everything is safely out of the way before our bombers arrive, and they'll undoubtedly organize an exceedingly hot reception for our aircraft. But whether or not the air raid takes place, you're under arrest for treason in time of war."

Longstreet's untrammeled fury started to return. "I've never ever heard such consummate drivel in all my life. That's perfectly absurd."

"Is it?"

"Yes, it is. It's completely and utterly ridiculous. The governors of the school have no problem with my composing crosswords. In fact, they rather encourage my activity—it gives the headmaster

15

something to boast about to prospective parents. And heaven knows, Stragham College has a distinct shortage of features that are worth flaunting. But during the school term they require me to be a full-time schoolmaster; I have to work on my puzzles during the holidays. I sent yesterday's crossword to *The Sunday Intelligencer* before the current term started at the beginning of September, three and a half months ago. I know nothing of modern warfare—I was too old to fight in the last war—but I very much doubt that this Rouen air raid you mentioned was scheduled that long ago."

The elderly schoolmaster stared at each man in turn for a few seconds, his sallow face suffused with rage and unconcealed contempt. Johnson and Carlyle looked at one another.

"Sir," Johnson asked respectfully, "can you prove that?"

"Of course I can, you stupid oaf. I board with Mrs. Bunting in Upper Stragham, at Number 36, Thornhill Street—I've been there for years. Go to my room. You'll find a folder in the drawer of my desk in which I place a copy of every crossword I compose. On the back, I make a note of when I posted the puzzle to *The Sunday Intelligencer* in London, when they published it, and when they paid me for it. And if it's not in the current folder, it's in one of the earlier folders in the bookcase. They're all labeled. Even an ignoramus like you will have no trouble finding it."

"Actually, sir," Johnson said, clearly embarrassed by the turn of events, "we obtained a search warrant before we arrested you at the school. All your folders are downstairs, together with the rest of the contents of your room. I'll just go and fetch the one from your desk drawer."

Johnson walked to the door of the almost empty room and knocked softly. Someone standing outside unlocked it and let him out. Carlyle and Longstreet sat in silence; Carlyle was too embarrassed to engage in any small talk, Longstreet far too angry. After a few minutes, Johnson returned. The schoolmaster noticed that this time the men outside left the door unlocked.

"Is this the folder, sir?"

"Wonders will never cease; you were actually able to locate the correct one. Well, well, well. Now, this looks like yesterday's crossword. Look over here, both of you. At the top of the page I've typed 'Grid Number 7.' Each newspaper has its own set of standard grids that we have to use, fifteen squares by fifteen squares. That makes the typesetting quick and easy. All that the compositors have to do is insert the correct grid into the page as they make it up.

"When I've finished composing a crossword, I type the clues on one piece of paper, and the answers on another. I make two carbon copies of each. I send the original and the top copy of the clues and the answers to Enoch Waterson, the crossword editor of *The Sunday Intelligencer*, and I keep both second copies in the folder here. Here are the clues, and the answers are on the next page. Look at the back of the page with the clues, and you'll see that I posted the puzzle to Waterson on the fourteenth of July. That's Bastille Day in France, of course. It would, in all probability, have arrived at the newspaper offices in London on the sixteenth of July."

Carlyle looked at the notebook. "Sir, with all due respect, anyone with a typewriter can type up a page of clues and a page of answers, insert them into a folder and write on the back that he composed the puzzle nearly five months earlier. Do you have any supporting evidence?"

Longstreet looked at him with undisguised derision. "Of course I do, you half-witted lamebrain: the register at *The Sunday Intelligencer* ... and Melinda Gascombe."

"Could you tell us about the register, please, sir?" Johnson asked.

"Like all national British newspapers, *The Intelligencer* receives hundreds of postal items every day, and every piece is logged in a huge register. Go to London, look at the register entries for the sixteenth of July, and you'll find that they received a crossword from me on that day."

"But is the information recorded in the register sufficiently detailed to show that they specifically received yesterday's puzzle on the sixteenth of July?"

"No, and that's where Melinda Gascombe comes in."

"Melinda Gascombe, sir?"

"Haven't you heard of her?"

Both men shook their heads. Longstreet rolled his eyes.

"She was the most brilliant astronomy student at Cambridge ever. Melinda was appointed Reader in Astronomy at the age of only twenty-two—

unbelievable. Sir Arthur Eddington has been the Plumian Professor of Astronomy and Experimental Philosophy since 1913, and it was all but certain that Melinda would be appointed to the chair on the day that Sir Arthur chose to retire. One evening she went home after delivering a truly brilliant lecture and stabbed her husband to death with a kitchen knife. She then calmly walked to the nearest police station and announced, 'I am Galileo Galilei and I've killed Pope Urban VIII.'"

"Pope Urban VIII?" Johnson asked diffidently.

"Galileo's nemesis, you ignorant fool. At the age of twenty-seven and with no previous warning of any kind, Melinda Gascombe had suddenly gone mad. What a tragedy—one of the greatest minds of this century. Well, she was clearly unfit to plead, and the judge committed her to Broadmoor, the hospital for the criminally insane."

Carlyle was bewildered. "What does this have to do with crossword puzzles?"

"I'm not a psychiatrist and therefore I can't explain it, but parts of Dr. Gascombe's mind are still in perfect working order, including the part that does crossword puzzles. Almost all the major newspapers send a copy of each puzzle to her for checking before they put it in the paper. She solves it and sends it back to the crossword editor, who compares her answers with those supplied by the composer. If they're identical, the editor publishes the puzzle; if not, the editor has to resolve the issue, returning the puzzle to the composer for correction, if necessary. He also sends it back if Melinda can't solve it in under ten minutes—everyone agrees that, if she can't complete it in that time, the crossword needs to be fixed. The newspapers pay Broadmoor for each puzzle that she checks, and the money is used to make the inmates' lives more comfortable. Anyhow, Melinda Gascombe logs each crossword she receives and meticulously audits the account books to make sure that Broadmoor receives every penny the newspapers owe the hospital. Go to Broadmoor and check her records, damn it, you pair of boneheaded baboons."

He turned to Carlyle. "I know exactly what you're going to say, that Dr. Gascombe is brilliant enough to easily construct a logbook that purports to show that I composed the puzzle five months ago. True. But I don't have the slightest shadow of a doubt that my records showing when I posted the puzzle; the newspaper's records regarding when they received the puzzle from me and sent the copy to Melinda Gascombe for checking; her records, together with the Broadmoor crossword financial records; the newspaper's register showing when they received the puzzle back from her; and the files of Enoch Waterson, the crossword editor of *The Sunday Intelligencer*, together constitute an unassailable level of proof of my innocence."

And Hector Longstreet sat back with a look of triumph on his face that quickly changed to a vicious stare of loathing.

Johnson and Carlyle looked at one another again. Neither had the faintest idea what to say next. Then suddenly Carlyle had a brainwave.

"Sir, do you have a security clearance?"

"Of course not! Why would I have such a thing? I'm a schoolmaster. I teach Classics to lazy and disobedient boys who would rather be doing anything else other than learning Latin and Greek, and you don't need a security clearance for that. Are you out of your mind?"

"Well, sir, in addition to falsely accusing you of being a Nazi spy, we've inadvertently divulged information regarding a military operation that's due to take place in five days' time. Consequently, we can't release you until then, even though I'm absolutely confident that you wouldn't mention anything about it to a living soul. But I think we have a solution that you'll like. You're in an MI5 safehouse. The Special Branch brought you here for the purpose of interrogating you over a period of days to discover who the Nazi agent is who gave you the information about the forthcoming air strike on Rouen."

Carlyle gave a brief embarrassed smile and continued. "We can't put you in prison, sir, because you're clearly innocent. We could play games with you and claim that we need to check out your story in every detail, and then release you in five days' time. Instead, here's what I suggest. We'll give you the run of the house until Saturday morning. MI5 has no one under guard in this building at the moment, and the staff live here permanently. That means you can admire the artwork and the furnishings, spend as much time as you wish in the library, and wander through the grounds. I know you'll enjoy your meals, and the cellar is extremely well stocked. The only restriction on your movements is that you have to stay away from the inner fence; it's electrified. The bedrooms are comfortable. And we've brought your belongings here from Mrs. Bunting's house.

"We'll contact your headmaster and tell him that we need your brilliant mind, as evidenced by your crossword-composing skills, to assist us in solving a critical problem that has arisen. He'll be delighted that you can serve our country in this way, and you'll have a five-day midterm break. All we ask in return is that you never tell anyone the real story."

The generous offer seemed to placate Longstreet. He nodded slowly. "Yes, I think that's fair. Naturally I wouldn't dream of mentioning anything to a soul. But what about the school secretary? In her own way, Miss Harrington is as crazy as Melinda Gascombe, but didn't she see your men leading me away in handcuffs? And what about Mrs. Bunting? You showed her the search warrant, and you took away my notebooks and everything else in the room."

"Well, sir, we'll replace everything at her house just before we take you back on Saturday morning, and as soon as we leave here we'll return to Upper Stragham and inform Mrs. Bunting that you needed your books and other possessions for the vital work you're doing for the government. And as for Miss Harrington, we'll tell her that we had to get you here as quickly as possible because the task you're undertaking for us is extremely important, and that meant arresting you— your devotion to the teaching profession is so strong that otherwise we'd never have got you out of your classroom. Will that work, sir?"

Hector Longstreet thought for a while. "I think it will. Although with Miss Harrington, one never quite knows what's going on her brain—I often wonder if she actually has one."

"Fine, sir, then that's settled. We'll take you downstairs and introduce you to the staff. Enjoy your holiday, sir!"

***

As they returned to their car, Johnson turned to Carlyle.

"That was a truly brilliant idea of yours, letting him think that he got away with it."

Carlyle smiled. "Thank you. But what else could we do? Interrogating him for days would be pointless. All we'd learn is who his contact is, and even though he's blissfully unaware of it, he's already given us that piece of information."

"Have you warned the staff that they're to watch him every second of every day?"

"Of course. And I've already contacted Air Commodore Pankhurst. We have to cancel the air raid. Not only will the Nazis empty the Rouen area of any military equipment that they can drive or drag away, but they'll also bring in every anti-aircraft gun within hundreds of miles in order to protect the city and its rail network, especially the marshalling yard. We'll lose a horrendous number of planes and aircrew."

"Agreed. Now, all we have to do is find out who's providing the information to the Nazi spy ring."

CHAPTER THREE

MI5 Headquarters, London
Tuesday, December 14th, 1943

As Big Ben chimed a quarter past nine, Air Commodore Archibald Pankhurst entered the basement conference room, closing the door behind him. His craggy face was as grim as always, and his perennial scowl lowered his bushy salt-and-pepper brows down to the level of his hooded eyes. Soon after the outbreak of the Second World War, the War Department moved the prisoners out of Wormwood Scrubs Prison to enable MI5 to use the building as a secure headquarters. The small conference room in the basement of "The Scrubs" was where Pankhurst met every morning with the members of his team.

As they heard his familiar precise footsteps, the five British military officers and two MI5 intelligence officers seated around the table rose swiftly to their feet. They stood to attention until Pankhurst nodded to indicate that they should sit. As they settled down, they heard a knock.

"Come!"

The door opened, and a woman on crutches entered clumsily. She was wearing the uniform of a female British military officer, with a major's crown on her shoulders. She appeared to be unused to manipulating her walking aids; it took her two attempts before she was able to successfully close the door behind her. Her tall, lithe body was topped by wavy auburn hair, of regulation length and pinned back. She wore no lipstick or other makeup of any kind.

"Come in, Limberg. Gentlemen, this is Senior Commander Limberg of the Auxiliary Territorial Service, attached to the Royal Corps of Signals. Limberg is an expert on strategies of military deception. And in case you're wondering why she's on crutches, two days ago she was walking through Pimlico when a delayed-action German bomb exploded in a pub two blocks away from her. She single-handedly rescued three badly injured men from the burning building as it was collapsing; they've recommended her for a medal. How's your banged-up knee, by the way?"

"I'm sure it'll be right as rain in a few days' time, sir."

"Let's hope that's the case. Now let me introduce my team to you. This is Lieutenant Wallstead of the Royal Engineers."

A tall red-headed man with freckles reached across the table and shook hands with her.

"Lieutenant Commander Chulmleigh from the Royal Navy and Squadron Leader Harkness from the Royal Air Force."

The two men grinned broadly. Limberg noticed Chulmleigh's wide forehead and prominent jaw, whereas her first impression of Squadron Leader Harkness was his piercing black eyes staring out over a Roman nose.

"Next, Major Tupman of the Royal Marines, and Captain Marks of the Royal Army Medical Corps."

Tupman was half a head taller than Lieutenant Wallstead. Even though he was seated far from her, it was easy for him to reach over and shake her hand. Marks, being decidedly shorter, decided that a smile would be an adequate greeting. His whole face lit up; he really seemed pleased that she had joined the team.

"The two civilians are Johnson and Carlyle."

Seated on either side of her, both men shook her hand. They noticed that Senior Commander Limberg's handshake was surprisingly strong. Johnson wondered idly if she had specially strengthened her hand muscles in order to make it clear to fellow officers that—even though she was a member of the Auxiliary Territorial Service, the female division of the British Army—her woman's rank of senior commander was fully equivalent to that of a male major and she was in every way as capable as a man holding that rank.

"The reason why Limberg is here is that she's the vice-president of the British Cruciverbalist Society. I'm sure you all know that a cruciverbalist is a person who composes crosswords, from the Latin words *crux* meaning a cross and *verbum*, a word. She's here to help us with the situation regarding the puzzle in *The Sunday Intelligencer.*

"You may be wondering why I've called in the vice-president and not the president. I had two good reasons. First, Limberg has the necessary security clearance, and the president doesn't. And second, the president of the society for the past ten years has been Hector Longstreet.

"Well, Limberg, before we look more closely into the situation, what can you tell us about him?"

"He's not a nice person, sir. He went up to Oxford to read Classics, intending to follow an academic career, but it turned out that he just wasn't quite good enough for that. Yes, he obtained a First, but so many brilliant people choose to study Latin and Greek that 'merely' first-class honors isn't enough. As a result, he was forced to take a position as a schoolmaster.

"He's an outstanding teacher, but he makes no secret of the fact that he despises himself for not having obtained a position at a university. Also, he hates schoolboys, and that shows, too. As a result, he started off teaching at a top school, and he's slowly come down in the world. Now he's at Stragham College. It's not quite as bad as Dotheboys Hall, rather it's your typical fourth-rate private school. All the parents are arch snobs who wouldn't dream of sending their sons to a local grammar school, where they'd receive a far superior education.

"Hector Longstreet turned seventy in 1941, but he's still teaching because the younger men have been called up, and he feels that educating the young is his contribution to the war effort. He's in perfect health, as far as I know, so I expect that he'll continue at Stragham until we've won the war.

"He has only one interest in life: cryptic crossword puzzles. The first ones appeared in British newspapers around 1925. He solved as many as he could lay his hands on, but then he realized that composing a puzzle is much more fun than solving one, particularly if you have a sadistic mindset, and Hector certainly does. His pupils hate and fear him in equal measure, and with good reason. Interestingly enough, unlike most schoolmasters, he never uses the cane; his vicious tongue is a far more painful instrument of punishment."

"How did a man like that attain the presidency of your organization?" Chulmleigh asked.

"He's the best crossword composer in the world," she replied. "It's as simple as that. Incidentally, he came up with the Fairness Rule for cryptic puzzles: you can try to mislead the solver as much as you like, but the clue must contain a fair definition, fair wordplay—and nothing else. You see, some inferior composers try to make their clues more difficult by adding extraneous pieces. But for all his faults, Hector is fair. His clues are often really hard; for example, he was the first person to use the word 'flower' in a clue to refer to a river. But when you see the solutions to his puzzles, you realize that he adheres to the Fairness Rule.

"He's very British. I might set a clue that involves a city abroad or a foreign language, like **Nice friend (3)**. The answer is **AMI**, the word for a friend in the French city of Nice. But Hector would never do that. He uses only English words in his puzzles, and any city that appears in either the clues or the answers is invariably in Great Britain."

"Which means," Carlyle stated, "that Longstreet broke one of his own rules when he composed 17-across; Rouen is a city in France."

"Yes, you're quite right. I missed that."

"And what about clues that require some familiarity with Latin and Greek?" Major Tupman asked.

Limberg thought for a moment. "That's a most interesting question. Now that I come to think of it, he never seems to include clues that require any knowledge of Classics, unlike certain crossword composers for *The Daily Recorder* who expect you not only to have a post-graduate degree in both those languages, but also to know the name of every single minor Greek and Roman deity. Plus the name of every nymph, naiad, dryad, satyr, faun, titan, and centaur. Of course I'm exaggerating, but not by much. In reply to your question, I think that Hector Longstreet has two sides to his personality, the classicist and the cruciverbalist, and they never overlap. How extremely perspicacious of you!"

"And yet," Captain Marks said, "Look at 4-down in this week's crossword. The clue is **Largest flower for classical lady warrior (6)**. The answer is **AMAZON**. In the Greek myths, the Amazons were a nation of female warriors. It seems that Longstreet has broken another of his rules. If he's a Nazi agent and was communicating with Germany via crossword puzzles, then he had no choice; he had to include the answer

AMAZON, notwithstanding what you've just told us. How significant is this, in your opinion?"

Senior Commander Limberg carefully shifted her position in her chair; it was obvious to everyone that, despite her best attempts to hide it, her injured knee was hurting her considerably. "I certainly can't claim to have seen every single puzzle that Longstreet has composed. But at the same time, I can't recall ever seeing a clue of his that relates to his encyclopedic knowledge of Classics and Classical Culture— AMAZON was the first. Have you asked him about it?"

"Well, Carlyle and I didn't know until now that he excluded Greece and Rome from his puzzles," Johnson said, "Also, we told him repeatedly that his arrest was a huge mistake on our part, to lull him into a state of false security. When we interview him again, we'll certainly raise the issue."

"I want to start at the beginning," Pankhurst said. "Carlyle, what put you and Johnson onto Longstreet?"

"I have an elderly aunt who lives for Longstreet's puzzles in *The Sunday Intelligencer*. He composes under the pen name Ramirez."

"Why?" Pankhurst asked.

"The inventor of the cryptic crossword, Edward Mathers, used the pseudonym 'Torquemada' for the puzzles he set for the Sunday newspaper, *The Observer*—Tomas de Torquemada was the first Grand Inquisitor of the Spanish Inquisition, an institution infamous for the infliction of excruciating pain. His successor at *The Observer* was Derrick Macnutt, who composed under the name 'Ximenes.' That was because the first Grand Inquisitor of the Inquisitions of Castile and Aragon was Francisco Ximenez de Cisneros, Cardinal Archbishop of Toledo."

"And Ramirez? Another torturer I assume?"

"Yes, sir. The third Grand Inquisitor of Spain was Diego Ramirez de Guzman, Bishop of Catania."

"Limberg," Pankhurst continued, "I assume that you haven't had time to compose crossword puzzles since the start of the war."

"No, sir. Unfortunately not."

"In the light of what you've just told us I'm a little afraid to ask you, but what was your *nom de plume* when you set them?"

"Do I have to answer that question, sir?"

The expectant looks on the faces of the eight men around the table made the answer unambiguously clear to her.

"Well, sir, it was Königsberg."

A long silence ensued while everyone waited respectfully for the senior officer present to ask the obvious question. Eventually the air commodore complied.

Before she could answer, Lieutenant Wallstead spoke up. "It's the seven bridges of Königsberg, isn't it?"

She smiled shyly, and then nodded. The even more obvious question was not long in coming, and this time Pankhurst asked it immediately.

"Limberg, what in the name of heaven are the seven bridges of Königsberg?" he demanded.

"Sir, the city of Königsberg in East Prussia started on two large islands in the Pregel River and then quickly spread to both banks. The two islands are connected to the mainland and to each other by a total of seven bridges. The problem is to find a way to walk through Königsberg crossing each bridge once and once only."

"And?" the air commodore asked impatiently.

"Well, sir, in about 1750 the great Swiss mathematician Leonhard Euler proved that it couldn't be done."

"You see, sir," Wallstead chimed in helpfully, "she chose as her crossword composer *nom de plume* the name of a famous puzzle that cannot be solved."

"How come you two know about the seven bridges of Königsberg?" Tupman asked.

"I'm an engineer, so I had to study mathematics, and I learned about Euler's negative result regarding the seven bridges of Königsberg when I studied Graph Theory," Wallstead said.

"And I read Mathematics at Cambridge," Limberg added.

"Actually," Pankhurst said quietly, "she was Senior Wrangler."

Gasps of admiration followed that announcement.

"I've never had the honor of meeting a Senior Wrangler before," Captain Marks said. "How did it feel as you stood below the balcony in the University's Senate House waiting tensely for the examiner to throw the printed copies of the results of the Mathematics Tripos examination down to the waiting students below, then grabbing a piece of paper as it floated past you and seeing that you were the top mathematics undergraduate at Cambridge? For many people, no higher distinction exists."

Senior Captain Limberg blushed furiously and looked down at the table.

"Let's go back to where we were," Archibald Pankhurst said. "Carlyle was telling us about his aunt who really enjoys Longstreet's puzzles."

"Yes, sir. She invited me to dinner this Sunday. When she opened the door, I could see she was concerned about something. 'I do hope that Ramirez is well,' she said as she took my coat.

"I asked her what she meant. 'Look at today's puzzle,' she said. 'I've left it on the coffee table. Follow me.'

"Lying on the table, opened at the crossword page, was *The Sunday Intelligencer*. Aunt Matilda never reads a word of it; she buys *The Intelligencer* solely for the puzzle. She said, 'The answer to 17-across is ROUEN, of course. ROUÉ attached to N for north. But that's not right.'

"I didn't see what she was getting at, so I said, 'It looks correct to me.'

"'But can't you see?' she asked impatiently. 'ROUÉ has an accent on the last letter, but ROUEN doesn't.'

"I still didn't follow. 'Aunt Matilda,' I said, 'Surely the accent doesn't matter?'

"'Of course it matters,' she replied, sounding exactly like a professor pointing out to a promising student that he'd split an infinitive on the penultimate page of an otherwise truly excellent essay. 'Ramirez would never do a thing like that; it's a violation of his Fairness Rule. The poor man must be ill.'

"I looked at Aunt Matilda's answer to 17-across, and then I noticed what she'd filled in for 17-down. In my role as liaison officer with the French Resistance movements in Normandy, I sat in on one of the Operation AMAZON briefings four days ago, so the juxtaposition of the number 17, **ROUEN**, and **RAID** immediately jumped out at me. Of course, I couldn't let my aunt know that I'd spotted a serious security breach.

"'Aunt Matilda,' I said in an offhand way, 'I see you've finished the crossword. May I take it?'

"'Of course, dear boy. But why do you want it? I never knew that you shared my love of crosswords. You'll have to tell me all about it over dinner.'

"'Please forgive me,' I said, 'but I have to take this puzzle and run. Right now, I'm sorry to say. I can't tell you why, but I hope you'll understand. I'll come to dinner some other Sunday, if you're still keen to invite your favorite nephew to a meal after this.' And I grabbed my coat and rushed here as quickly as I could. In the Underground, I studied the rest of the puzzle, and I noticed 4-down."

"Well," Pankhurst said, "now we know that this puzzle is atypical for three reasons: the accent, the French city, and the clue from Greek mythology. What does this tell us?"

"That he composed the puzzle in a great hurry," Squadron Leader Harkness suggested.

"Agreed, and that tells us that, in all probability, this puzzle is not the one he submitted on the fourteenth of July. Johnson, what do you think happened?"

"I'm pretty sure that he posted a puzzle to *The Sunday Intelligencer* on the fourteenth of July, as he said. That puzzle must have followed the usual route, that is, someone logged it in the mail register and forwarded it to the crossword editor who sent to Melinda Gascombe in Broadmoor, and so on. But my guess is that that wasn't the puzzle that appeared in the paper two days ago.

"Once Longstreet found out about the air raid on Rouen, and I have no idea how that happened, he quickly composed another puzzle, which he rushed to London. He couldn't have sent it by post, because that would have resulted in a clerk making an entry in the register. Instead, he found some other means to get it into the hands of the crossword editor, who substituted it for the one he received from Longstreet on the sixteenth of July."

"But every paper has military censors," Wallstead said. "How could they let it pass?"

"How could they not let it pass?" Johnson replied. "What they saw was a standard blank puzzle—Grid Number 7—plus a set of cryptic clues. It was impossible for a censor to have noticed anything. And the solution would appear the following Sunday, after the air raid."

"Just a minute," the air commodore said, "you've just raised a key point. If we were to accuse Longstreet of espionage, he'd point out what you've just said. He'd claim that the whole thing was simply a coincidence and, even if it wasn't, the solution would appear too late to be of any use to the enemy."

"But sir," Captain Marks insisted, "each morning several copies of the first edition of the major newspapers go to Portugal on the first plane out. The crossword would be in the hands of the *Abwehr* officers in Lisbon by noon on Sunday."

"Are you saying, Marks, that the Germans take every London paper and then solve the crossword in the hope that the composer has hidden military intelligence somewhere in the grid?"

"Not at all, sir. As far as I know, the only paper that would be of any interest to them is *The Sunday Intelligencer*, unless they've found another crossword composer who's also a traitor to our country. Also, Ramirez must have some way of indicating to the Germans that the puzzle hides a secret."

"That's easy," Carlyle said. "During the summer holidays, Longstreet composes a year's worth of puzzles. When the next school term starts, someone takes a copy of each of those puzzles to Lisbon and delivers them to the *Abwehr*. Each week they compare the printed puzzle with the next one in Longstreet's collection. If the puzzle is different, it means that it's been specially composed at the last minute, and therefore contains hidden information for the Germans. They solve the puzzle and extract the information, in this case that on Friday night the Royal Air Force is going to conduct an air raid on Rouen, code named AMAZON."

"But is it that simple?" Harkness asked. "Cryptic puzzles aren't easy to solve, and Longstreet's are especially difficult. Remember, the man's a sadist who composes crosswords under the name of a Grand Inquisitor known to have ordered his victims to be tortured. I've no doubt that Carlyle's Aunt Matilda would agree that solving a Ramirez puzzle can take all day, if not longer. And that's for someone who attempts those crosswords week after week and has therefore grown familiar with Longstreet's tricks and quirks. And if it's that hard to solve one of his crosswords when your first language is English, how can we expect a German to solve the puzzle at all, let alone quickly enough to inform their High Command that we're about to raid Rouen on the seventeenth?"

"What exactly are you saying?" Pankhurst asked.

"I'm saying two things, sir. First, I think we need to check whether the puzzle two days ago is indeed the one that Longstreet submitted on the fourteenth of July, or whether, as we've surmised, it's a new puzzle he threw together at the last minute. And second, even if it is a brand-new puzzle, unless we can come up with an explanation as to how the *Abwehr* is able to solve Longstreet's crosswords so quickly, we have to put the whole thing down to coincidence."

"Four coincidences, Harkness? The accent in ROUÉ, the French city, the word AMAZON with a Classics clue, and the Rouen air raid scheduled for the seventeenth? Four? Aren't you asking us to suspend rationality?"

CHAPTER FOUR

Crowthorne, Berkshire, England
Tuesday, December 14th, 1943

"We were lucky that we managed to get on that train to Wokingham just as it was leaving Waterloo Station," Johnson said. "Maybe we'll have time to interview both Dr. Melinda Gascombe and the crossword editor of *The Sunday Intelligencer* today."

"Maybe, maybe not," Carlyle responded. "The fact that we've arrived outside Broadmoor Hospital for the Criminally Insane doesn't necessarily imply we'll get inside at any time soon. Despite the name, this isn't a hospital; it's a prison. The nonmedical staff members are prison warders. That means that it takes time to get in, and even longer to get out. Let's hope that Archie's phone call to the Chairman of The Board of Control for Lunacy and Mental Deficiency did the trick; they're the people who're in charge of the treatment of the mentally ill."

"I thought they were called the Commissioners in Lunacy."

"That used to be the case, but it changed a while ago, before the First World War, I think. Anyhow, the main thing is whether we'll get to see Melinda without having to jump through innumerable time-consuming hoops."

Waiting for them at the red brick gatehouse with its clock tower was a short plump pompous-looking man in a morning suit: black coat with knee-length tails, gray waistcoat, and black-and-gray striped trousers. He introduced himself as Sir Edgar Makepeace, Dr. Gascombe's psychiatrist.

"The Medical Superintendent informed me that you're here on a matter of national security," he said in a high-pitched voice. "I have to say that that surprises me. Melinda has been in Broadmoor for more than five years, since before the start of the war. I can't imagine how she could possibly help you. Well, it really isn't my business, of course."

The two MI5 officers said nothing.

"In any event, your visit poses a practical problem. I fully appreciate the need for secrecy. But I cannot leave you alone with her; two attendants have to be present at all times."

"Surely that won't be necessary, Sir Edgar," Johnson replied.

"I assure you that it is. She slips almost instantaneously from her persona as a calm, highly intelligent woman into a state of murderous rage. In that frenzy, her adrenaline level rises sharply and she becomes capable of acts of almost superhuman strength. I'm still not sure what triggers this aggressive state, but when it starts it takes two trained men to prevent her from committing physical violence that could well result in serious injury or worse. No, Mr. Johnson, I'm afraid I have to insist on it. The only acceptable alternative would be to confine her in a straitjacket during your interview. Based on previous experiences, however, I doubt that she would talk to you under those conditions."

"May I consult with my colleague?" Johnson asked.

"Of course. Please go ahead."

Johnson took Carlyle aside. They stood some ten yards from the psychiatrist, with their backs to him. "The only thing we want to ask her is whether she's seen the crossword before."

"Yes, that's true, but the ensuing conversation may include the three critical words." Even though he kept his voice low, he was careful not to say those words aloud, just in case Sir Edgar had extraordinarily good hearing.

"I agree. But can we take the risk?"

"We have no alternative," Johnson said.

"Should we swear the attendants to secrecy?"

"I think that might be counterproductive. If we simply pose the question to her in a casual way, they'll surely not realize the importance of what's going on."

"I suppose you're right. But as you said, we have no alternative," Carlyle said.

They rejoined the psychiatrist.

"Sir Edgar," Carlyle said, "we believe we can obtain the information we need without divulging anything that we shouldn't in front of your attendants.

Please could you arrange for someone to take us to Dr. Gascombe."

The psychiatrist summoned an attendant in a white uniform, who led the way past the Female Airing Court, a large garden with a gazebo and extensive lawns, to the Female Quarters. He unlocked and relocked a series of heavily barred doors, and finally opened the metal door to a prison cell. In front of them a woman of about thirty sat on a wooden chair; on each side of her stood a man in a prison warder's uniform. Her face was a mask; her skin was pallid, as if she had not been outdoors for months. The bars on the small window behind her were as thick as those on the doors in the Female Quarters.

Carlyle entered first. He smiled at her. "Good morning, Dr. Gascombe."

She smiled back. She had a perfect set of pearly white teeth. Johnson now squeezed into the cell. The door clanged shut behind him, and the two MI5 officers heard their escort lock it firmly behind them.

"I'm Carlyle, and this is Johnson. I wonder if you can help us. I have here a photograph of a crossword puzzle. We wondered if you've seen it before."

She studied the puzzle for no more than seven seconds and then handed it back to him. "Why do you ask?"

Carlyle was sure that she would ask that question, and gave the reply that they had agreed on in the train on the way to Broadmoor. "Some doubt has arisen regarding its authenticity."

"I'm not surprised. I wrote to Enoch about it."

"Enoch Waterson? The crossword editor at *The Sunday Intelligencer*?"

"Yes. I told him that two clues made me wonder if Hector Longstreet really was the composer."

"You're referring to the accent, the foreign city, and the classical reference?" he asked, hoping that she would not say any of the words with a hidden military meaning in front of the attendants.

"Obviously."

He breathed a silent prayer of thanks.

"And how did Enoch reply?" Johnson asked.

"He assured me that Hector had composed the puzzle. Enoch said that he'd raised those issues in a letter to Hector, who informed him that the items weren't mistakes; he'd deliberately included them to make the puzzle harder. It's true—everything else is relatively straightforward.

"By the way," she added, "I noticed that someone has tried to solve the crossword. Who was it?"

"My Aunt Matilda," Carlyle replied. "She subscribes to *The Intelligencer*. The first thing she does every Sunday morning is solve the puzzle. Then she throws the rest of the paper away, or more precisely, she puts it aside for the schoolchildren when they come around for the next paper salvage collection."

"Well, next time you see her, you'd better tell her that her answer to 11-down is wrong. She wrote PEACE; the correct answer is PLACE."

Johnson glanced at Carlyle, who instantly knew what his colleague was thinking: Dr. Gascombe had studied the puzzle for no more than a few seconds, but in that time she had somehow checked all of Aunt Matilda's answers.

"Do you happen to recall when you received that crossword?" Johnson inquired.

"Hector sets all his puzzles for the academic year during the preceding school holidays. I think the governors of his school insist on it, to enable him to devote himself to teaching Classics full time. That crossword arrived here towards the end of July, I think. Would you mind passing me that large black notebook on the table, please?"

From the way she spoke and her body language as she sat in the chair, Johnson deduced that she was not permitted to stand up, let alone retrieve the book and hand it to her visitors. He walked over to the table next to the narrow bed, fetched the notebook, and gave it to her. She quickly found the entry she sought.

"I received the puzzle from Enoch on the twentieth of July. I solved it that day, and sent it back to him with the letter that I just told you about. I received his reply on the third of August. The money for my work was paid at the end of July, as per our arrangement. *The Sunday Intelligencer* is particularly good about payments, unlike a certain daily newspaper I could mention. Surprising, really—I've heard that *The Intelligencer* has been in financial difficulties for years.

"Do either of you have any further questions?"

Johnson shook his head. She handed him her notebook and he replaced it where he'd found it on the table. He turned to thank her and say goodbye when Carlyle asked, "Dr. Gascombe, what can you tell us about Hector Longstreet?"

"He's undoubtedly the best crossword composer in the world, and he's an excellent teacher of Latin and Greek. But that doesn't in any way make up for the fact that he's a vicious, evil man. He gets his jollies from publicly humiliating and shaming schoolboys."

"And who's the cruciverbalist who composes under the name 'Königsberg'?"

"Oh, that would be Vanessa Limberg. She's quite delightful. You'd never guess it if you met her, but she's one of only a handful of lady Senior Wranglers. And she's multitalented; Cambridge University awarded her a blue in fencing."

"Is she one of the top composers?" Johnson asked.

"Before the war, she composed crosswords for one of the better provincial newspapers—I'm afraid she never reached the ranks of the national dailies. I've heard that her war work now makes it impossible for her to continue setting crosswords; she simply doesn't have a spare moment. Of course, our leading woman cruciverbalist is Bridget Hawkesbury. The newspapers don't publish her crosswords either, but for a different reason."

"Oh?"

"She and a friend were unfortunate enough to be hiking in the mountains of Bavaria when the war broke out. They're in an internment camp somewhere in Germany. She's allowed to send occasional letters, but not crosswords she's composed; I suppose that the authorities are worried that she might use the puzzles to convey secret information."

Looking Johnson straight in the eye she added, "That's the sort of thing intelligence officers worry about."

He was unable to hold her gaze.

She smiled again. "Don't worry, Mr. Johnson—if that's your real name, which I doubt. I won't give the game away."

Carlyle glanced at the attendants. They both looked bored, almost asleep on their feet. He assumed they were used to nonsensical ramblings from Broadmoor inmates and would treat Melinda's remarks as coming from an unsound mind.

"I receive a letter from Bridget every few months or so. Recently she told me that she's keeping sane by composing cryptic crosswords every minute of the day."

As she spoke the word 'day' her facial expression became distorted. Her hands turned into two talons. She lunged out of the chair, which toppled noisily onto the cement floor. Melinda rushed at Johnson and tried to strangle him. But the two attendants were far more vigilant than Carlyle had thought. They grabbed the frenzied astronomer before she could reach Johnson.

"Bang loudly on the door," one of them shouted as he struggled to hold Melinda. "He'll let you out."

***

"I have to apologize to you, Sir Edgar," Johnson said. "You were quite right about the need for those two attendants. They probably saved my life."

"I'm just glad they stopped her in time. What did you say that set her off?"

"I'm not really sure. We were asking her about cruciverbalists, and she was telling us about a woman now in a German internment camp. That's when Melinda suddenly flew at me. As far as I can tell, her rage was entirely unprovoked. On the contrary, in fact. Earlier in that part of our conversation she told us about a crossword composer who's a really nasty piece of work. She became indignant when she described his character, perhaps even annoyed, but in a socially acceptable way. When I asked her about another cruciverbalist, she immediately returned to her previous cheerful mood and said some extremely nice things about her. Then Melinda started talking amiably about a third composer. For no apparent reason, at least not apparent to me, she suddenly exploded and tried to kill me."

"Yes, that's what seems to happen every time; I've not been able to find an ostensible trigger. A violent rage suddenly consumes her for no apparent reason. I wish we knew more about the human mind and how it works; it really would be wonderful if we could cure Melinda and return her to the world outside. By the way," he asked in an offhand manner, "did she give you the information you came here for?"

"You were correct in that respect, too, Sir Edgar. I'm afraid our visit was completely fruitless. However, thank you for your help."

"Not at all, Mr. Carlyle. I'll arrange for one of the attendants to escort you to the gatehouse, and I'll phone for a taxi to take you back to the station."

***

"Inquisitive, isn't he?" Johnson remarked as they climbed out of the cab at Wokingham Station and waited for the next train to London. "Even though I told him that we'd learned nothing from poor Melinda, I'm absolutely certain that he's going to interrogate the two attendants to try to find out the object of our visit. And he'll probably subtly try to extract information from her, too. But I think she's too clever for him."

"How scrupulous is he? Do you think he'll use sodium pentothal or some other truth serum on her to satisfy his curiosity?"

"Perhaps. But why does it matter? In my opinion, it's incontrovertible that the crossword was composed in July—and that's even before we've verified the correspondence between Melinda, Longstreet, and Enoch the editor."

"Yes, of course," Carlyle said. "But I think that she was trying to tell us that she suspects that someone is sending secret information to Germany in crossword puzzles, and that Bridget Hawkesbury is solving those puzzles for them, possibly unknowingly, perhaps under duress."

"I had the same impression, but I put it out of my mind because I thought if that was what she wanted to tell us, she'd simply say so."

"I was wondering about that in the taxi," Carlyle said, "and I've come up with three possible explanations. From what she said to you about intelligence officers, she suspects that we're from MI5, but she has no way of telling for sure, and therefore she decided to restrict herself to dropping a hint. As far as she's concerned, we may be enemy agents trying to find out how much she actually knows."

"I agree with that."

"Then the attendants were present. I don't think she wanted to speak openly in front of them."

"Yes. And did you notice how careful she was not to say aloud any of the words from the crossword, other than PEACE and PLACE, which are obviously harmless. It's clear that, despite their casual stance, they're listening carefully to everything she says, waiting for that irrational rage to take control of her."

"True. And finally, she's an academic. She was Reader in Astronomy for five years before she fell ill. Cambridge follows the European tradition of having only one professor in each department and consequently a reader is all but a professor. I think she was trying to instruct us by making us think; that's the approach they use at Cambridge."

"All three reasons make sense. Of course," Johnson added, "we have to consider a fourth possibility."

"You mean that she's mentally unbalanced and what we believe to be a warning is in reality an irrational remark from an insane person?"

"Yes. Sad, isn't it? We've just had the privilege of meeting one of the finest brains in the world, and we've no idea whether to place any credence at all on what she told us."

"But what if she's right?" Carlyle asked. "What if her suspicions aren't the ravings of a diseased mind? Surely we have to make certain that Sir Edgar Makepeace isn't allowed to talk to her?"

"And what about the attendants? That psychiatrist may ask them questions that would get them to begin thinking about our conversation. Next thing they'll start talking about our conversation to all and sundry."

"Would that really be a problem?" Carlyle asked. "What possible harm could that do?"

"Let's suppose that Melinda is right and a cruciverbalist somewhere in Britain is using crosswords to send information to Germany. If we could find the man or the woman, we could use that route to send disinformation to the Nazis. For example, we could tell them that the Royal Air Force has planned to bomb Rouen whereas the air raid is actually going to take place against Amiens, some sixty miles away. The Germans would move all their mobile anti-aircraft guns to Rouen that night, leaving Amiens relatively undefended.

"But more importantly," Johnson continued, "what about the forthcoming invasion of Europe? Hitler needs to know where we're going to invade. I hear that he's pretty sure that it's going to be the Pas-de-Calais, with diversionary attacks at other places. But we need to convince him beyond all doubt. That crossword conduit might be just the thing. But if news about the activities of the puzzle gang gets out as a consequence of our visit to Broadmoor, we'll have lost a wonderful opportunity to mislead the Nazis."

"You're quite right," Carlyle said. "Let's get to a phone and tell Pankhurst what we've learned. I'm sure he'll find a way to get that psychiatrist out of Broadmoor immediately and keep him away, probably by playing on the man's vanity. For instance, Archie could arrange for the Medical Superintendent at Broadmoor to tell Sir Edgar that his country needs him right away to help shell-shocked soldiers in a military hospital overseas. What do you think about sending him to North Africa?"

"Or Sicily? Either would do," Johnson said. "Where's the nearest phone booth? It doesn't matter if we miss our train—we can talk to the crossword editor tomorrow. But we have to stop Sir Edgar right now."

CHAPTER FIVE

Fleet Street, London
Wednesday, December 15th, 1943

Before the war, an impressive horde of uniformed porters, receptionists, and pageboys thronged the foyer of the palatial office building on Fleet Street that housed *The Sunday Intelligencer.* But as Johnson and Carlyle entered through the brass and glass revolving door, they immediately noticed that the marble-lined hall was empty, with the exception of two older women who sat behind a plain wooden desk in front of an ornate art deco pillar coated with gold leaf. Carlyle approached them.

"May I help you, sir?"

"We're looking for Mr. Waterson, the crossword editor."

"I'm afraid that Mr. Waterson isn't in today. He comes here twice a week, on Tuesdays and Fridays, between the hours of nine and twelve. Would you care to see his secretary?"

The two men looked at one another. Johnson nodded. Carlyle turned back to the receptionist. "Yes, please, if we may."

"Miss Frobisher is in Room 49, on the fourth floor." She smiled apologetically. "I'm sorry to have to tell you that, after the last bombing raid two weeks ago, we've had to resume printing the paper in Manchester, and we haven't been able to repair any of the lifts yet. The stairs are in that corner."

She smiled again as the two men thanked her and walked toward the imposing staircase. By the time they reached the fourth floor, neither of them felt like smiling. The stairs were more ornamental than functional; employees and visitors to the building alike were supposed to use the elevators, which currently were out of service. Carlyle and Johnson were young and fit, but the distance between successive steps was just too large for anyone to be able climb the stairs comfortably. They arrived at Room 49 somewhat out of breath.

Johnson tapped politely on the frosted glass insert of the opened wooden door, then entered. "Are you Miss Frobisher?"

"Yes." The woman was in her late thirties, but her long bleached hair was backcombed, pinned and curled into a victory roll, a style that, as a rule, only considerably younger women sported.

"I believe that you're Mr. Waterson's secretary," Johnson continued.

"Actually, I'm the secretary for all five of the part-time editors: crosswords, chess, gardening, motoring, and bridge. They're here every Friday morning and on one other morning; Mr. Waterson is here on Tuesdays. That means that if you need to see him, you'll have to come back on Friday."

"Miss Frobisher, if we return on Friday, we'll have to climb those stairs again, so I sincerely hope that you'll be able to help us."

She smiled sympathetically. "I can try."

"First," Johnson said, "Let me show you my identification card."

Her eyes, the lashes heavily coated with mascara, opened wide when she saw the words "Military Intelligence."

"How can I assist you, Mr. Johnson?"

"Do you know a man called Hector Longstreet?"

She took a short breath. "He's the bane of my life. Every letter to him I have to type and retype again and again. The worst was in July or August. Mr. Waterson dictated a letter to Mr. Longstreet that contained a French word. He spelled the word for me, and pointed out that the last letter had an accent on it. But he didn't say which kind of accent. Knowing that every communication to Mr. Longstreet has to be perfect, I took the greatest care to ensure that I made no mistakes. But when I took it to Mr. Waterson, he said that I had typed the wrong accent—it had to go the other way. That meant I had to retype the whole thing. This time I got the accent right, but I somehow managed to misspell Mr. Waterson's name under the signature line. Finally, I had everything correct the third time. All that fuss over a French word, and I can't even remember what it was."

"Miss Frobisher, was the word 'roué' by any chance?" Carlyle asked in a kindly voice.

Her eyes opened wide again. "How did you know that?"

"Could you show me the letter, please?"

She was too stunned to ask him anything more and obediently trotted over to a large wooden filing cabinet. After a few minutes of fruitless searching, she suddenly shouted, "I've found it!"

She took a manila folder out of the cabinet, extracted a carbon copy of the letter she had typed, and handed it to Carlyle.

"Thank you, Miss Frobisher. And that folder should also contain a letter to Mr. Waterson from Dr. Melinda Gascombe, as well as a reply from Hector Longstreet to the letter you've just found for me. Oh, you should also find a letter from Mr. Waterson replying to Dr. Gascombe."

"Yes, the others are right here. Would you like to see them, too?"

"Yes, please."

She handed him three more pieces of paper. Carlyle glanced at each of the four documents, checked the dates, and then said, "Miss Frobisher, I'd like to take these letters with me. I'll give you a receipt, of course."

She looked doubtful. "I really don't know. Mr. Longstreet would be most upset if he found out."

"Mr. Longstreet? What's he got to do with it? Don't you work for Mr. Waterson?"

"Yes, of course I do, but if Mr. Longstreet gets upset with me he'll leave *The Sunday Intelligencer* and take his crosswords to some other paper, and then they'd immediately fire Mr. Waterson and he'll fire me. You see, Mr. Longstreet's crosswords sell thousands and thousands of copies of the newspaper. If he stopped sending his puzzles here, our circulation would go way down and people would rather buy the paper he moves to in order to get his crosswords."

"I see. Well, perhaps it won't be necessary to take them away if Johnson and I read them carefully here in your office. Let me see now."

He handed two of them to his colleague, and started reading a third, the letter from Waterson to Longstreet asking him about the uncharacteristic clues. By the time he reached the second paragraph, he realized that the tone of the letter was most odd; it certainly was not what he would have expected from a crossword editor to a contributor. He took a shot in the dark.

"Miss Frobisher, was Mr. Waterson a former pupil of Mr. Longstreet?"

She turned a fiery shade of red and looked away. "Please don't make me answer that question, sir," she begged.

"Miss Frobisher, we're at war with Germany, and this may be a matter of national security. I'd be most grateful if you'd tell me."

She looked back at him with a look of fear on her face. "Sir, they made me promise never to tell," she whimpered.

"Who's 'they'? Who made you promise?" Carlyle asked.

"The managers here. As I told you, Mr. Longstreet's crosswords are most important to the financial success of the paper. Many, many people love doing his crosswords. It's the challenge, you see. Also, several of the clues each week are really extremely clever, and people enjoy that. And the best thing about those puzzles is that, even if you left school at the age of fourteen, you can still solve them. All the answers are straightforward—you don't need to know those fancy ten-shilling words or the names of obscure Greek goddesses like in the other crosswords. You just have to think clearly to be able to solve his crosswords, tough as they are, and almost anybody can do that if they try hard enough."

"Yes, I see, but what did they instruct you not to tell?"

She swallowed and then took a deep breath. "The newspaper hasn't been doing at all well since the Depression, and it's been getting worse year by year. The proprietor can't afford to pay Mr. Longstreet what those puzzles are really worth. As a result, they've set up an arrangement."

"An arrangement?" Carlyle asked.

"Do I have to tell you, sir?" she begged.

"Please, Miss Frobisher."

She took another deep breath.

"Well, the arrangement is that Mr. Longstreet chooses his own editor, who reports to him. And it's always someone that Mr. Longstreet used to teach. The crossword editor then hires a secretary to work for all five of the part-time editors, which effectively means that Mr. Longstreet is my boss's boss. In return, Mr. Longstreet charges the newspaper only the standard amount for his puzzles; he doesn't insist on being paid the large fee he really should receive for his crosswords."

Johnson wanted to be certain. "Are you telling me, Miss Frobisher, that Mr. Longstreet is willing to take less money than he deserves in return for having full control over his crossword puzzles?"

"I don't know anything about that sort of thing, sir. All I know is that Mr. Waterson is terrified of Mr. Longstreet, and he does everything that Mr. Longstreet tells him to do. And so do I."

And at that, Miss Frobisher burst into tears. Johnson waited patiently until the sobbing stopped.

"Miss Frobisher," he said, "we certainly didn't mean to upset you. We're both very sorry. And we don't want to get you into trouble with anyone, least of all Mr. Longstreet or Mr. Waterson. Suppose you get the photographic department on the phone and ask them to please send someone over here to take pictures of the letters. We'll take the prints away with us, and you can then replace all four items in the manila folder and put the folder back in the filing cabinet exactly the way everything was. Will that work?"

She smiled through her tears. "That would be fine, sir."

CHAPTER SIX

MI5 Headquarters, London
Thursday, December 16th, 1943

"**G**entlemen," Air Marshal Archibald Pankhurst said, "the situation regarding tomorrow's Rouen raid needs to be resolved once and for all."

Senior Commander Limberg had been a member of Pankhurst's team for two days now, but Pankhurst apparently was still unaware of her gender. Or perhaps it was hard for the air commodore to change his ways after more than forty years of using the word *gentlemen* to address his officers.

"In my opinion," he continued, "it's now certain that Hector Longstreet composed the crossword containing the words **ROUEN, RAID**, and **AMAZON** in July this year. The evidence is overwhelming, especially the copies of the four letters that Carlyle and Johnson brought us.

"Bomber Command proposed the raid last Friday. If you want to convince me that Longstreet is an enemy agent, you'll have to explain to me how he and the rest of his gang of Nazi secret agents managed to forge the letters in such a short time. The evidence we found in Longstreet's own folder, in the *Intelligencer* register, and in Melinda Gascombe's notebook is somewhat weaker, but all that would have to be forged, too.

"Furthermore, despite her overall mental condition, Melinda Gascombe's recollections regarding the puzzle are hard to challenge, as are those of the secretary at the Sunday newspaper. What was her name again? Oh yes, Violet Frobisher. As far as I'm concerned, what we're dealing with here is nothing more than a remarkable coincidence. Does everyone agree?"

Eight heads nodded, almost in unison.

"Excellent. I shall inform Bomber Command that we haven't found any reason why the raid should not go ahead tomorrow night. However," he went on, "in the course of clearing up the Great Rouen Raid Crossword Mystery, we've possibly uncovered something else."

He cleared his throat briefly.

"Both Johnson and Carlyle believe that Dr. Melinda Gascombe may have hinted that a person or persons unknown are somehow using crossword puzzles to send information to the Nazis. She also mentioned that a top lady cruciverbalist named Bridget Hawkesbury is in German hands. If that's the case, the Nazis could be using her to quickly solve puzzles containing secret military information, possibly against her will or perhaps without her even realizing what they're up to.

"When we meet tomorrow morning I want to hear your ideas as to how we should proceed in response to this possible threat to our national security."

***

"Well, gentlemen? You've had twenty-four hours to consider the matter. What are your thoughts about crosswords and military secrets? Let's go around the table clockwise. Wallstead?"

"Sir," the red-headed Royal Engineer replied, "each day a few planes fly from here to neutral Portugal. On the first flight, they take with them several copies of the first edition of specific newspapers: nine national dailies, thirteen Sunday papers. As far as I've been able to determine, no other newspapers leave our shores openly. So, if crosswords are getting to the Germans via that route, we need to check only sixty-seven crosswords each week. I believe the military censors could do that."

"Anything else, Wallstead?"

"Yes, sir. It's regarding the puzzles in the daily papers. Suppose that a crossword appears on a Monday. The solution is printed on Tuesday, together with the next crossword. That means that if something is hidden in a daily puzzle, the Germans don't need to solve it—they can look at the solution twenty-four hours later."

"Sir," Chulmleigh interrupted, "does anyone check that the solution corresponds exactly to the puzzle? If I wanted to inform the *Abwehr* office in Lisbon regarding a raid on Rouen on the seventeenth of December, I wouldn't bother to compose a special puzzle that day. Instead, all I would need to do is list the word **ROUEN** as the answer for 17-across and **RAID** for 17-down. After all, the solution doesn't appear as letters filled in on a grid; they just give a numbered list of the answers to all the 'across' clues first, and then the 'down' clues."

"But that wouldn't work," Marks said with a smile, his whole face lighting up once again. "Readers would write to the newspaper pointing out the mistakes in the solution, and you'd be found out."

"Not if it's a one-time only strategy," Chulmleigh insisted. "If I were a Nazi spy and I'd found out that the invasion of Europe this summer was going to take place on, say, the fourteenth of May at Le Havre, I wouldn't hesitate for a second. I'd change the answers to the puzzle to reflect the information I'd found, and then I'd flee the country as quickly as I could. Yes, readers would write numerous letters to the editor, but my information would get through to Berlin."

"And when the authorities discover what you've done from the torrent of letters, they'd alter the date and location of the invasion," Tupman said. "No, Marks is right. Changing the answers wouldn't work. You'd need to compose a new puzzle incorporating your information, and your crossword editor would have to cooperate and allow the switch."

"Which probably means," Johnson said, "that the only person who could do it would be our friend Hector Longstreet. It seems most unlikely that two crossword composers both control a personal editor who does precisely what they demand."

"Just a minute, gentlemen," Pankhurst said. "We're saying two things. We've all agreed that Longstreet is innocent regarding the Rouen raid tonight. But, if a crossword composer is actually leaking information to the Germans, as Melinda Gascombe apparently hinted, then it has to be Hector Longstreet. In other words, we've arrested a criminal before he's had a chance to commit the crime. If he's a criminal. And if he decides to commit a crime."

"Sir," Tupman inquired, "can we try an experiment?"

"What exactly are you asking?"

"Well, sir, suppose we ask Limberg to compose a puzzle in the style of Longstreet and arrange for *The Sunday Intelligencer* to publish it. Ideally it should give away the date and location of some operation, and preferably the code name as well—just like with Operation AMAZON and the Rouen raid tonight. Then we see if the Germans react."

The air commodore looked at Limberg. "Could you do that?"

"You mean compose in the style of Longstreet?"

"Yes."

"Sir, I think it would be better if I just made a few modifications to one of Hector's as yet unpublished crosswords, but to only the clues that relate to the operation. That way, any discrepancy in style could be put down to drawing the Germans' attention to the military intelligence concealed in the puzzle. I'd have to include a foreign place, of course, the location that we're going to attack. And I'd probably include a truly obscure classical reference, like the name of one of the over a hundred lost plays by Sophocles."

"What you're saying," Marks said, "is that the Krauts will know that your crossword contains hidden information from things like accents and foreign cities and classical references."

"Yes, that's what I meant."

"They received Longstreet's puzzle on Sunday," Marks continued. "Suppose that Bridget Hawkesbury solved it for them and that they noted the foreign city and the classical reference, and possibly even the accent. And they interpreted the crossword as meaning that tomorrow night we're going to bomb Rouen."

Turning to face Air Commodore Pankhurst, he said quietly, "Sir, don't you think that you ought to advise Bomber Command to call off the Rouen raid tomorrow night?"

"Marks, do you still agree that the crossword was composed in July?"

"Yes, of course, sir."

"Then why on earth would you want me to call the raid off? I'm absolutely certain that the whole thing is a series of coincidences."

"Yes, but perhaps not the ones you mean, sir."

"Explain."

"Sir, suppose that Longstreet isn't an enemy agent at all, but an extremely nasty British patriot. Remember that Limberg told us that Hector Longstreet never allows foreign languages or foreign places to enter his crosswords; he's a John Bull, a personification of all that is good and great about our country.

"Suppose further that he's somehow made contact with the *Abwehr*, possibly through one of his ex-pupils, and he's told them that he'll send them secret military intelligence via his crosswords. The way they'll know that a specific puzzle contains hidden information is if it contains a classical reference and a reference to a foreign location.

"My guess is that in July he took the greatest pleasure in composing a crossword that would send the Germans off on a wild goose chase. Perhaps as a consequence of that fiasco of a Dieppe raid last July, in which more than half of our six thousand men were killed, wounded or captured, he dreamed up the idea of a fictional air raid on Rouen and embedded the information in a crossword. Yes, sir, there were coincidences, but only three, not four as you suggested at Tuesday's meeting."

"And what were they?"

"The first coincidence was that he used 17-across and 17-down to highlight the imaginary raid, and we've scheduled the air bombardment for tonight, the seventeenth. Actually, December has thirty-one days, giving him a chance of one in thirty-one of getting the date right just by chance."

"And the second?"

"His choice of the name AMAZON for the operation."

"And what was the third coincidence?" Pankhurst asked.

"He selected Rouen as the location for the raid."

"Just a minute, Marks. When Carlyle and Johnson interviewed him, they told him about this evening's raid. If he's such a true-blue patriot, and if he knew that the Germans believe that we're going to bomb Rouen tonight, why didn't he speak up then?"

Johnson raised his hand. "Sir, I suspect that, by successfully warning the Nazis about tonight's raid, he'll acquire great credibility, and the next time he can fool them into doing more than just moving a few antiaircraft weapons around."

"Like convincing them beyond all doubt as to the date and location of the forthcoming invasion of Europe?"

"Precisely, sir," Johnson said.

"What do we do now?"

"Sir, I urge you to call off the Rouen raid. At the very least they need to reschedule it for a different date. And with your permission, sir, Carlyle and I need to pay a visit to Hector Longstreet right now."

CHAPTER SEVEN

Wycombe District, Buckinghamshire, England
Friday, December 17th, 1943

Carlyle and Johnson stood by the battered ancient desk as an MI5 officer ushered Longstreet into the large bare room with the splendid ceiling. They greeted him somewhat coldly. Carlyle suggested that they all sit.

"I understand that you've enjoyed your stay here," Johnson said.

"Yes, indeed, it's been most pleasant. I only wish I could stay longer, but I understand that I have to return to Stragham tomorrow."

"Mr. Longstreet," Carlyle said, "that may not happen. Unless you can completely clear up the matter of last Sunday's crossword puzzle, we're taking you off to jail."

Longstreet glared at him contemptuously as if Johnson were a schoolboy in his Latin class who had failed to identify an ablative absolute. "Have you been drinking?" he demanded to know. "We settled that four days ago."

"You may think you settled the matter, Mr. Longstreet. But we couldn't find any evidence to back up your story."

"Are you insane? I showed you the crossword in my folder. Why didn't you check the register at *The Sunday Intelligencer* and then talk to Melinda Gascombe?"

"We did," Johnson said, "and they don't support your story, any more than your folder does."

Longstreet rolled his eyes. "Unquestionably I am dealing with the two most incompetent investigators in Britain, perhaps in the entire universe. Before I make an official complaint to your elders and betters to ensure that neither of you bunglers will ever be in a position to bother an honest citizen again, perhaps you would be kind enough to explain to me how you arrived at your idiotic conclusion?"

"Mr. Longstreet," Carlyle said, "you've produced rock-solid evidence that indicates that on the fourteenth of July you sent a crossword to *The Sunday Intelligencer*; that the crossword editor forwarded it to Melinda Gascombe; and that she returned it to Enoch Waterson. But we haven't found anything to show that on the fourteenth of July you sent *the crossword in question*. On the contrary, we believe that you composed last Sunday's puzzle as soon as you learned about the Rouen raid, rushed the crossword to London, and ordered your editor to publish it."

"And am I supposed to dignify that load of utter balderdash with a reply?"

"It's entirely up to you," Johnson replied. "But unless you wish to spend the rest of your life in prison for treason in time of war, you probably should respond."

A long silence followed. Then Longstreet said, "Well, what about the letters?"

"The letters?" Johnson asked.

"Yes, the letters, damn it. The insolent letter from that crazy bitch Gascombe suggesting that someone else had composed my puzzle. The letter Waterson sent me because the incompetent fool doesn't have enough brain cells to be able to formulate a coherent response to that moronic woman. And my reply informing him of that fact in no uncertain terms."

"Do you have a copy of any of those letters?"

"A copy? Why should I keep a copy? The letter from Waterson merely confirmed my opinion of his inability to run a meat raffle in a country pub. I've no idea how that inept ignoramus got his job at the newspaper, and even less of an idea how he manages to keep it."

"Yes, you do, Mr. Longstreet," Johnson said firmly.

"How dare you contradict me!"

"We're well aware of your arrangement with the proprietor regarding your accepting lower fees in return for being allowed to appoint your own editor. I think it would make a most amusing story in this Sunday's *Intelligencer*."

"They'd never do such a thing. If such an article were ever to appear in print, that would be the last time I'd let them publish one of my crosswords."

"It would be the last time *any* newspaper published one of your crosswords."

But Longstreet still had some fight left in him.

"You poor ignorant fool, Johnson, don't you know that every other newspaper in Britain is fighting to get my crosswords? It means thousands and thousands more in sales to them."

"Mr. Longstreet, the story in question, which would probably appear on the front page above the fold, would focus on the following clues: 17-across, 17-down, and 4-down. The article would state, without mincing words, that your puzzle revealed to the Germans, well ahead of time, that we were planning to bomb Rouen tonight. It would include an interview with a source in the Air Ministry indicating how many aircraft the Jerries would have shot down and how many Allied lives would have been lost, had we not cancelled the raid at the last minute. Yes, Bomber Command has cancelled Operation AMAZON.

"And after that article has appeared, do you really think that any newspaper anywhere in the world would ever accept a crossword from you? Also, you know full well that the governors of Stragham College would meet that very night and dismiss you on the spot. And do you think that any school, no matter how desperate, would even think of hiring you?

"Most of all, your former pupils whom you've tormented over the past fifty years would be laughing their heads off. The one thing that you cannot tolerate under any circumstances is ridicule, especially public ridicule. In this case, the derision, mockery, and condemnation of a traitor would be nationwide. Or more likely, worldwide."

Longstreet suddenly realized that he had no cards left to play. He started to shake. His whole body shuddered and convulsed. And then he burst into tears. Carlyle and Johnson sat stony-faced and waited. They had both felt bad the previous day when they unintentionally upset Miss Frobisher. But neither felt the slightest qualm of conscience when they saw Hector Longstreet weeping piteously like a schoolboy tormented by his schoolmaster.

Eventually the deep sobbing subsided.

"Mr. Longstreet."

The schoolmaster did not respond, so Carlyle tried again. This time his voice was louder and firmer.

"Mr. Longstreet!"

The man in the chair opposite him looked at him with red eyes.

"Mr. Longstreet, construe: *Et cognoscetis veritatem et veritas liberabit vos.*"

In a shaky voice, still filled with tears, the Classics teacher replied, "'And ye shall know the truth and the truth shall set you free.'"

"Correct. Now identify."

"Vulgate translation of the Bible from Greek into Latin: The Gospel According to John, Chapter Eight, Verse 32."

Carlyle nodded, and then waited for a few seconds before continuing.

"Mr. Longstreet, we're prepared to make a deal with you. If you're willing to tell us the truth and cooperate with us fully, no one will ever know what you've done."

"Yes, yes, I'll do whatever you say. What do you want from me?"

"Two things. First, a full confession. And I mean the truth, the whole truth, and nothing but the truth. Including all the details regarding your consorting with the enemy."

"You know about that?"

"We know everything," Carlyle said. "Then, once you've confessed in detail, we'll ask you from time to time to compose a puzzle for us. We'll tell you the answers we want you to include in the grid. And then you'll set appropriate clues involving foreign places and classical references."

At this, Longstreet's mouth fell open. He was unable to speak for a while. Then he said hoarsely, "You know about that, too?"

"As I just told you," Carlyle said, "we know everything. And if you lie to us, two things will happen. You'll go to jail for the rest of your life, and *The Sunday Intelligencer* will tell the world why. Do you understand me?"

"Yes." His voice revealed that Hector Longstreet was a broken man.

"Start at the beginning."

"You mean when I bumped into Rudolf Walton?"

"Yes," Carlyle said, "start then."

"Well, you know what happened in the train."

"Mr. Longstreet, perhaps I was a little unclear. We require a full and detailed confession from you, omitting nothing and concealing nothing."

"Yes, I see. Well, one day I took the train to London. I was on my way to the British Museum to see the newly opened Duveen Gallery displaying the Elgin Marbles, and that means it must have been in the summer of 1938. Seated opposite me in the compartment was a face I recognized. I never forget the name of any of the pupils I've taught. And I certainly hadn't forgotten Rudolf Walton in the twelve years since he left the school.

"You see, unlike almost all other the boys I've taught at Stragham College, Walton is intelligent and creative. I took a particularly strong dislike to him when I learned that he despised Classics and intended to waste his God-given gifts writing novels. Novels!

"He recognized me, too. We politely exchanged pleasantries. Then I asked him what he was doing. He said that he'd just published his fifth spy thriller. Now, novels are bad enough, but spy thrillers! For a moment, I wondered if he'd said that just to annoy me, but the look on his face was perfectly innocent. We maintained a dignified silence for the rest of the journey. When we reached London, I shook hands with him and wished him well.

"I spent two glorious hours in the Museum in thrall to the matchless statues of Phidias. But on my way home on the train, I started thinking about Walton and wondering why he was wasting his life writing spy thrillers when he could do something worthwhile, like composing crosswords. And then the thought struck me that perhaps I could do my country a service by combining spies and crosswords.

"Like all intelligent people, I knew that war was inevitable after Hitler marched into the Sudetenland in March 1938. And I wanted to serve my country. I knew I couldn't fight, of course, but I could certainly use my skills as a crossword composer to fool the enemy. And another idea came to me: perhaps I could feed false information to the Germans via a puzzle.

"A week later I contacted Sir Herbert Sically, one of the governors of Stragham College. Sir Herbert is an avid hunter. He never stops telling people that he once went to shoot foxes in East Prussia, where he met Hermann Göring, *Reichsminister* of Aviation and Commander-in-Chief of the *Luftwaffe*. They hit it off so well that Göring invited Sir Herbert to become a member of the *Deutsche Jägerschaft*, the German Hunting Brotherhood.

"I wrote to Sir Herbert and asked him if he could arrange for me to meet with Prince Ludwig von Hesse-Darmstadt, the German honorary cultural attaché in Britain, to discuss crossword cooperation between Germany and Britain. Ten days later I found myself in a room in the Germany Embassy at Number 9, Carlton House Terrace. Prince Ludwig was quite charming until I told him the real purpose of my visit. At that point, he rose and asked me to accompany him. I gathered from his sudden coldness that he didn't like the concept of espionage.

"He took me to Captain Albrecht Soltmann, the Assistant Military Attaché, and then excused himself. I explained to Captain Soltmann that I was a strong admirer of Hitler. I quoted verbatim two or three times from a copy of *Mein Kampf* that I'd bought at a second-hand bookshop in Charing Cross Road, and that seemed to be enough to satisfy him regarding my unconditional commitment to Nazism.

"Next, I informed him that one of my former pupils was attached to the Imperial General Staff. But then I claimed that he shared my disillusion with Britain as a whole and British values in particular, and that he would pass classified information on to me so that I could incorporate top-secret military intelligence into the answers of my crosswords. All the Germans had to do was look through the clues for a classical reference and a mention of a location outside Britain. If both were present, they should solve the puzzle and extract the information I'd provided. Soltmann said that this was an excellent idea, and that we should keep in touch.

"On the train back to Stragham, I suddenly realized how stupid my plan was. People whose first language is English almost always find my puzzles hard to solve, even after many years of practice. How could I expect Germans, who had no experience of cryptic puzzles, to be able to find the answers to my clues? Captain Soltmann had clearly been humoring me.

"Then another thought struck me. In order to ingratiate myself with Captain Soltmann, I'd declared myself to be a fascist and an unbridled admirer of Adolf Hitler. Sir Herbert had given my name and address to the embassy to arrange my meeting with Prince Ludwig. That meant that the Germans had proof that Hector Longstreet was a Nazi sympathizer. How long would it take for that information to reach MI5? When a war breaks out, all enemy aliens are interned. Would I be treated that way, too? And if I were arrested, would anyone believe my story? Probably not—it was too unlikely to possibly be true.

"And how would my puzzles reach the Germans? Once hostilities commenced, travel of all kinds between Germany and Britain would cease. Perhaps they would send newspapers by mail. But that would be too slow; the false information hidden in my crosswords would be out of date before the Germans could use it. Accordingly, I resolved to put the whole incident behind me, and I made up my mind to try as best I could to forget that I'd ever done anything that stupid.

"Then, after the war started, three things happened. First, in my capacity as president of the British Cruciverbalist Society, I learned that the Germans had interned Bridget Hawkesbury. The irony didn't escape me. I'd feared, for good reason, that my own people would lock me up as a fascist supporter. Instead the Germans put Bridget in a civilian prison camp while I went scot-free. Perhaps, I thought, they might come up with some pretext that would encourage her to solve my puzzle every week, without telling her that one day they'd use her solution to a crossword against her own country. Of course, the whole idea was that I would feed false information to the Krauts, but neither they nor Bridget would be aware of that.

"Then I read about the amazing coincidence. As I'm sure you know, on the seventeenth of August last year, two days before the disastrous Dieppe raid, the word **DIEPPE** was the answer to a clue in *The Daily Telegraph* crossword. That really shook me. I was sure that the Nazis knew about that, too, and perhaps Captain Soltmann would remember my meeting with him and the plan I'd put forward.

"Finally, I learned that every day they fly a few copies of the early edition of the major British newspapers, including *The Sunday Intelligencer*, to Portugal. That meant that I could put my plan into action. You must believe me that I made up the name Operation AMAZON for a nonexistent air raid on Rouen."

"Yes, we're aware of that. As a matter of interest, why did you choose that name?" Carlyle asked.

"I needed a classical reference because, as you know, that was one of the two signposts to alert the Germans that I had hidden military secrets in the puzzle. I thought of Bridget. She knew that I was the first person who'd used the word 'flower' in a clue to refer to a river. In case they asked her, she could assure them that I had indeed composed the puzzle."

"Thank you. Would you please continue?" Carlyle said.

"Certainly. In July, I composed a puzzle in which I hid the words **ROUEN**, **RAID**, and **AMAZON** and sent it off to Waterson at the newspaper. I had no idea when it would be published. And nor did I care, of course—I was alerting the enemy to a nonexistent raid to waste their efforts and fuel in moving military equipment to the wrong place, and hopefully weakening them elsewhere.

"Then the Special Branch men came to arrest me. In the car, I decided that the best way to handle the questions that I feared I was about to face regarding my visit to the German Embassy in 1938 was righteous indignation at the stupidity of the police arresting an innocent citizen."

"Are you saying that your anger was all an act?"

"Only partly. The rage I exhibited towards the two of you—for which I sincerely apologize—was put on. But I was genuinely incensed with myself, at *my* stupidity at what I had done. Consequently, it was easy for me to direct my anger against you. Also, I admit that I frequently lose my temper in the classroom. As a result, feigning fury towards the two of you wasn't hard; anger is an emotion with which I am all too familiar.

"When you informed me that my nonexistent raid on Rouen was genuine in every way, I knew that I should have confessed everything, but I was terrified that you wouldn't believe the truth, just as no one initially believed that the **DIEPPE** answer in *The Daily Telegraph* crossword last year was pure coincidence. And I might have had to tell you about my visit to the German Embassy in 1938. Believing that attack is the best form of defense, I increased the level of my anger."

"But weren't you concerned that we might believe that you knew nothing about the Rouen raid and allow it to proceed, with immense loss of life, never mind the scarce planes destroyed?" Johnson inquired.

"I was too concerned about myself to think that far ahead. My sole concern was to convince you that I had indeed composed the puzzle in July. I'm sorry."

Johnson and Carlyle exchanged looks. Carlyle nodded.

"Mr. Longstreet," Johnson said, "tomorrow they'll drive you back to Upper Stragham. They'll return all your possessions to your room in Mrs. Bunting's house in Thornhill Street. Furthermore, you may tell anyone who asks that while you were away you were doing work for the government, but you're to give no details of any kind—not that anyone would ask that sort of thing these days. Is that understood?"

"Yes."

"I have here a copy of the Official Secrets Act 1939. I require you to read it and initial each page to indicate that you have done so. Then you are to read and sign this document, which states that you agree to abide by the restrictions of the Official Secrets Act. Take your time."

Longstreet took a pair of spectacles out of an inside pocket. One lens was cracked; both were smeared with grime. Then he took a fountain pen out of another pocket, unscrewed the cap, placed it on the back of the pen, and laid the pen carefully on the large wooden desk. Finally, he held his hand out to Johnson for the documents. Having read, initialed, and signed as instructed, Longstreet returned the papers to Johnson. Then the elderly schoolmaster replaced his pen and glasses in their respective jacket pockets.

"Now, Mr. Longstreet," Johnson said, "I wish to officially inform you that every aspect of this matter is Most Secret. You are not to talk to anyone about it, and especially not to the members of the British Cruciverbalist Society. If someone exhibits undue curiosity of any kind, contact us at once; the telephone number is printed on this card. If you lose it, you can get hold of us via your local police station, of course.

"Next, you need to be aware that the government may require your services at any time to compose a puzzle to our specifications. To this end, we need you to provide us with a list of the reference books you use to compose crosswords. If any of them aren't in the library here, we'll acquire them for you. And you'll also have a typewriter at your disposal.

"When we bring you here, you'll need to be able to get to work right away. Always remember that we won't be able to hold the presses at *The Intelligencer* while waiting for you to finish composing a crossword."

Longstreet nodded as Johnson continued.

"We'll make your headmaster and the governors of the school fully aware that the war effort needs you, and I'm sure that they'll be most cooperative in every way. In fact, I believe that, as far as Stragham College is concerned, you're going come out of this with greatly enhanced stature. I think you'll find that the whole school will treat you with genuine respect."

Johnson had to bite his tongue to prevent him adding the words *until the salutary effect of this interview wears off and you start being nasty to everyone again.*

CHAPTER EIGHT

MI5 Headquarters, London
Saturday, December 18th, 1943

"Gentlemen, the Prime Minister has assigned a new task to us. At the Tehran Conference held about two weeks ago in the Soviet Embassy in Persia, Mr. Churchill, President Roosevelt, and Marshal Stalin decided that the invasion of Europe across the English Channel is going to take place next summer. They've confirmed the appointment of General Eisenhower as commander of SHAEF, the Supreme Headquarters Allied Expeditionary Force. The current plan is to land in the French province of Normandy, whereas Hitler believes that we're going to invade a different province, the Pas-de-Calais, which is situated directly opposite the Straits of Dover and is therefore the area of France closest to Britain.

"Now, gentlemen, bear with me while I impart secret information to Limberg that you're all familiar with: MI5 controls all the German spies in Britain."

From the look of surprise on her face, it was clear that Senior Commander Limberg had been completely unaware of the situation. The Air Commodore continued explaining to her.

"We believe that we've captured every single spy that the *Abwehr*, the German military intelligence agency, has sent to Britain before or during the war. Several of them surrendered as soon as they landed in our country, and almost all the others quickly gave themselves away by making the most elementary mistakes. The standard of training of spies in the *Abwehr* is deplorably low, thank heavens, and most of the agents they send here are quite stupid.

"If we think that a captured *Abwehr* agent could be of some use to us, we give him a choice: execution or becoming a double agent. Almost all choose to betray their country—most spies are craven cowards. Currently our Double-Cross System controls thirty-seven agents who regularly transmit messages by radio to Nazi Germany. I know it's hard to believe, but the Germans haven't cottoned on to the fact that we composed every word of every single report, without exception, that they've received from their agents in Britain. Our messages consist of a mixture of irrelevant facts; information that we know the Germans already have; critically important information, such as the date of an assault, but delivered too late to be of any use to them; and disinformation. And that's where you come in, Limberg."

She nodded in acknowledgment.

"In addition to the agents that the *Abwehr* sends to Britain equipped with radios for transmitting reports back to Germany, they also have the PICKFORD network, the one we set up."

Seeing the men exchanging glances, Senior Commander Limberg listened extremely carefully to what the air commodore said next.

"In mid-1937, an MI5 officer, calling himself PICKFORD, sent a package to the German consul in Edinburgh containing the plans for the Muir bombsight. Of course, we knew that they already had the detailed blueprints; the idea was to establish in the minds of the Nazis the existence of a British traitor willing and able to supply Germany with top-quality information. Over the next two years, several equally valuable packages arrived at the Edinburgh consulate. Then, just before the war broke out, we sent a radio message to the *Abwehr*, ostensibly from agent PICKFORD, asking them to send him an assistant. Someone in the *Abwehr* got confused and, in his response, referred to the agent as 'Pickwick.' That gave us an idea—in PICKFORD's reply, he insisted that his new assistant's code name had to be a character from the works of Charles Dickens. The network has been so successful that the *Abwehr* people keep sending subagents to Britain to help PICKFORD. Arresting them is then child's play because they tell PICKFORD precisely when and where the new subagent will arrive. We interrogate them and, after we've learned everything that they're prepared to tell us, we hang them.

"Every day or two, PICKFORD sends a lengthy radio message to Berlin, incorporating the information he's obtained from his many Dickens subagents—I think that by now he has at least twenty-three. Of course, the subagents that the *Abwehr* have sent here are all dead, and the subagents that PICKFORD has recruited in Britain are figments of MI5's imagination. We have a whole team of officers whose sole job is to compose the PICKFORD bulletins, checking that nothing contradicts any earlier reports from his many subagents, and ensuring that we don't accidentally give away secret information. Best of all, we know with certainty that Admiral Canaris, the head of the *Abwehr*, believes every word that PICKFORD transmits, and almost all his staff are equally credulous."

"Sir, how do we know that?"

"Senior Commander Limberg," Pankhurst replied in a surprisingly mild voice, "this is your fifth day on my team. If you intend to be back here for a sixth day, you'd better not ask any more questions like that."

Her peaches and cream complexion reddened to a deep shade of crimson. "I'm terribly sorry, sir. It won't happen again, sir."

"It had better not. I'm sure that you appreciate the fact that if you were cleared to know that information I'd have answered your question before you asked it. The fact that I didn't should have told you something."

"Yes, sir." Her cheeks were starting to return to her normal color, but she looked mortified.

"Limberg, we have two ways to send deceptive information to Germany by radio: via the double agents, or in agent PICKFORD's regular reports. If

Hitler and his minions absolutely have to believe an item of disinformation, we need to use PICKFORD."

Tupman put up his hand. "Sir, don't we have a possible third way? What about Hector Longstreet and his crosswords?"

"Well, after the cancellation of last night's raid, will they believe him in the future, assuming that they're even checking his puzzles?"

"Sir, this morning before the meeting, I contacted the Met Office. Heavy cloud shrouded Normandy all of last night, including Rouen. Typical winter weather. Bomber Command would've had to cancel the air strike in any event; our bombardiers wouldn't have been able to see the railway lines. Consequently, Longstreet's credibility is probably unchanged. Regarding your point as to whether they even look at his puzzles, let alone examine them carefully for military intelligence, that's something we don't know. Maybe we should run a trial."

"Such as what, Tupman?" Pankhurst asked. "If you warn the Germans that we're about to do something, they'll be there in full force, which we certainly don't want. And if we tell them about a nonexistent operation, they'll never believe Longstreet in the future."

"Sir, let me think about that."

"Yes, do that," Pankhurst said. "It's a good idea, so see if you can come up with something. Now let's return to our current problem. As I said, Hitler is convinced that we're going to attack the Pas-de-Calais, whereas we're actually planning on invading Normandy. This raises two issues. First, the Allies have to ensure that, from now on until the moment we land on the beach in Normandy, Hitler continues to be absolutely certain that the target is the Pas-de-Calais. Second, once we've landed in Normandy, Eisenhower requires at least three days to establish a lodgement, and preferably longer. During that time, Hitler has to believe that the invasion of Normandy is a feint, a diversionary attack designed to decoy his forces away from the Pas-de-Calais. If at any time he starts to realize that Normandy is the real target, he'll send in his mobile reserves located in the area, especially tanks. If they were to arrive at the landing beaches during those first three days, they'll wipe out every last man on the ground, and I anticipate that means at least a hundred and fifty thousand soldiers, probably tens of thousands more than that. The disaster will delay the end of the war by at least a year, more likely two.

"In particular, Hitler has placed several large tank formations around Paris and Rouen for deployment in the relevant part of the Pas-de-Calais when the invasion starts in that area. We have to make sure that Hitler orders all those tanks to stay firmly put during the Normandy invasion so that he can bring them into action when what he believes to be the actual invasion begins somewhere in the Pas-de-Calais.

"At the Tehran Conference, 'The Big Three' decided that the code name for the invasion plan is to be Operation OVERLORD. They also decided to draw up a deception plan, Operation BODYGUARD, with the objective of misleading Hitler with regard to both the time and the place of the invasion. Our task is to come up with ideas that we'll forward to the steering committee.

"Well, gentlemen. How do we fool Hitler?"

No one said anything for more than a minute. Then Senior Commander Limberg raised her hand.

"Sir, about three months ago at the headquarters of the Royal Corps of Signals we had a visit from a colonel who said he'd been one of the planners for Operation HUSKY."

"You mean our highly successful invasion of Sicily last July? It took only a month to drive all Axis forces off the island and reopen the sea lanes in the Mediterranean."

"Yes, sir. Well, sir, that evening in the officers' mess, the visiting colonel tried to seduce me. His technique was to try to impress me with how brilliant he is. He told me that during the invasion of Sicily the Allies had only a fraction of the anticipated casualties because of a clever stratagem he'd thought up and carried out. According to him, he arranged for the Royal Air Force to drop the body of a dead British officer from a plane just off the coast of Portugal. It floated ashore. The local German agent got to hear of it and discovered that the officer had a briefcase chained to his wrist. The *Abwehr* officer bribed various Portuguese officials to get his hands on that briefcase. Inside it he found plans for our invasion of Greece, with a feint against Sicily. He forwarded the plans to Berlin. As a result, Hitler fortified Greece as strongly as he could, leaving Sicily relatively undefended. When we attacked Sicily, we also attacked Greece, but that was only a feint. As a result,

Hitler continued to believe that the real attack was the one against Greece, and he didn't send any reinforcements to Sicily until it was far too late, which is why it fell within a month.

"I didn't know what to say to the colonel. It sounded as if he might have been revealing military secrets to impress me. Consequently, I excused myself and went to bed, and the next morning I reported him, just as a precaution. Four days later I was ordered to go to London to give evidence at a closed court-martial where I testified as to what the colonel had told me. I've no idea what happened subsequently. The only reason I've mentioned this incident at this meeting is that one approach might be to drop the body of a dead British officer from a plane off the coast of France with a briefcase containing plans for an assault on the Pas-de-Calais, with a feint against Normandy."

Another long silence followed, this time because the air commodore was trying to decide how to respond to her. Eventually he came to a decision. "At his court-martial, Colonel Digby-Smith tried to argue that he hadn't violated the Official Secrets Act because he'd changed many of the facts regarding the deceptive operation. It didn't help him; he's been reduced in the ranks to private and is serving a five-year sentence in a military prison.

"Limberg, it's going to be a few more days before you'll be cleared to know what really happened, so let me just make some remarks. As an expert in disinformation, you're well aware that a critical factor when evaluating the reliability of a document is its provenance. If a German agent in Portugal had come home and found a briefcase lying on his doorstep containing detailed plans for an invasion of, say, Greece, with a feint against Sicily, without a doubt the *Abwehr* would've advised Hitler that this was a British disinformation trick. Furthermore, the Germans would probably have deduced that the reason why we dropped the plan into their laps was that the real attack was to be against Sicily, with a feint against Greece. Consequently, Limberg, we would never put plans inside a briefcase for the Germans to find.

"On the other hand, what we might have done, if we'd actually carried out such an operation, would be to put a personal letter from one senior staff officer to another senior staff officer in a briefcase, and allowed the Germans to deduce from hints in the contents of the letter that we were about to invade Greece with a feint against Sicily. For example, we might have included a clumsy reference to grease, knowing that the Germans expect us to make excruciatingly weak puns whenever possible.

"As you also know, the best disinformation is the kind that reinforces what the enemy already believes. For example, if we knew that Hitler and his inner circle were pretty sure that we were on the point of invading Greece, and for various reasons they thought that an invasion of Sicily was unlikely, then a deception along the lines I've outlined might have been successful. Successful beyond our wildest dreams, in fact.

"Now, suppose that, as Colonel Digby-Smith suggested to you that night, we dropped a dead body out of a plane off the coast of Portugal to fool the Germans and it floated ashore. Not all Nazis are fools. In fact, some of them are very clever indeed. Consequently, if you were now to arrange for the body of a second British officer to drift inshore, this time off the coast of France, I strongly suspect that the Krauts will smell a rat. In fact, I'm certain that they'll jump to exactly the right conclusion. That is, they'll deduce that we intend to invade Normandy, with a feint attack in the Pas-de-Calais."

Once more a long silence ensued. Then Squadron Leader Harkness spoke up.

"Sir, in my opinion the key issue is provenance. If we can arrange for disinformation to fall in the hands of the Germans in such a way that no *Abwehr* officer can possibly claim that we planted it, it'll be believed."

"I agree, Harkness, but perfect provenance is all but impossible to achieve."

"Certainly, sir. But we can try to make it as near perfect as possible."

"What exactly do you have in mind?"

"Well, sir, dead bodies tend to pose a problem. If you float a body ashore, it has to appear to have drowned. If the person actually died in, say, a road accident, even the most clueless of doctors performing the post mortem will surely be able to detect that we're up to something. Now, bodies of drowned military officers are pretty thin on the ground. But, sadly, road accidents do happen. Perhaps we could do a parachute drop of one such road victim. To the Germans, it will appear that the soldier died as a result of a bad fall from a plane."

"Harkness, how are you going to guarantee that the body is going to fall into the hands of the Germans? After all, the body may end up in a field. Suppose that a farmer finds the body, searches it, finds the secret information, and then does everything he can to get the papers into our hands or the hands of the Free French, which is just what we don't want."

"I have an idea," Lieutenant Commander Chulmleigh said. "Suppose we drop the body in an area where a Resistance group is active. Once the corpse has hit the ground, a member of the group runs to the police to report what's happened. The police call in the German military, and the first individuals who touch the body are German soldiers. Perfect provenance!"

Yet again no one said anything for a long while. Then Major Tupman spoke up.

"Sir, one of the oldest French Resistance groups operates in the vicinity of Saint-Auban-sûr-Lot. I know about it because an elderly cousin of mine lives in the village. The local schoolmaster, a man named Jean-Michel, founded the group. The Free French provided them with a radio. And it's a good thing they did, because that was the group that obtained the plans of Operation BARBAROSSA twenty-four hours before the invasion. Mr. Churchill tried to warn Uncle Joe Stalin that Hitler was about to break the Molotov–Ribbentrop Non-Aggression Treaty and invade the Soviet Union, but Stalin wouldn't listen. Shortly after their success, someone betrayed Jean-Michel and his radio operator to the Germans. The rest of the group managed to evade capture. Somehow or other they obtained another radio, and they've been sending information to us from time to time. Their leader is a man called François."

CHAPTER NINE

Abwehr *Headquarters, Berlin*
Saturday, December 18th, 1943

"Colonel Donndorf," Admiral Canaris, head of the *Abwehr*, said to his aide, "I've just flown back from *Herr* Hitler's headquarters in Rastenberg in East Prussia. The *Führer* has assigned a new and most important task to the *Abwehr*. As we both know, Churchill, Roosevelt, and Stalin met about two weeks ago in Tehran. Our spies in Persia learned that 'The Big Three' agreed that planning is to continue for the cross-channel invasion of Europe scheduled to take place in May. They confirmed General Eisenhower as commander of the Supreme Headquarters Allied Expeditionary Force, or SHAEF as they call it. Churchill and Roosevelt first agreed to this invasion of Europe at the Third Washington Conference—that was in May this year. At that time, *Herr* Hitler decided that this was mere bravado, a stunt designed to raise the spirits of the people of Britain. After all, our *Luftwaffe* has bombed them into all but total submission. But in the last two weeks, virtually every message our spies in Britain have sent us has contained references to a forthcoming assault on Europe. The *Führer* has therefore ordered us to answer this question: When and where are the Allies going to invade?"

Canaris paused to collect his thoughts. Donndorf said nothing, but his long, manicured fingers idly adjusted the position of the rimless monocle set in his right eye socket. A thin black cord passed through a hole near the corner of the glass and looped around his neck.

"The precise date of the invasion is important, of course, but not quite as vital as the location. Once we know where the assault will take place, we can heavily fortify the area, bring in masses of troops and weapons of all kinds, and then wait. But where will they attack?

"Our agents in Britain have provided us with a large quantity of information. It all points in the same direction: the invasion will take place in the Pas-de-Calais. The target makes perfect sense militarily. The Pas-de-Calais is situated directly opposite the Straits of Dover and is therefore the area of France that's closest to Britain. The English Channel is notoriously rough, and the shorter the distance that their troops have to cross, the easier it'll be for them. Also, the region has several good ports, including Calais and Boulogne—and possibly even Étaples—that they can use to bring in men, vehicles, and supplies to support the invasion. That's unlike the situation in, say, Normandy, which has no harbors that an invading force can use.

"Of course, the Allies will carry out feint attacks against other targets, to try to fool the *Führer* into moving his forces away from the Pas-de-Calais. For example, *Herr* Hitler expects assaults against Belgium and also elsewhere in France, including Bordeaux and the French Riviera.

"One idea of his is that the British will direct a major diversionary onslaught against Dunkirk, for emotional reasons. He thinks that they'll bomb the Dunkirk area and launch commando attacks in the vicinity, in the hope that we'll fall for their stratagem and move our tanks and the rest of our mobile strategic reserve over to Dunkirk. Once we've fallen for their trick, they'll attack a relatively undefended area of the Pas-de-Calais.

"He's also concerned that, simultaneously with the invasion of France, the allies will also invade Norway. With two landings, the *Führer* will have to split his defensive forces. As a result, it's even more vital that we make no mistake in determining where the invasion or invasions will take place to enable us to concentrate our limited resources on precisely those locations."

"I understand, Admiral. But what if we get it wrong?"

"That's the whole point, Donndorf. And therein lies the genius of *Herr* Hitler's plan. Everyone knows about the Atlantic Wall. The men constructing it are valiant 'volunteers,' forced laborers from the conquered territories. The Wall stretches from the northernmost tip of Norway, along the Atlantic coasts of Norway, Denmark, and northern Germany, and then along the coast of France all the way to the Spanish border. Well, the *Führer* has informed the world that the Wall will repel any Allied invader. Yes, it's true that we've laid numerous underwater landing craft obstructions and we've placed hordes of antitank obstacles on the sand. Further up the beach, an invading force will encounter reinforced concrete pillboxes with machine guns and antitank guns, and even light artillery. Behind them are fortified gun emplacements. And we've laid mines in the water and on the beaches; we've constructed forests of sharpened metal poles in places where paratroopers or gliders might land; and we've flooded estuaries and low-lying rivers, ideal areas for an Allied sea-borne landing."

"That all sounds excellent."

"Yes, Donndorf, it certainly sounds excellent. In practice, however, we're facing some serious problems. First and foremost, the Atlantic Wall is nowhere near complete yet. Also, *Herr* Hitler has decreed that one-twelfth of the steel and concrete used in the Atlantic Wall has to go to the Channel Islands. Now I understand the motivation behind his decision. The islands are the only area of Britain that we control, and from a propaganda viewpoint, the *Führer* will not allow the British to recapture them. But one glance at the map will convince you that the Allies can simply bypass the Channel Islands—they're of no strategic importance at all. Finally, and most important of all, even when we've completed the Atlantic Wall defenses, by themselves they'll be inadequate. The only way we can hold off an allied invasion is if those tanks and the other mobile strategic reserve units I mentioned to you can be brought to bear to fight off the enemy before they can establish a lodgement on the landing beach."

"And that means that we have to know for certain where the Allies are going to invade—the real assault I mean, not the feints."

"Precisely, Donndorf. But suppose we can persuade the British and Americans not to invade in 1944, but rather to wait a year. During that year we can fortify the Atlantic Wall, and Europe will become impregnable. The *Reich* will indeed last a thousand years!"

"But Admiral, you've just told me that two weeks ago in Tehran the Allies agreed to invade in May. How can we possibly expect them to wait another year?"

"That's another aspect of the brilliance of the *Führer*'s plan. If we can make them believe that the Atlantic Wall is complete and fully fortified, it will take them another year to build up a sufficiently large army in Britain to cross the English Channel and successfully invade Europe. And by that time, the Atlantic Wall will indeed be impregnable.

"On the other hand, if they don't believe our disinformation then they'll invade. And if we can determine where that will be, we'll cut them down on the landing beach. Either way, the invasion will fail.

"And the reason that the *Führer* met with me today was to charge the *Abwehr* with two tasks. We have to determine with absolute certainty where the actual landing will take place, so that the *Führer* will know where not to respond to feints. And we need to convince the Allies that the Atlantic Wall is impregnable. From aerial reconnaissance, they obviously know the places where we haven't even started to build the Wall, but our Army will soon solve that problem by constructing defenses along the entire length of the French Atlantic coast. It'll certainly take time for us to build sufficient reinforced concrete gun emplacements that can withstand intense Allied bombing, time that we don't have. And we don't have enough of the necessary materials, either. But we can transport enough slave laborers from the concentration camps to the French coast to construct wooden buildings covered in a thin layer of cement designed to look like reinforced concrete gun emplacements. My point is this: if we can succeed in just one of the two tasks, Germany will win the war.

"By the way,' Admiral Canaris added, "perhaps I shouldn't have used the term 'slave laborers'—a directive came through last month informing us that the correct term is *Gastarbeitnehmer* (guest workers)."

Colonel Donndorf thought it would be safest to ignore that last remark and instead respond to the matter at hand. "Admiral, the first task, finding the place where the Allies intend to invade, is relatively easy. All we have to do is continue to analyze the reports we receive from our two sets of agents in Britain."

"Just how many do we have now, Donndorf?"

"Well, Admiral, if I recall correctly we currently receive radio messages, usually once a week, from thirty-seven agents. And then we have agent PICKFORD. I believe that he has twenty-three subagents reporting to him. After we've won the war, I certainly intend to go to England and meet him."

"Or her."

"Her, Admiral?"

"Yes, Donndorf, her. Remember that I once told you that your predecessor, Colonel Tobler, thought that agent PICKFORD is a woman. We don't have a photograph of PICKFORD in his personal file. In fact, we don't even have a personal file, because we know absolutely nothing about him. Or her. When I asked Tobler why he thought that PICKFORD was a female, he replied, 'Intuition.' That's not how we operate in the *Abwehr*. Nevertheless, I respect Tobler and his views. Maybe he's right. But it doesn't matter. What's important is that for years now agent PICKFORD has sent us regular reports that time after time have proved to be correct. Not in every single minor detail, of course. But the key points of his radio messages have been absolutely invaluable to us."

"Yes, indeed, Admiral. And that's why I said that determining where the landings will actually take place should be straightforward. And we may have a third conduit for acquiring information from the British."

"Oh? And what's that?"

"As you know, plenty of British people support *Herr* Hitler. I'm not referring to the riff-raff in the British National Socialist Party led by Forbes Penthwick—they're just street fighters of the worst kind. What I'm talking about are the intellectuals. Unfortunately, the British have arrested almost all of them and put them in jail or internment camps. But a few somehow escaped the dragnet, including a teacher of Latin and Greek named Hector Longstreet. His hobby is composing crossword puzzles.

"Longstreet visited our embassy in London in 1938, promising to use his crosswords to pass on information from a contact of his on the Imperial General Staff who shares his views. It's all in the file here. It seems that Captain Albrecht Soltmann, the Assistant Military Attaché who met with Longstreet, was suspicious that he might be an MI5 agent trying to plant disinformation; his story seemed too fantastic to be credible. So Soltmann arranged for a private detective who'd previously done work for the embassy to perform a detailed background check on Longstreet. The investigator was able to confirm everything that Longstreet had said. The detective even discovered a former pupil of Longstreet's on the Imperial General Staff."

"Why have we never followed through on this most promising conduit?"

"But we have, Admiral. I won't bore you with the details, but we've been monitoring Longstreet's crosswords and have so far found just one with hidden military intelligence. He informed us that the British had scheduled a bombing raid on Rouen for last night."

"I don't seem to recall any such raid, Donndorf."

"No, Admiral, it never took place. The cloud cover over that part of France was one hundred percent the whole night; the British planes couldn't possibly see the ground from the air, and they had no choice but to cancel the raid. Of course, we were ready for them. We brought in every mobile anti-aircraft weapon we could, and we emptied the railway marshalling yards."

"Do you think they'll try again tonight?"

"Perhaps, Admiral. Our air defenses will be staying in place for another few days, just in case. But maybe they have a different target already lined up. And we can't bypass the Rouen rail complex indefinitely. It's a wait-and-see situation. But at least we know that Longstreet is operational. Perhaps we should pay Mr. Longstreet a visit and tell him what information we need."

"That sounds like a good idea. Should we ask agent PICKFORD to send a subagent to meet with him?"

"I've looked through the file. The private detective stated in his report to Captain Soltmann that Longstreet is arrogant and self-opinionated, and does precisely what he wants to do."

"Would a honey trap work?"

"You mean sending a beautiful woman to ensnare Longstreet in a compromising situation? I wouldn't advise that approach, Admiral. The investigator wrote that Longstreet is totally asexual, what the British call 'a cold fish,' so nothing along those lines would work. And it's likely to be counterproductive. Instead, we have to find a way to make him want to obtain details of the forthcoming invasion and send them to us. I have an idea, and with your permission, I'd like to think it through for a day or two."

"By all means, Donndorf. Go ahead, but keep me informed. This could be the key to saving Germany. But what about our second task? How do you propose to fool the Allies into believing that the Atlantic Wall is as impenetrable and unassailable as the *Führer* claims?"

Colonel Donndorf thought for a moment. "Admiral, that's a lot harder. But I've had an idea. Do you remember that, at the end of April, a British plane en route from London to Gibraltar crashed just off the coast of Spain, near the town of Huelva? The body of a British officer, a Major William Martin if I remember correctly, drifted to shore. A leather-covered chain was looped around the belt of his trench coat and the other end was fastened to a briefcase.

"We eventually managed to get hold of the briefcase; *Abwehr* officers in Spain had to bribe the relevant officials. Inside the briefcase were three letters. Our people in Madrid managed to extract the letters without breaking the official wax seals on the envelopes; they wound the paper around a narrow probe that they inserted in the gap under the top of the flap. They copied the letters and then carefully re-inserted them into their respective envelopes. The British couldn't possibly tell that we'd read the letters, so we returned the briefcase and its contents to the Spanish authorities. They followed the relevant international law appertaining to the belongings of deceased foreign nationals in neutral countries and handed the briefcase to the British military attaché. That was fully two weeks after the air crash.

"One letter was important. It was a personal communication from Lieutenant General Sir Archibald Nye, Vice Chief of the Imperial General

Staff, to General Sir Harold Alexander, commander of the Eighteenth Army Group in Algeria and Tunisia. We deduced from that letter that the Allies were going to invade Greece and Sardinia, with a feint toward Sicily. The letter explicitly mentioned Greece and included a clumsy reference to sardines—hence Sardinia."

"But the invasion of Sicily turned out to be the real thing," Admiral Canaris remarked.

"Yes. We think that they changed the whole plan around because, immediately after the crash, the Allies feared that we'd acquired the briefcase and read the letters. After all, they had more than two months in which to reorganize."

"Donndorf, in your opinion, could the whole affair have been a British disinformation operation?"

"Admiral, I don't think that's the case. I firmly believe that the letter from the one general to his friend was genuine. After all, the other letters that the dead officer had in his briefcase tied in with and supported the important one, even the one from his fiancée. Also, it's unlikely that MI5 could have collected the stuff they found in Major Martin's pockets. It included a photograph of his bride-to-be, two love letters, a bill from a jeweler for an expensive engagement ring, a letter from his bank manager regarding his overdraft, and a paid bill from the club where he stayed. We even found a letter from his father, written from some hotel in Wales. And there was more. Let me think now. Oh yes, a book of stamps, a St. Christopher medal, and a silver cross.

And stubs from theatre tickets, keys, a bus ticket—the list goes on and on."

"But the British could have assembled those items," Canaris insisted.

"True. But they all fitted together so seamlessly. Major Martin's identity card was a replacement for the one he'd lost. He hadn't renewed his headquarters pass—it had expired. In other words, this was a careless man, one who bought an expensive engagement ring despite an overdraft."

"Again, the British could have put all the pieces together."

"Admiral, I can only suggest with the greatest respect that you get the files and read the various letters. I believe you'll find that everything seems to be part of a genuine whole."

"I've read them, as you very well know. I went over every single item, multiple times. You forgot about the letter of introduction for Major Martin from his commanding officer, Vice-Admiral Louis Mountbatten, Chief of Combined Operations, to Admiral of the Fleet Sir Andrew Cunningham, Commander-in-Chief Mediterranean Fleet and Allied naval commander in the Mediterranean. That tied in with everything else, too.

"Donndorf, I have to tell you that everything looked one hundred percent consistent to me, too. We found no mistakes; all the pieces hung together naturally. The MI5 people are good, but they're not that good. Yes, you're quite right; this wasn't a British plot. But why did you raise the subject?"

"Well, Admiral, what if we were to present the British with a fictional map that shows that the Atlantic Wall is invincible? And our map will have even better provenance than the Major Martin letter, which we both agree is genuine."

"And how would you achieve that?"

"We give the map to one of our dispatch riders, and arrange with a French Resistance group to put a wire across the road—you know the drill. We arrange for the leader of the group to get the information to London. He can use his radio to summon a plane to take the map there."

"But why should the leader of a Resistance group help us?" Canaris asked.

"His name is François, and he's on our side. He's been sending disinformation to the British for more than two years, ever since we shot the founder of the group and his radio operator."

"What does this François do?"

"He's a carpenter's assistant."

"Donndorf, are you trying to tell me that a carpenter's assistant has the sophisticated skills essential to head a Resistance group that actually is working for us, without the other members finding out about it?"

"You're quite right, of course. But even though the members of the group think that François is their leader, the person who's actually calling the shots is the elderly parish priest, Father Patrice."

"But will Father Patrice help us?" Canaris asked.

"He probably won't object too strenuously to the death of the dispatch rider, but when our men arrest at least ten Frenchmen at random and shoot them in retaliation for the death of a German soldier, he'll lose parishioners, some of whom may be his close friends."

"I thought they did the reprisal executions at Fort Romainville in Paris. We have plenty of members of the Resistance locked up in the prison."

"I thought that, too, but it seems that they've run out of hostages, and now they choose men at random from the area where the German soldier was killed, and sometimes women as well."

"Surely we can instruct the *Gestapo* to leave the locals alone?" Donndorf suggested.

"Not without telling them in advance that we've ordered a French Resistance group to kill a German dispatch rider, and that'll almost certainly blow the whole plan."

"I've just had an idea," the colonel said. "Suppose we arrange for François and his group to set the trap for the dispatch rider. When the wire throws him off his motorcycle, they notice that someone has sealed the dispatch case he's carrying—they notice red sealing wax all over the place. The members of the Resistance group take the greatest care not to open the case; they leave the seals intact. Then they radio London, tell them that they've found a message that's so important that even the leather dispatch case has been sealed. Clearly the case has to go to London, and they ask for a Lysander to land in a nearby field to pick it up. Then, when the plane lands, they insist that the pilot takes both the dispatch case and the rider, because if the Germans find the soldier they'll do reprisal killings."

"And what'll they do with the motorcycle?" Admiral Canaris inquired.

"They'll take it apart and then hide all the pieces in various places, possibly in workshops. The authorities won't find anything to connect François and his people with the disappearance of the dispatch rider: no dead body, no vehicle, and therefore no reprisals. But the provenance of the fictitious map will be unimpeachable. It'll be sealed in a leather bag, still fastened around the body of the dead dispatch rider. And a French Resistance group will deliver it on a plate to London."

CHAPTER TEN

Civilian Internment Camp Ilag VIII,
Tost, Upper Silesia, Germany
Wednesday, December 22nd, 1943

"You asked to see me, Major Froschtümpel?" Bridget Hawkesbury asked. She was a compact woman of about forty, her prematurely gray hair neatly arranged in a bun.

"Yes, Miss Hawkesbury. I have some good news for you. Please sit down. As you know, we do our best to assist enemy aliens interned in this camp who have artistic and creative skills. You'll no doubt remember Mr. P. G. Wodehouse. Not only did we provide him with everything he needed to write highly amusing stories about life in an internment camp, including locating a typewriter with an English keyboard layout for him to use, but we also encouraged him to present the material in the form of five radio talks from Berlin. They were extremely well received, by the way, especially in America. And we supplied him with whatever he required to write a comic novel during the year he was here. He even sent me an autographed copy. Here, please take a look. It's called *Money in the Bank.*

"When he turned sixty we released him under the Geneva Convention. I was most sad when he left in 1941; his humorous monologues enriched the lives of everyone here, including myself. Do you not agree?"

"Yes, Major Froschtümpel," Bridget said, wondering where the conversation was leading. She decided to make a neutral sort of remark. "We miss Mr. Wodehouse."

"Everyone in the camp administration," the major said, "still talks all the time about his hilarious remark about Tost: 'If this is Upper Silesia, one wonders what Lower Silesia must be like!'"

Bridget smiled out of politeness; even the wittiest remarks are no longer funny after hearing them too many times.

"When you came here," Major Froschtümpel continued, "you asked me if you could continue to compose crossword puzzles for British newspapers. You'll recall that I asked my superior officer. Not knowing anything about cryptic puzzles, Lieutenant Colonel von Krägelheimer was concerned that you might use them to send hidden messages, though how you would learn any secret military information locked up in Ilag VIII is beyond my comprehension. However, he later agreed to a compromise. Here in Germany we get copies of the major British newspapers. He gave me permission to give you the crosswords in *The Sunday Intelligencer*, provided that you sat and solved them here in the commandant's office, and that I checked the solution before you returned to the camp to ensure that no messages were hidden. Of course, I never found any. Nor did I expect to."

Bridget smiled politely again, wondering what was coming.

"Well, Miss Hawkesbury, as I said, I have some good news. As you are well aware, morale in our camps is a high priority for us. Lieutenant Colonel von Krägelheimer has assigned me the task of thinking up ways of raising the spirits of our internees, and I've come up with an idea. Believe it or not, the colonel is still concerned that, if you were to compose a puzzle, you might somehow embed military intelligence into the answers. But he's conceded that, if someone else were to supply you with a completed puzzle, it would be impossible for you to compose clues for those answers that might divulge a top secret.

"Well," Major Froschtümpel continued, "on this squared paper here I've provided you with a puzzle solution that I've put together, obviously with the aid of this English dictionary and that encyclopedia over there that the colonel gave me. All you have to do is to come up with a set of cryptic clues. We'll then circulate your puzzle to the other camps with British internees, especially prisoner of war camps.

"I know what you're thinking. You're a loyal Englishwoman, and you're wondering if composing cryptic puzzles for the Germans would at best be cooperating with the enemy, and at worst an act of treason. Am I right?"

She nodded.

"Well, before you do anything, please consult the members of the Camp Committee. I'm sure they'll tell you that composing puzzles for your fellow Britishers would be most meritorious and greatly appreciated by one and all. Thank you for coming to see me."

As Bridget Hawkesbury turned to go, Major Froschtümpel said, "By the way, I'm sure you'll be interested to know that I'm working on something else as well. Wouldn't it be wonderful if your puzzles appeared once again in a newspaper?"

Seeing the look of horror on her face he quickly added, "I mean a British newspaper, of course. After all, what would be the point of publishing a cryptic puzzle in English in a German paper? Can you imagine the look on the *Führer*'s face as he opens his copy of the *Völkischer Beobachter* (The People's Observer) and sees one of your puzzles on page fifteen? The problem, Miss Hawkesbury, is finding a way of getting your puzzles to London, but please be assured that I'm working on it. British newspapers come to Germany via the early morning flight from Britain to Portugal, and therefore it's certainly reasonable for your puzzles to be on the return flight. Anyhow, as I said, I'm giving the matter my full attention. I'll let you know as soon as I've made more progress. And I look forward to seeing your first puzzle soon."

As soon as a guard had escorted Bridget back into the camp, Major Froschtümpel picked up the telephone on his desk. "Get me Colonel Donndorf at the *Abwehr*. Yes, right away. It's urgent."

After a wait of a few minutes, the phone rang.

"Colonel Donndorf? It's Froschtümpel at Ilag VIII. I did exactly what you said. I used that squared paper you sent me to copy the black squares and the numbers in the crossword grid in Monday's *The Daily Recorder* and then I wrote in the solution that I found in yesterday's paper. I hope she believes that I found those words in the dictionary and encyclopedia you provided and that I showed her. One answer was SESQUIPEDALIAN—but I don't remember what that long word means. Another was SYZYGY. I wouldn't know how to pronounce it, but apparently it's an astronomical term of some sort. And one of the answers was CARMENTA. I thought it was a disease, but it turns out that she's the Roman goddess of childbirth. And another answer was a Greek satyr, SILENUS."

"Never mind all that, Froschtümpel. Did she fall for it?"

"I think she did, Colonel. As you suspected, she was worried that she might be aiding the enemy, but I told her to talk to the Camp Committee, and I've no doubt that they'll approve it. But it was your idea of having her crosswords published in British newspapers once more that sold her on your plan."

"So, if I send you a grid and a puzzle solution, you'll use your squared paper for 'your' crossword, and she'll compose a set of clues for the puzzle?"

"I'm confident that this will work."

"Excellent. You'll receive the puzzle in the next few days. As soon as she's come up with the clues, send them to me by messenger.

"By the way, Froschtümpel. You've been working on this ever since we interned Miss Hawkesbury. Your whole plan depends on the totally irrational belief of Lieutenant Colonel von Krägelheimer that she might use crosswords to convey secret information. You've agreed with her that it's impossible for her to acquire such information and that no one in a camp who receives one of her crosswords could make use of any information that isn't in the puzzle in the first place. She believes you're on her side, that you see her point, but you've insisted that you can nothing about that obdurate old fool, Lieutenant Colonel von Krägelheimer. That's all been excellent. But now that your plan is finally about to come to fruition, I urge you to take the greatest care to ensure that Bridget Hawkesbury never even suspects that Lieutenant Colonel von Krägelheimer is a figment of your imagination."

***

"Sir Lucius," Bridget Hawkesbury said, "I think that Froschtümpel is up to his old tricks again."

"Really? What's he come up with this time?"

"You obviously remember how he suggested to P. G. Wodehouse that he write a humorous account of his life here in Tost. That was fine. You and the members of your Camp Committee invited Mr. Wodehouse to read his material aloud to the internees, and those evenings of hilarity boosted everyone's morale. But then, playing to the man's vanity and also his naïveté, Froschtümpel persuaded the fat-headed fool to present the material in the form of those five radio broadcasts from Berlin."

"Yes, that was terrible. The outcry from Britain was so loud that we could hear it from here. Everyone denounced him as a collaborator and a traitor. It was a Nazi public relations triumph. What does Froschtümpel want you to do?" Sir Lucius asked.

"Well, he's trying the same sort of thing on me. The first step is that he wants me to compose cryptic crosswords for circulation amongst English-speaking prisoners held in internment and prisoner of war camps. Of course, that senile old moron Lieutenant Colonel von Krägelheimer is still concerned that I might use the answers to transmit secret military information. To solve the problem, Froschtümpel has given me a completed grid, and I have to compose a set of clues for his answers.

"My initial reaction was that the whole thing seemed a bit dodgy. But before I could protest, he told me to consult with you and the Camp Committee. He assured me that you'd all think it was an excellent idea. And on reflection, I have to admit that perhaps I was wrong. Like Mr. Wodehouse's original article, it does seem to be good morale booster."

"I fully agree," Sir Lucius said. "I, for one, would love to try my hand at solving one of your brainteasers. And I'm sure that holds for everyone else, too, especially the POWs. I'll have to discuss it with the others on the committee, of course—we run everything on strictly democratic lines here, as you well know. But I'd be most surprised if the outcome were anything short of unanimous enthusiastic support."

"That's most reassuring to hear. But it's the second part that worries me. Just as with Mr. Wodehouse, Froschtümpel tried to play to my vanity. As I was leaving, he mentioned that he's trying to arrange for my crosswords to be published in a British newspaper. My concern, of course, is that once I've composed a puzzle and handed it to him, I have no control at all about what he does with it."

"That's true, of course," Sir Lucius answered. "But what's the worst thing he could do with your puzzle? Even if he arranged for it to be published in the *Völkischer Beobachter,* what harm could that do? Cryptic crossword puzzles are certainly not the same thing as radio broadcasts from Berlin that make light of British prisoners in German hands. We'll obviously look closely at the possible repercussions but, again, I think you'll get unanimous approval. Personally, I can't see a possible downside, but one of the others may be more astute. We'll certainly get back to you in a day or two but, if I were you, I'd get to work right away on that first puzzle."

CHAPTER ELEVEN

Upper Stragham, Buckinghamshire, England
Wednesday, January 12th, 1944

The young man standing on the doorstep of Mrs. Bunting's house at Number 36, Thornhill Street was dressed in a navy-blue barathea blazer and gray flannel trousers. His white shirt gleamed in the morning sunlight. Around his neck he wore a navy-blue, red, and silver striped Royal Air Force tie.

But Mrs. Bunting noticed none of this. As she opened the door she observed his six-inch wide handlebar moustache, the style that many of the air force pilots now sported. Then she saw that he was wearing a black patch over his left eye. He smiled, turning his head slightly to the right at the same time. Now she was shocked to see an angry red scar running vertically from the corner of his eye patch, past the tip of his moustache, and down into his neck. Smaller horizontal cicatrices led away from the left and right sides of the broad main scar. Mrs. Bunting tried to tear her eyes away from the disfigured left cheek, but was unable to.

"Does Mr. Longstreet live here?"

"Yes, he does."

"My name is Blenkenship. May I see him, please?"

"I'm afraid he's at Stragham College, Mr. Blenkenship. That's where he teaches. He usually comes back in the late afternoon. If it's urgent, perhaps you should go to the college. It's only a fifteen-minute walk from here. But I see you have a car."

He smiled again.

"I have a letter for Mr. Longstreet. May I leave it with you?"

"Certainly."

As he handed the letter to her she looked down and saw that he was wearing cotton gloves. *He burned his hands in a plane crash*, she thought.

"I'll put it here on the hall table," she said. "He'll see it when he comes in."

"Well, it's a very important letter. I'd be happier if you handed it to him personally."

"Yes, indeed, Mr. Blenkenship. I'll give it to him as soon as he gets here."

***

When Mrs. Bunting heard her lodger's key clanking in the front door lock she took the envelope from the kitchen table and greeted Hector in the hallway.

"A Mr. Blenkenship was here this morning. He left this letter for you."

"I don't know any Blenkenship. And I've never had a pupil with that name."

"I think he's a pilot. He has a pilot's moustache. And a huge red scar runs right down his face; I think he was injured in the war."

"I certainly don't know anyone like that. But please give me the letter."

"He came in a black car. He parked it on the other side of the road, outside Mrs. Metcalfe's house. I heard him drive off after he left here."

Longstreet had to struggle not to roll his eyes. "And my letter, Mrs. Bunting?"

"Here it is, Mr. Longstreet."

You've probably steamed it open, you evil witch. "Thank you for keeping it for me."

"Not at all, Mr. Longstreet. I hope it's not bad news?"

"I'm sure that everything's fine, thank you for asking," he said.

With a show of reluctance, Mrs. Bunting returned to her kitchen. Hector Longstreet climbed up the stairs to his room, unlocked the door, and bolted it behind him. Only then did he examine the long envelope.

It was made of cream-colored bond paper, now almost unavailable in England; before the war, all the letters he received from parents were on cream bond, to show their wealth and their exquisite taste. The name typed on the envelope read "H. Longstreet, Esq., M.A." No address. No return address. Intrigued, he took a paper knife from the small wooden tray on the top of his desk and slit open the envelope. Inside was a sheet of paper, also cream-colored bond, folded in three. He opened the paper, and a newspaper clipping fell out onto the floor. Longstreet picked it up and unfolded it. It proved to be a crossword grid. Someone had meticulously cut it out of a newspaper, probably using a knife and straightedge, because he couldn't see any scissors marks. He turned the grid over and immediately realized that it had come from *The Daily Recorder*. He placed the clipping on the desk, face up.

Now he examined the sheet of paper. Typed on it were crossword clues.

Longstreet abhorred novels of all kinds, especially crime novels. But he read newspapers voraciously, including reports of court cases, and he therefore knew all about the importance of fingerprints. He dropped the paper onto the desk as if it was infested with lethal germs.

He rummaged through the pile of newspapers neatly stacked in one corner of his room for the next paper drive until he found one with a crossword that had the same grid; he was delighted to see that it was from *The Daily Recorder*. As far as Longstreet was concerned, one used a pen when solving a crossword; pencils and erasers were for children and the feebleminded. He extracted his fountain pen and spectacles out of their respective jacket pockets and, taking the greatest care not to touch the typed page again, solved the puzzle in a few minutes.

The style of the crossword seemed familiar, but at the same time somewhat unfamiliar. Then he realized why. Bridget Hawkesbury had unquestionably composed the puzzle, but the answers were not the sort of words she usually chose. For example, 4-across was a Shakespearean character, **FALSTAFF**. This was most irregular; he knew that Bridget detested everything to do with Shakespeare, including his plays, his sonnets and, above all, his characters. Then, 7-down was **FIND**, sharing the second to last letter of **FALSTAFF**. That also seemed wrong to him. Bridget hated answers that were both nouns and verbs, probably because she found it hard to come up with sufficiently challenging clues.

Then he looked more closely at the remaining answers. He noticed that 9-down was **INVASION** and 17-down was **LOCATION**. He searched his pockets for the card that Johnson had given him, and for change for the public telephone. Then he rushed out of his room, heading for the telephone booth outside the post office on Mason Road.

***

"I've spoken to your Mrs. Bunting," Carlyle said, seated behind the wooden desk in the bare room with the painted ceiling. "All she can tell me is that the man in the black car had a huge scar on one cheek, but she's not sure which one; a black eye patch, probably covering his left eye, but possibly the right one; and what she described as a Royal Air Force pilot's moustache. I drew a handlebar moustache for her, and she nodded. However, I'm certain that, if the man came back to her house without his eye patch, his false facial hair, and his exaggerated stage makeup scar, she wouldn't recognize him at all."

Longstreet and Johnson nodded.

"Also, I went to the school and asked the school secretary, Miss Harrington, whether she received any phone calls this morning. After nervously fiddling with those lethal-looking hairpins for a while, she told me that someone had phoned to speak to you, Mr. Longstreet. When she said that you were teaching and asked if she could take a message, the caller said no and hung up the phone. I'm pretty sure that her caller was the same man, checking that you were safely at Stragham College so he could leave the letter for you with Mrs. Bunting; there was no danger that he'd have to give it to you personally."

"Danger?" Hector Longstreet asked, raising one eyebrow. "Does MI5 consider me to be dangerous?"

"Only in the sense you're dangerously intelligent," Johnson replied with a laugh, "and you might have seen through his disguises."

Longstreet smirked ostentatiously.

"What we need to find out," Carlyle said, "is whether the man who came to the house is a German agent or an unwitting innocent man whom an agent paid to deliver the letter. My guess is the latter. But how would we find him? The man wore gloves and the only fingerprints on the envelope matched those we took from Mrs. Bunting and from you, Mr. Longstreet. And the same applies to the letter and the grid."

"Aha!" Longstreet said. "I was right. The Bunting bitch steams my letters open and reads them."

"I'm glad you told us that," Johnson remarked. "Now we know that any correspondence that we might have to send to you would have to go to the school. Does Miss Harrington also open other people's letters?"

"Probably not. But it's easy to fix the Bunting problem. When I get back I'll inform her that you fingerprinted today's letter, and that you're going to fingerprint all future letters. That should do it!"

"I agree. But that doesn't solve the problem of finding who delivered the letter," Carlyle said. "Any ideas?"

"All we know," Johnson said, "is that it was a man of conscription age. That means that either he was on leave, or the authorities have excused him from military service for some reason."

"And," Longstreet added, "he probably has acting experience."

"Although," Johnson replied, "someone else might have applied the moustache and drawn the scar on his cheek."

"And what about the phone call?" Hector Longstreet asked. "Can you trace it?"

"Not even if we'd had the necessary equipment connected," Carlyle replied. "The call was far too short."

"Was that done deliberately to avoid possible tracing?" the schoolmaster continued.

"I've no idea," Carlyle said. "I'd answer one way if we knew that he's a German agent, another way if he's just an innocent participant.

"Something else just occurred to me," he added. "How did they know where you work and where you live?"

"I think I know the answer to that," Longstreet said. "When I went to see Captain Soltmann, the German Assistant Military Attaché, I gave him my work and home addresses. I've been at the school since 1921, and all that time I've rented a room from Mrs. Bunting."

"That would certainly explain it," Carlyle replied. "Now, let's get down to business. Mr. Longstreet, it's clear that your German contacts—I can't think of a better way to describe them—want you to find out from your former pupil on the Imperial General Staff where we're going to invade. That means that we need you to compose a crossword puzzle to tell them."

For once, Hector Longstreet was rendered totally speechless. Finally, he managed to utter a few words. "But ... but I can't do that. I've signed the Official Secrets Act. And, whatever else you may think of me, I'm a loyal Englishman. I could never reveal any military secret, let alone that one. And I—"

"It's all right, Mr. Longstreet," Carlyle said. "We're not asking you to tell the Germans where we're going to attack Nazi-occupied Europe. We've found out where Hitler thinks we're going to invade. All we want you to do is to reinforce his belief."

"But I have a problem with that, too."

"What problem?" Johnson asked.

"Well, suppose Hitler has decided that our troops are going to land in, I don't know, let's say Le Havre. If you tell me to put Le Havre in a crossword, then

I'll know for sure that Le Havre is not the real target. And suppose further that someone slips up and they find out that I'm actually giving false information to the enemy, then they'll realize that Le Havre isn't actually the target and Hitler will—"

"Mr. Longstreet," Johnson said, "it's not like that at all. We need you to include two locations in your puzzle: Southern Norway and the Pas-de-Calais. Suppose that we're going to invade, say, Hardangerfjord, just to the south of Bergen. Reinforcing Hitler's belief that Southern Norway is the target won't change anything—the whole coastline consists of fjord after fjord where we might stage the invasion. And similarly, for the Pas-de-Calais—the *Führer* knows the numerous possible sites where we might land. The only thing we're asking you to do at this stage is convince the Germans that you're a traitor who's willing and able to give them the information they need in order to win the war. And to achieve that, all you have to do is include the names of those two places."

"I think I understand," Longstreet said. "Somehow or other you have a way of determining what Hitler is thinking. I'll tell him we're going to invade Southern Norway and the Pas-de-Calais, to strengthen his belief. Once you've found out that he's taken the bait, you'll want me to be more specific by providing him with a region in Southern Norway and one in the Pas-de-Calais. And as soon as he's reinforced those areas, I'll give him additional details, and so on."

"Exactly," Johnson answered.

"Good. But I have another problem. The answer **PASDECALAIS** is eleven letters long, and Grid Number 18 has four words of that length. It's the only grid with eleven-letter words. But it doesn't have any words with six letters, such as **NORWAY**. Do you want me to create a new grid, which will undoubtedly cause problems at *The Sunday Intelligencer*, or compose two puzzles, one with each of the two words? In that case, of course, both puzzles would have at least one classical reference. My concern is that the Germans won't realize that the newspaper has no grids that will accommodate both words, and they may therefore conclude that the second target replaces the first, or possibly is an alternate target whereas, as I understand the situation, Hitler believes we're going to invade the two locations simultaneously. Which do you want: a new grid, or two puzzles?"

Johnson looked at Carlyle, who shrugged his shoulders. In the ensuing silence, Longstreet spoke up.

"Perhaps I should contact Enoch Waterson, my crossword editor, and ask him to find out whether it would be feasible for the paper to use a new grid of my invention that includes both eleven-letter words and six-letter words. It's Wednesday afternoon, but I have his home number. Do you have a telephone I could use?"

Johnson escorted Longstreet to a phone in an office downstairs but conveniently omitted to tell him that all conversations on that line were recorded; he wanted to hear the interaction between Waterson and his former teacher. Johnson stood outside the office and listened until he was sure that the schoolmaster was talking to his editor. Then he rejoined Carlyle.

"We'll have to be careful," he said. "Longstreet started off cooperating nicely. However, as I'm sure you've noticed, now he's starting to try to take charge. When he gets back—"

As Johnson said those words, Longstreet reentered the room. "I've spoken to Waterson. He says that one of the typesetters is a crossword aficionado. He's been nagging Waterson for months to ask me to design a new grid, for the sake of variety. For some reason, Waterson never passed on the request. Accordingly, I'd be delighted to design a new grid and a puzzle with … oh, I've been unutterably stupid! Grid Number 12 has two twelve-letter words and two six-letter words. All we have to do is replace the last letter of 1-across with a black square, and the same with the first letter of 28-across to preserve the symmetry, and I'll have exactly what I need."

"But with two more black squares than usual, won't the puzzle look a little strange?" Johnson asked.

"It might," Longstreet replied. "But that would be all to the good. It would indicate to the Germans that this is a special puzzle of some sort, which it certainly will be. Fine, that's what I'll do. Now I'm off to the library; I hope you bought all those books I requested. I'll get the completed puzzle to you as soon as I can."

Longstreet rose to his feet and walked to the door, totally in control of the situation.

CHAPTER TWELVE

MI5 Headquarters, London
Thursday, January 13th, 1944

"Right, gentlemen," Air Commodore Pankhurst said, "how do you propose that we go about fooling the Germans?" Captain Marks raised his hand. "Yes, Marks?"

"Sir, I know a man called Appleby. He was a general in World War I, extremely successful in the East African campaign, and before that in the German West African colonies of Togoland Protectorate and Cameroon. Anyhow, after the war he retired to Devon. With the rise of Hitler, he became obsessed with pigeons."

"Did you say 'pigeons,' Marks?"

"Yes, sir. Homing pigeons. Both sides used them to carry messages during the First World War. They can carry a weight of up to two ounces. That means that you write a message on a piece of paper, place it in a small canister, fasten it to the bird's leg, and release the bird, which immediately starts to fly to its home loft. During the First World War, soldiers used to try to shoot down any pigeons they saw flying up from enemy trenches, realizing that officers would use homing pigeons to carry only truly important messages. However, once a bird has reached a height of a few hundred feet, the chances of hitting it as it flies at a speed of fifty miles per hour are miniscule.

"After the war, a few Britishers got involved with pigeon racing. That's where they release a number of birds the same distance from their home lofts and measure how long it takes each one to get back; the fastest bird wins. I was surprised to learn that our Royal Family takes part in these races; King Leopold II of Belgium gave them breeding stock more than forty years ago. Britain is hardly overrun with pigeon aficionados. But Germany has tens of thousands of enthusiasts.

"General Appleby realized that war was coming, and wondered about communications. The fact is that no one has yet managed to come up with a really safe way to send a report. A radio message can be detected and decoded. Letters mailed to neutral countries are subject to inspection by censors who look for secret ink and microdots. And letters are slow; in fact, they sometimes deliberately keep letters sent overseas from England for a week or even a month to try to ensure that any hidden military information will be out of date by the time the letter finally arrives at its destination. But a trained homing pigeon released behind enemy lines will immediately fly to its home loft, up to a distance of seven hundred miles. Those birds are fast and dependable. And it's really hard to intercept one.

"The Krauts apparently have realized this. They've put German homing pigeons in the lofts of French collaborators. When we invade, the French will release those pigeons from behind our lines. The birds will fly home to Germany bearing intelligence that the Nazis can use against us. And short of killing every pigeon in France, we simply cannot stop them.

"Since the fall of France, General Appleby has been trying to persuade anyone who'll listen to him that we need to drop crates of trained homing pigeons to members of French Resistance groups to enable them to safely send messages to us—German radio detectors are becoming more and more effective."

"Yes, yes, Marks, but what has all this to do with Operation BODYGUARD? May I remind you that our job is to deceive the Germans?"

"Yes, sir. I realize that. My suggestion is to use homing pigeons for deceptive purposes."

"And how, pray?"

"Well, sir, er ..." Marks swallowed nervously before continuing. "I was thinking we could use, um, stupid British homing pigeons masquerading as French homing pigeons."

He paused, waiting for the explosion. It began instantly.

"What the—?" But before he could complete his sentence, Archibald Pankhurst suddenly remembered that one of the "gentlemen" seated around the table was an officer who was a member of the fairer sex. Exercising extreme self-control far above and beyond the call of duty, he slowly inhaled. Then he exhaled equally slowly and asked, as pleasantly as he could manage under the circumstances, "Yes, Marks?"

Captain Marks spoke quickly, before the air commodore's legendary temper could take precedence over his impeccable manners. "Sir, every homing pigeon has a light-weight band fastened to its leg that bears a unique identification number. They circulate lists of those numbers amongst the pigeon racing fraternity to enable them to return the occasional lost bird to its owner. General Appleby has constructed a number of bands bearing French-style identification numbers. The idea is to choose really stupid birds, and—"

Seeing a dangerous look in the air commodore's eyes on hearing the phrase "stupid birds," Marks's voice tapered down to silence. Then he looked meaningfully at Senior Commander Limberg and continued.

"Sir, a well-trained homing pigeon will try its utmost to return to its home loft. An untrained bird will simply fly to the nearest loft. Suppose we write a disinformation message in French, encrypt it using an easy-to-break code, fasten it to, er, an unintelligent pigeon and drop the bird over Germany. On finding a strange bird in his loft bearing a message in code, the loft owner will undoubted take the paper to the nearest *Gestapo* office, where they'll decrypt the message and immediately deduce that the pigeon was released from France. After all, the bird will have a band on its legs that unambiguously and incontrovertibly identifies the location of its home loft as somewhere in France. And the message will be in French, putting the whole matter beyond any doubt."

And Captain Marks sat back nervously in his chair, waiting to see whether the air commodore's earlier tirade was over or had merely been put on temporary hold pending receipt of further ammunition.

"A very clever idea," Pankhurst said. "On paper. Will it work in practice?"

"Well, sir, General Appleby has thought of a way of testing it. As I said, he has constructed several pigeon bands that appear to be French. In fact, he now has more than a hundred. He proposes to take a hundred, er, a hundred pigeons with somewhat lower IQs and—"

"Just how do you measure the intelligence quotient of a pigeon, Marks?" asked the air commodore in the low, calm voice that all the men around the table knew from bitter experience almost inevitably meant that a major explosion was about to erupt.

"I'm not sure, sir. Perhaps you could ask the general, sir. He seems to be extremely knowledgeable regarding bird brains."

Marks tried to bite back those last two words, but it was too late. Air Commodore Pankhurst seized them the way a peregrine falcon snatches a homing pigeon out of the sky with its talons.

"Actually, Marks, this morning I'm starting to become equally knowledgeable on the subject of birdbrains."

Captain Marks somehow managed to produce a small grin in response to the witticism.

"Marks, what sort of message did you and the general have in mind for transmission by a weak-minded *Columba livia*?" the air commodore asked, thereby revealing yet another facet of his extensive general knowledge.

"Sir, one idea was a warning that a major German armaments and munitions train would pass through a specific railroad junction at a certain time and date. If we observed a buildup of flak weapons at the time and place in question, even though no train of that kind was due to pass, we'd know that the Nazis had received the message. A useful side effect is the Germans would have moved some of their air defense systems from where they should have been located to the site of this spurious train. And the fact that no air raid took place wouldn't cause the Germans to disbelieve future pigeon-based warnings; the Krauts would simply conclude that they had the only copy of the message, and the incorrect tip from the French Resistance never reached England."

"How do you propose to get the pigeons to Germany?"

"General Appleby has designed a cardboard box to be dropped by parachute. When it hits the ground, it opens, and the bird flies off."

"Actually, that's quite a good idea. Do you have other messages for the birds?"

"Yes, sir, we have a whole set. One is—"

"That's fine, Marks. Our job is to come up with ideas and you've certainly done that. I'll arrange a meeting between the relevant members of the steering committee and General Appleby. That's not his real name, is it, Marks?"

"No, sir, it isn't."

"You were hoping to protect him if I disliked his idea."

"Yes, sir."

"Marks, as you well know I can read you like a book. Fortunately for you, this time I enjoyed the book in question—it was a good read. And by the way, Marks, on the one hand I admire you for shielding a certain retired general with a bee in his bonnet, or perhaps I should say a bird in his bowler hat. On the other hand, just how many pigeon-obsessed retired generals do you think we have who go around plaguing the rest of mankind? And in case you're wondering, he's a member of my club. And he's by no means the most annoying member.

"Let's get back to our agenda."

CHAPTER THIRTEEN

Abwehr *Headquarters, Berlin*
Thursday, January 13th, 1944

"Donndorf," Admiral Canaris said, "About two months ago, the Allied invasion seemed all but inevitable. The *Führer* decided to put Field Marshal Rommel in charge of the French coastal defenses. At that time, it was an extremely frustrating appointment. Almost all the members of our High Command felt that Allied naval firepower was now so overwhelming that it would be futile even to try to defend against an assault. Instead, they informed Rommel that we should let the Allies land and then destroy them on the ground by counterattacking with our armor—they wanted to keep our tanks in reserve some distance from the beaches, probably somewhere near Paris, to enable them to mount a concerted onslaught by rushing all of them to the Allied beachhead, wherever it might be. As a result, the only thing that the person in charge of defending the French coast could do was sit back and wait for the Allies to invade.

"Then, as I told you, a month ago *Herr* Hitler came up with his two-part plan, namely, if we can find where the Allies are going to invade or if we can persuade them that the Atlantic Wall is impregnable, we win the war. Field Marshal Rommel, being a most practical man, asked the question: how do we make the Atlantic Wall impenetrable? And he came up with the answer: we need to duplicate the Lindemann Battery within range of all likely landing places."

"What's the Lindemann Battery?"

"We've constructed a naval battery at Sangatte, just to the west of Calais. It consists of three sixteen-inch SK C/34 guns, originally designed for use as heavy armaments on battleships. Those guns aren't just sinking Allied ships in the English Channel. Their range is thirty-five miles, but the Straits of Dover are only twenty-one miles across. That means that we're hitting targets in Kent, including the cities of Folkestone and Dover. The British now refer to that part of England as 'Hell Fire Corner.' The Allies have repeatedly tried, in vain, to bomb the battery to try to put our artillery out of action, but we've constructed concrete casements twelve feet thick, and they provide adequate protection for those naval guns. And in case you're wondering about the name, the battery honors Ernst Lindemann, the captain of the *Bismarck*.

"In other words, Rommel is going to repel the invasion in two phases. First, when Allied warships appear off the coast of France and start to bombard the defenses of the landing beach, the nearest Lindemann Battery will respond in force—that's his answer to the fears of the High Command regarding Allied naval firepower. Second, when the Allied troops land, Rommel's tanks will immediately advance *en masse* and mow them down to the last man."

"But Admiral, if Rommel insists on keeping his tanks right by the Wall instead of far enough behind the coast to be able to move them to wherever the invasion may take place, he has to know where the Allies are going to land."

"Precisely, Donndorf. Precisely."

"And he also needs to know which attacks on France are going to be feints and which onslaught is the real thing."

"Of course."

"Admiral, does Field Marshal Rommel have an opinion as to where the Allies are going to land?"

"I met with him this morning. He told me that he thinks that the most likely target at this time is the Pas-de-Calais. He gave me the usual two reasons, namely, shortest route and good port facilities. And then he added a third one: the distance from there to the border of Germany is relatively short."

Donndorf blanched visibly when he heard that, but he said nothing as Admiral Canaris continued.

"But he's by no means certain that the landing will be in the Pas-de-Calais. On the contrary, he's busy reinforcing the Atlantic Wall along its entire length, with Lindemann Batteries within range of the likely sites. But we have a problem."

The admiral paused as he decided how best to explain the situation without sounding defeatist. Then he threw caution to the wind.

"Donndorf, we cannot manufacture any additional heavy naval batteries before the invasion if it takes place in 1944. The American B-17 bombers are carrying out precision bombing by day. They're systematically destroying our means of production. Those Flying Fortresses aren't just wiping out our factories; they're going after our power plants and steel mills, too. And if we manage to manufacture weapons, their attacks on our transportation networks, especially railroad yards and junctions, make it hard to get the armaments to where we need them. And if that weren't enough, the British are destroying what's left in night raids.

"Field Marshal Rommel hid nothing from me. As far as he's concerned, it would be impossible to make the Atlantic Wall even remotely impregnable along its length if the Allies invade in May 1944—we need at least another year. The best we can do for now is to attempt to reinforce those areas that we consider to be likely landing places.

"The *Abwehr* strategy is therefore as laid down by *Herr* Hitler. We need to discover where the Allies are landing, and we need to convince them that the entire Atlantic Wall is strongly defended."

"Did you suggest to him that we should let a fake map of the Wall defenses fall into the hands of the Allies?"

"Yes, I did. But for some reason he seemed to be unhappy with the idea. He said he wanted to think about it and would get back to me."

"Admiral, are you saying that the Desert Fox is opposed to the use of disinformation? Before the Battle of El Alamein, he sowed half a million landmines, then created what appeared to be well-used tracks through those minefields by repeatedly dragging an axle and tires through the fields at the end of a long wire in the hope of luring Allied vehicles into his minefields. That doesn't sound like a man who's opposed to the use of deception to win battles."

"No, Donndorf. His objection seemed to be to some specific aspect of our strategy."

"Did he say what it was? Could we modify certain details to meet his misgivings?"

"As far as I could tell, he likes the idea in principle, but he appears to have a fundamental objection of some kind, one that he didn't care to share with me today. He said he'll get back to me soon, but he wouldn't give a precise date."

"Should I start working on an alternative approach to fooling the Allies as to strengths and weaknesses of the Atlantic Wall?"

"I don't think that's a particularly good use of your time, Donndorf. Instead, let's wait for a few days to hear what Rommel has to say. On the other hand, if you just happen to come up with an even better alternative, don't keep it to yourself."

***

"Why the long face, Donndorf?"

"Admiral, I've been talking to Lieutenant Hammermann."

"Rommel's aide-de-camp? What did he say?"

"It seems that after you left Rommel yesterday morning, he told his aide why he objects to our proposal. Hammermann told me about a large-scale map of the entire Atlantic Wall, all 1,650 miles of it. The *Abteilung für Kriegskarten- und Vermessungswesen* (Military Mapping and Survey Agency) produced it. The map consists of fifty-six detailed sheets depicting every blockhouse, trench, tunnel, bunker, artillery emplacement, machine gun post, watchtower, barracks, fortified artillery battery, antitank obstacle, and minefield, and a lot more besides. It also shows where the Wall is undefended and where we have no Wall at all. Of course, they continually update the map as we extend the Wall and fortify it. As far as we know, the Allies are ignorant of the existence of the map.

"I don't have to tell you, Admiral, that if the Allies were ever to lay their hands on that map, Germany would be done for—the invasion of Europe would succeed beyond the wildest dreams of the enemy. Fortunately, the *Abteilung für Kriegskarten- und Vermessungswesen* falls under the Army General Staff, which means that the mapmakers are military officers. They all know exactly what would happen if they were to breathe a word about the true state of affairs regarding the incomplete Wall. Nevertheless, Field Marshal Rommel is highly conscious of security, and he's constantly aware that our map of the Wall needs to be guarded at all times.

"Now, suppose you were to commission a 'modified' map, one showing a completed Atlantic Wall, with every conceivable defensive component in place. The only people who could supply such a map are precisely the mapmakers at the *Abteilung für Kriegskarten- und Vermessungswesen*, the military geographers who are responsible for the actual map. And that's why the field marshal objects to your idea. If just one of those mapmakers working on the forgery were to mention its existence to anyone, we're done for. Eventually the Allies would learn that the map we're going to plant on them is fictional. And the result of that would be as catastrophic as giving them a copy of the actual map. More so, perhaps; if you know for certain that a document is disinformation, you can often learn more about your enemy's intentions than from correct information.

"According to his aide-de-camp, Field Marshal Rommel thinks that your plan is excellent. But he feels that the security risk as a consequence of constructing a false map for deceptive purposes outweighs any possible advantage to be gained."

"What a pity he didn't tell me this yesterday," the admiral responded. "The problem is easily solved. We just make use of Operation BERNHARD."

"I'm not sure I know about Operation BERNHARD, Admiral."

"Sorry, Donndorf, I forgot that you joined me only in mid-1941. Early in this war, the Royal Air Force dropped tens of thousands of forged German food and clothing ration coupons all over our country, severely disrupting any attempt to control those parts of our economy. SS-Major Bernhard Krüger decided to take revenge. In a brilliant flash of inspiration, he realized that if we were to drop hundreds of millions of forged Bank of England banknotes over Britain, we would totally destabilize the enemy's economy; people would use the counterfeit notes to buy goods, and eventually the pound would become valueless. Furthermore, British notes are in circulation all over the world, especially in the countries of the British Empire, and flooding other enemy countries with fake notes would eventually destroy the economies of those Allied governments, too.

"The problem, of course, was how to produce counterfeit pound notes of various denominations—£5, £10, £20 and £50—that would be indistinguishable from the real thing. And that's really difficult to achieve. You see, just before the war started, two British traitors in the Bank of England gave us details of nearly a hundred and fifty different security features that the British incorporate in their banknotes. For example, Bank of England notes include a medallion in the top left-hand corner that depicts a helmeted Britannia with olive branch, spear, and shield. The medallion alone has three secret marks: a group of five tiny dots on the back of her right hand, a shading line down the length of her spear that stops just short of the base of the handle, and a hairline break across the shading lines in the upper-right section of foliage surrounding the figure. And to make matters worse, on some issues of certain denominations—but not others—her shield is irregularly curved. And that's just a few of the countless tricks that the British build into their currency."

"And what did SS-Major Krüger do?" the colonel asked.

"He recruited about a hundred and fifty prisoners in concentration camps and extermination camps with skills in forgery, printing, engraving, typography, and graphic art and put them to work counterfeiting Bank of England currency."

"But how could he know who has the necessary skills?"

"Simple. After *Herr* Hitler became Chancellor in February 1933, he announced that Germany would hold a national census; the real reason was that he wanted to be able to identify Jews, gypsies, and members of other ethnic groups he deemed undesirable. Thomas J. Watson, head of an American company called IBM, traveled to Germany in October 1933 to assist in setting up a German subsidiary, Dehomag. He even invested over a million United States dollars in the new company to ensure that it would be successful. The *Führer* used the IBM machines Dehomag supplied to analyze the census data and thereby identify individuals with only one or two Jewish ancestors—but that's enough to throw them into an extermination camp.

"In fact, the IBM machines have proved to be even more useful. When new inmates arrive at a camp, the guards ask them if they have any special skills. The prisoners eagerly tell the guards everything they can do because they think that they'll be able to stay alive if they can be of some value to Germany. And that information is encoded on IBM punch cards; every concentration camp has its own department for doing that. As a result, all SS-Major Krüger had to do was to use the IBM punch-card machines to find every Jewish inmate who has skills that could contribute toward counterfeiting British banknotes. He then transported them to Sachsenhausen concentration camp; it's just outside Oranienburg, no more than twenty-five miles to our north. Inside the camp he constructed two special barracks, Barracks 18 and 19, surrounded by three concentric rings of barbed wire fences electrified to one thousand watts. And there the Jews toil away."

"Admiral, why only Jews? Surely members of many other races could do an equally good job?"

"Of course. But you have to consider the issue of sabotage. It would be so easy for a counterfeiter to make a subtle change to the banknotes. No one would notice it until we distributed the money, and by then it would be too late. Well, Krüger has warned all his workers that if anyone makes the slightest attempt of any kind to undermine the program, every single worker in Barracks 18 and 19 will go straight to the Sachsenhausen gas chamber and ovens that Commandant Anton Kaindl constructed in March 1943."

"I still don't see the point. Surely SS-Major Bernhard Krüger would issue the same warning to non-Jewish workers, and they would all suffer the same fate if anyone tried to sabotage the counterfeiting operation in any way."

"Yes, but Jews believe in the sanctity of human life. They wouldn't do anything that would result in our killing innocent people, Jews or non-Jews, as reprisals. For that reason, he chose only Jews, knowing that they would do their best to try to save their own lives and refrain from any action that could result in mass executions of others."

"But don't they realize that the SS will kill them all when the job is done?"

"I'm sure they do. But once they've finally mastered British banknotes, their next task will be to print perfect American dollars, and so on. And they're engaged in other work as well; I'll tell you about that in a minute.

"In any event, SS-Major Krüger treats them well. Unlike the inmates of any other concentration camp, they have adequate food. They wear white laboratory coats instead of striped concentration camp uniforms; they have soft beds with clean sheets. They work eight-hour days and have Sundays off—everywhere else, the guards make the inmates work twelve hours or fourteen hours or more every single day and they beat them brutally if they slacken off for even a second. In contrast, Krüger has even installed four ping-pong tables for their recreation. But no infirmary."

"What happens if one of them needs medical attention that can't be supplied inside the two barracks?"

"Surely you realize, Donndorf, that in the opinion of the SS, maintaining the secrecy of Operation BERNHARD is infinitely more important than the life of a Jew. No one is ever allowed to leave those two barracks. So what do you think happens if someone needs to go an infirmary, Donndorf?"

The colonel did not reply.

"Anyhow, they've made lots of progress with the counterfeit banknotes already," Canaris continued. "An SS officer took a hundred of the very first batch over the border to a Swiss bank, in Basel I think it was, and asked if they were forgeries. The expert at the bank identified twenty-five of the notes as genuine. And that was before the prisoners started to incorporate the subtler security features. The notes are all but perfect now, and they're printing about four hundred thousand of them every month."

"But Admiral, if we're flooding Britain with these counterfeit banknotes, why hasn't agent PICKFORD mentioned this in any of his messages? Are the forgeries so perfect, so undetectable that the British don't realize what's going on?"

This time it was Canaris who decided to say nothing. But then he changed his mind.

"Donndorf, I think you're well aware that the Allies are currently destroying the *Luftwaffe* on three fronts: the Eastern Front, the Western Front, and the Mediterranean. We just don't have the planes to drop the money over Britain."

"Admiral, may I ask what's happening to the banknotes?"

"The SS has them. They're delivering them to their spies in foreign countries, to pay their salaries and to remunerate their contacts and sources. For example, they used Operation BERNHARD money to pay for the rescue of Mussolini in the Apennine Mountains last September. And I can't prove it—yet—but I strongly believe that senior SS officers have 'borrowed' millions of the forged notes and deposited the funds in numbered bank accounts in Switzerland. It's their insurance policy, just in case we lose the war."

Donndorf looked stunned. Then he asked, "But what has all this to do with our creating a dummy map of the Atlantic Wall?"

"As I mentioned to you, in addition to counterfeiting British banknotes, the Jews are successfully forging all sorts of other things: passports, visas, ration books, civilian and military identity cards, marriage and birth certificates, rubber stamps. Their inventory comprises nearly seventy thousand items that they can copy and use as a basis for fake documents. They certainly have the skills to make any map we require. And because the forgers are safely behind three concentric electrified barbed wire fences situated inside the electrified perimeter fence of Sachsenhausen concentration camp, Field Marshal Rommel will be able sleep well at night; the secret will stay inside Barracks 18 and 19."

CHAPTER FOURTEEN

Civilian Internment Camp Ilag VIII,
Tost, Upper Silesia, Germany
Tuesday, March 14th, 1944

"Sir Lucius," Bridget Hawkesbury said, "I think that something odd is happening. I need to discuss it in private with you and two or three utterly trustworthy other internees. They need to be knowledgeable regarding the subtleties of the English language, and it would certainly help if they were crossword addicts."

Lucius Featherstone pointed at two short men dressed identically who were walking past the window of the hut in which they were standing. "How about the Bloxham twins? When the Germans invaded France, they were trapped while unwisely attending a conference in Paris on comparative linguistics, whatever that is."

"Can they be trusted?"

Sir Lucius looked shocked. "I was at Rugby with them," he declared indignantly.

Realizing that the issue of security was now settled beyond all doubt as far as the chairman of the Camp

Committee was concerned, Bridget resigned herself to dealing with the three old boys of the same prestigious British boarding school.

Sir Lucius Featherstone went to the window and called the two men inside. "Miss Hawkesbury, I believe you know Eldred and Titus Bloxham, though I'm damned if I know which is which."

The twins just grinned.

"Miss Hawkesbury says she has something to discuss in strictest confidence with experts in both crosswords and the English language, and you two certainly fit the bill. Go ahead, Miss Hawkesbury."

"As we all know," she began, "we're about to invade Europe. For obvious reasons, Hitler wants to know where we're going to land. And I think I've become an unwitting pawn in a major espionage conspiracy."

She looked at each of the three men in turn. None of their faces betrayed the slightest emotion. They knew and respected Bridget, and wanted to know more before reacting in any way.

She went on, "It started in 1940, when the Germans first interned me in Ilag VIII. The camp commandant, Major Froschtümpel, asked all the new arrivals if he could assist in any way to make our lives here more bearable—after all, unhappy detainees try to escape. I told him that I compose crosswords, and asked if I could continue to send crosswords to a British newspaper. He said he had no powers beyond the camp fence, and he would therefore need to consult his superior officer, Lieutenant Colonel von

Krägelheimer, to get permission to send my crosswords out of Germany.

"Lieutenant Colonel von Krägelheimer turned down my request because he was concerned that I might use puzzles to send hidden messages to the British. Froschtümpel was most sympathetic, agreeing with me that this was utter nonsense, but pointed out that he couldn't do anything. A few weeks later he called me into his office on a Monday and handed me a crossword. The composer's name, 'Ramirez,' at the top of the puzzle revealed that Hector Longstreet had composed it for *The Sunday Intelligencer*, though I'd have realized that fact as soon as I started working on the crossword; Hector's style is unique.

"Froschtümpel said that I had one hour to solve it in his office, and after I'd completed it he had to check to make sure that no secret messages were hidden in the puzzle. I finished it in less than ten minutes and handed the grid to him. He looked through it carefully and asked me a considerable number of questions about cryptic crosswords in general and that puzzle in particular. He'd never heard of anagrams and was unfamiliar with any other form of wordplay, either.

"The following Monday he called me in again and handed me Hector's crossword from the previous day. I believe that Froschtümpel had carefully studied my solution to the first puzzle, because when he looked through the second grid after I'd completed it, he asked far fewer questions and seemed to understand the key issues. And this continued Monday after Monday. I couldn't comprehend why he did this—my initial thought was that he fancied me. But everything was always conducted totally professionally. I really enjoy Longstreet's work, and going to Froschtümpel's office to solve a crossword was a welcome break in the boring life we lead here."

None of the men said anything, so Bridget continued. "At the end of last year, Froschtümpel called me in on a Wednesday—it was just before Christmas. He said that Lieutenant Colonel von Krägelheimer had given me permission to compose puzzles, provided that the Germans supplied the answers. That made perfect sense to me. Froschtümpel showed me his new English dictionary and encyclopedia and then gave me a hand-drawn grid into which he'd entered the answers. He said he'd put it together using those two books. Take a look and tell me what you think."

She handed the completed grid to the Bloxham twins. They looked at it briefly. Then they exploded.

"Froschtümpel didn't compose this."

"Of course not, Titus. It was that pompous twit, Admiral Sir Philip Henderson-Peacock, GCB, OM, GCVO who thinks that just because he saved Britain during the First World War by decisively winning the Battle of the Isles of Scilly he knows everything."

"And look at those pretentious words, like **SESQUIPEDALIAN**. That micro-brained muttonhead believes that if you use a long word that almost nobody knows it shows how clever you are. In actual fact, the man's a conceited moron who knows nothing about crossword puzzles."

"I don't understand," Eldred said, "why *The Daily Recorder* publishes his cretinous crosswords every

Monday week after week after week. It makes no sense at all. In my opinion—"

"Miss Hawkesbury," Sir Lucius interrupted, "what did you do when you discovered that Major Froschtümpel had lied to you?"

Both Bloxhams were instantly silent as they waited for her to answer. "Actually, Sir Lucius, I'm ashamed to admit that I was so delighted to be once again composing crosswords that initially I didn't notice that Froschtümpel hadn't put the puzzle together. I worked on it and handed him my list of clues. I woke up at three o'clock the next morning with the realization that he'd stolen the puzzle from *The Daily Recorder*. I lay awake until daybreak racked with guilt about what I'd done. And then suddenly I realized that no problem existed. I'd composed a set of clues for someone else's answers. So what?"

"I see," said the chairman. "And what happened next?"

"Well, the following week Froschtümpel told me how he'd made sure that the German authorities had distributed copies of my crossword to all the camps with British internees and prisoners of war, and how pleased everyone was with the first puzzle. Then he handed me a second grid that he claimed was also his work. It was obvious that the actual person who put the puzzle together was Joseph Garner, another of the six cruciverbalists for *The Daily Recorder*. But as I said, it didn't bother me at all. I just composed my set of clues and gave them to him. Then came the first bombshell. A week later he called me in yet again and handed me a third complete puzzle. Please take a look."

She handed the grid to the Bloxhams.

"FALSTAFF, eh? That must have made you very happy!"

"And then what about 8-down? Was he trying to drive you crazy? Didn't he know that you hate a noun/verb like FIND? And what about—"

Both the twins were silent for a second or two as it began to dawn on them that Major Froschtümpel had concealed a message in his puzzle. Then Eldred spoke.

"Great jumping Jehosaphat! FIND INVASION LOCATION. What did you do when you realized what was going on? Did you refuse to compose the puzzle?"

"What good would that have done?" she asked. "I'm totally powerless while I'm interned here in Ilag VIII. He would've just found someone else to compose the puzzle, someone who might not have caught on. Instead, I sent a message to whoever was going to receive the puzzle."

"A message? What sort of message?" Titus asked.

"Look at 27-across," she replied. "The answer is REPOSING. My clue read: P.S.: Ignore mess up or it looks like you're dead (8)."

"Of course! When you mess up the letters of P.S.: Ignore you get REPOSING. That's the wordplay—an anagram. And the definition is it looks like you're dead—when someone is resting with his eyes shut, it sometimes seems as if he's dead. But the hidden message that you sent was: You'd better ignore the message hidden in this puzzle, or we'll kill you."

Bridget nodded slowly. Once more silence reigned. Then Sir Lucius spoke. "What happened next?"

"Remember that every Monday Froschtümpel summons me to his office to solve Longstreet's crossword in the previous day's *The Sunday Intelligencer*?"

All three men nodded.

"Well, that continued. And then came the second bombshell. About ten days after I'd composed the **FIND INVASION LOCATION** crossword, Longstreet's puzzle appeared in an oddly shaped grid."

"What do you mean?" Sir Lucius Featherstone asked.

"It had an extra black square in the first row and the last row. Instead of the usual twelve-letter words at those places in the grid, the answers had eleven letters. But that wasn't the real surprise. One of the clues was **Diana? No! A nymph (5)**." The answer, of course—"

"—was **NAIAD**," Titus Bloxham said.

"Why?" Sir Lucius asked.

"The **No!**," Eldred said, "tells you to rearrange the letters of **Diana**, and you get **NAIAD**, a type of **nymph**."

"Precisely," Bridget said. "But Hector Longstreet never ever sets classical clues. Actually, he did once, a few months ago, but nothing else before or since. Returning to the puzzle I'm telling you about now, in addition to **NAIAD** he had two foreign locations among the answers. Again, he's done that only once before. Then the city was Rouen."

"What were the locations in this puzzle?" the chairman inquired.

"Norway and the Pas-de-Calais," Bridget said. "The answer **PASDECALAIS** is eleven letters long. That was why he modified the grid. And—"

"Merciful heavens!" This time it was Sir Lucius who interrupted. "Are you telling me that Hector Longstreet is a traitor? Has he somehow managed to obey the order **FIND INVASION LOCATION** and tell the Germans? So what did you do? Pretend that you couldn't solve the puzzle?"

"Again, they'd just have found somebody else. Instead, I solved the puzzle and handed the completed grid to Froschtümpel."

Both twins spoke simultaneously. Titus asked, "How could you?" and Eldred shouted, "You Judas!"

Bridget just smiled. "Longstreet is the greatest cruciverbalist ever. Yes, his puzzle included the words **NORWAY** and **PASDECALAIS**. But it also included the answer **DECEIVER** with the clue **Trickster received mess up (8)**. The definition is **trickster**, and when you **mess up** the letters of **received** you get **DECEIVER**. Hector was telling me that he'd **received** my message via one of my clues. In his clue, he echoed my warning to him by repeating my phrase **mess up**."

"And his clue told you not to worry because he's a **trickster** and a **DECEIVER**," Sir Lucius Featherstone remarked. "Aha! The information he gave the Germans was false.

153

"But why did you want to meet with us?" he continued. "It seems to me that you're handling the whole situation absolutely superbly. You haven't let on to Froschtümpel that you know that he's stealing solutions from *The Daily Recorder*, and, much more importantly, you're helping Longstreet to fool the Nazis. Why are you telling us what's going on?"

"Sir Lucius, for anyone who doesn't know all the details, I've been aiding and abetting the enemy. Wodehouse was just a naïve fool to make those five radio broadcasts, but our fellow countrymen have labeled him a traitor, a coward, a collaborator, a Nazi sympathizer—and worse. When this war is over and the messages-in-crosswords story comes to light, I don't want people to say those things about me."

"But Longstreet will certainly explain the situation. And you can tell everyone what you've just told us. You could even write a book about it—*Crossword Traitor* would be a most appropriate title. And an ironic one."

"Sir Lucius, Hector Longstreet is an elderly man. He may pass away before the war is over. And no one can guarantee that I'll ever leave Germany, especially if Froschtümpel finds out what I've done. The Auschwitz extermination camp is only about fifty miles from here."

She paused. Then she looked each man in turn straight in the eye. "I want you three to promise me that, should the need arise, you'll tell the people of Britain what really happened."

CHAPTER FIFTEEN

MI5 Headquarters, London
Tuesday, March 14th, 1944

"Gentlemen," an inflexible Air Commodore Pankhurst said, "we've received a request from the Operation BODYGUARD team. As you're all well aware, they've chosen two false targets for the invasion of Europe: one in Southern Norway and the other in the Pas-de-Calais. They've drawn up a plan, they call it Operation FORTITUDE, for deceiving the Nazis into believing that we're going to invade Europe in those two locations. A few hours before we start our assault on Normandy, we're going to make the Germans think that we've commenced our offensives against Southern Norway and the Pas-de-Calais. In preparation for our 'invasions' there, Resistance groups will sabotage railway yards and destroy bridges and railway junctions in the areas surrounding the false targets, making it hard for the Germans to bring in reinforcements.

"The Germans will waste a considerable amount of time and energy trying to find alternate routes to rush more defenders into the area. Best of all, we're hoping that Hitler will send his tanks from Rouen and Paris to the Pas-de-Calais. Every tank moved to the wrong site will save Allied lives on the Normandy beaches.

"Now, the members of the Operation FORTITUDE team have created two dummy armies. The 'British Fourth Army' or BFA, based in Scotland, is responsible for our imaginary offensive against Southern Norway; the 'First United States Army Group' or FUSAG will invade the Pas-de-Calais from South East England. One of the challenges of Operation FORTITUDE is that we have to convince the Germans that we have enough men and armaments of all kinds for two full armies when we actually don't.

"The members of the FORTITUDE team have apparently read everything available on the subject of dummy armies, starting with General Allenby's attack on the Gaza–Beersheba line in Palestine in 1917. Using that material, they've drawn up an outline of how they're going to proceed. For example, if we want to have an army in Scotland then we have to build camps to house them and train them. The soldiers in the camps have to be fed. And paid. Et cetera, et cetera.

"They've asked us to critique their outline. I want you to go away and read what they've produced. Come back here tomorrow full of ideas.

"Oh, wait a minute," he added, "we also have some unfinished business to attend to. Marks, what's the latest on those pigeons?"

Marks cleared his throat loudly.

"Well, sir, General, er, Appleby and I loaded twenty pigeons with appropriate messages. We liaised with the Royal Air Force—Harkness was a great help—and we made arrangement for the pigeons to be dropped over Germany en route to various bombing raids. We used those cardboard cages the general designed, each supplied with its own parachute. We even put a handful of corn in each cage."

"And?"

"Up to now, nothing, sir."

"Nothing?"

"No, sir, nothing. But eighty of our additional messages relate to fictional events scheduled for next week and the week after. Consequently, those pigeons haven't left Britain yet."

"What you're saying, Marks, is that the first twenty of your pigeons are either flying aimlessly around Germany, or hungry Germans have eaten them."

"Yes, sir, that's probably a fair assessment."

"Well, let's hope that at least one or two of the other eighty find their way to receptive lofts."

***

"Gentlemen, you've had twenty-four hours to study the Operation FORTITUDE material. How can we assist them? Let's go around the table clockwise. Wallstead?"

"Yes, sir. They've proposed two dummy armies. I agree that a dummy army has to have equipment, and dummy equipment is fine. In fact, it has to be dummy equipment as far as possible, because we're short of planes and tanks, even with the huge numbers that the Yanks are shipping here. Our factories are hardly coping, even with the limited German bombing as a consequence of our triumphs in the air, because their U-boats are sinking too many cargo vessels laden with incoming raw materials.

"Regarding the area in Kent set aside for FUSAG, I agree that we need to inundate it with dummy airfields, dummy landing craft, dummy barracks and the like. After all, some *Luftwaffe* planes still fly over that part of England, despite the successes of our Spitfire and Hurricane pilots. But it seems a waste of time and money to construct highly detailed dummy camps in Scotland; it's probably too far away for German reconnaissance planes to reach. If we locate the dummy camps in or near existing real camps, that should suffice."

"That makes sense. I'll include that in my report. Next idea?"

"The outline makes no mention of any electricity. Even with the blackout, we'll need some lighting. For example, we'll sometimes have to turn on runway lights at night. We're going to build those dummy camps in the middle of nowhere, and we're going to have to arrange a power supply for them."

"Fine. Keep going."

"Sir, maybe Chulmleigh would like to talk now."

"Chulmleigh?"

"Yes, sir. I'm concerned about the fake radio traffic for both dummy armies. Is it going to be encrypted, or will some of it be sent out in clear? In either event, they're going to need lots of radio operators. Do we have that many? And what are they going to use for scripts? They can't transmit any messages that the Germans may already have received."

"Those are important questions. Does anyone have any ideas?"

"Sir," Johnson said, "As I understand it, we have a genuine army in the vicinity of Portsmouth, ready to invade Normandy. That army is going to send out innumerable radio messages as all armies do, both encrypted and in clear text. We have a fake army in Kent. What if we routed those messages by landline from Portsmouth to Kent, and then broadcast them from there? The Germans have great radio detection skills, and they'll conclude that the genuine army is in Kent."

"That's a really good suggestion. I'll pass it on to the committee. Back to Chulmleigh. Do you have anything else?"

"No, sir."

"Harkness?"

"The dummy planes, sir."

"What about them?"

"I've seen one inflatable model, sir. It was made of rubber, I think, and it blew over in a fresh breeze. No more than twenty knots, sir. And the same problem will arise with dummy tanks made of rubber."

"Good point. More?"

"Yes, sir. What about the pubs in the vicinity of the dummy camps? They'll be most surprised that no serviceman ever drops in for a drink. And once word gets around—"

"Yes, of course. Well, we'll have to staff the dummy camps, if only to have someone to turn the landing lights on and off and make sure that the dummy planes and tanks stay fastened to the ground. And some radio technicians will have to be there, too, to make sure that the equipment in Kent is in full working order; Johnson was quite right, the Germans have certainly become experts in determining the location of a transmitter. I'll suggest to the FORTITUDE people that they ensure that the staff members of the dummy camps make themselves conspicuous in pubs. And in the High Street shops of the neighboring villages, as well. Limberg?"

"Sir, I feel that the emphasis in the outline is on physical things like planes and camps and soldiers, and not enough on the spread of disinformation. For instance, diplomats of neutral countries fly between Britain and Portugal, and I have no doubt that some of them are in the pay of the Germans. I suggest that we incautiously let slip a variety of misleading information in the ears of such people.

"Also, we need to arrange for top generals to visit the dummy camps so we can take their photographs there with the dummy equipment in the background, blurred of course. Then the pictures should appear on the same page as genuine photographs in service magazines and newspapers like *Union Jack* or *The Stars and Stripes*. For example, we need to photograph General Patton with FUSAG soldiers. The Germans are convinced that Patton is going to lead the invasion force. We know that they think that he's the most daring, determined, and decisive Allied general. That means that we have to have photographs of him in Kent, ready to lead his troops across the Channel. And we should send General Montgomery to Scotland for pictures, even if the members of the FORTITUDE team follow Wallstead's advice and don't actually construct a fully fledged dummy camp."

"Thank you, Limberg."

"I found one other issue, sir, but I'm not sure how to approach it."

"Go on."

"In my opinion, the best way to send disinformation to Germany regarding the two dummy armies would be to utilize the double agents and, of course, agent PICKFORD and his network. But I doubt that the FORTITUDE people have the clearance to know about those two channels."

"Yes, indeed. I'll handle that, Limberg. Anything else?"

"Yes, sir. Perhaps we could use Longstreet's crossword puzzles to inform the Germans of the location of the dummy camps. And if air reconnaissance over those areas increases, that would give us an indication that they're looking at his puzzles."

"That's an excellent idea. Tupman?"

"All my items have already been covered, sir."

"Fine. Marks?"

"The point you raised yesterday, sir. By May, we just won't have enough Allied servicemen in Britain to man two armies. We have to somehow convince the Germans that we already have more soldiers here than in reality, and that the rate of arrival of fresh troops, particularly from America, is greater than what we can actually achieve."

"Johnson?"

"Sir, I think we need to send a British traitor to Germany to inform the *Abwehr* about the dummy armies. I volunteer, sir."

Mouths dropped open around the table. For the first time in his long and distinguished career, Air Commodore Archibald Pankhurst was rendered speechless. But Carlyle had something to add.

"He's right, sir. But he can't report on both dummy camps—how would he possibly know about both of them? I volunteer too, sir, and I'll report on the other one."

Pankhurst recovered quickly. "Out of the question," he snapped. "General Eisenhower has issued a blanket order: no one with knowledge of Operation OVERLORD is allowed to leave Britain. No exceptions. And you two know far more about the forthcoming invasion than most. One injection of a *Gestapo* truth drug and you'll give away our most valuable secrets."

Major Tupman raised his hand. "Sir, maybe we need to approach the problem from a different angle. Our objective is to convince the Germans that the dummy army in the South East, opposite the Pas-de-Calais, is the real thing. But General Eisenhower is right; we can't send anyone who knows the real facts to meet with the Germans and try to fool them. But we also can't send anyone who hasn't personally visited the dummy army camps; the Germans will see through him instantly."

"Exactly what are you suggesting, Tupman?"

"We're looking at ways to fool the Germans. Instead, let's look at ways to fool the person we'll send to meet the Nazis."

"Go on. This sounds interesting."

"Suppose we order someone to inspect that vast marshalling camp in the vicinity of Southampton; it's on Southampton Common, just to the north of the city. By the end of April, they'll have nearly ten thousand American troops stationed there waiting to cross the Channel, and about a thousand vehicles. But suppose we tell that someone that he's actually 150 miles away at Dover, across from the Pas-de-Calais."

"Tupman, not even one of Marks's preposterous pigeons would fall for that!"

"Yes, sir. But Limberg's reporter for *The Stars and Stripes* might, especially if he's young and gullible and freshly arrived in Britain."

Once again there was total silence. But this time it was because everyone around the table was thinking furiously. And once again it was the air commodore who spoke first.

"Tupman, let's go through this idea of yours step by step. A reporter from an American military newspaper would certainly visit a marshalling camp for United States troops. Let's suppose we find a reporter from the backwoods of the state of, I don't know, let's say North Dakota. We'll call him Hank— that's a good American name. In 1941, Hank starts to study journalism at the University of North Dakota.

Does such a university exist? Well, if not, he'll find one in some nearby state. Anyhow, halfway through his first year of study the Japs bomb Pearl Harbor, and Hank immediately volunteers for military service; he's patriotic and he's exceedingly brave.

"Now, as we all know, for the past two years the Americans have experienced severe manpower shortages in their essential war industries; the United States Army often transfers soldiers to civilian status in the Enlisted Reserve Corps in order to increase production. As a result, they put Hank to work in a widget factory in North Dakota."

"What's a widget, sir?" Chulmleigh asked.

"Be quiet, Chulmleigh. It's what they manufacture in North Dakota. As I was saying before we heard from the Royal Navy, with the invasion of Europe about to take place, the Americans call Hank back to active duty. They want to keep morale high all over the country, including North Dakota, and so they order Hank to write articles for various North Dakota newspapers about local boys in uniform, which he does with great success. And after a few months, we arrange with our American colleagues to send Hank here to write for *The Stars and Stripes.*

"Now, Hank has led a pretty insular life, and he knows as much about Britain and the war in Europe as I do about North Dakota. Then, soon after he arrives, we take him in a military train to Southampton. We travel at night, keeping the window blinds in the carriage tightly closed 'because of the blackout.' When we arrive, he sees a sign on the station platform that says 'North Dover'—that won't be too hard to arrange. In addition, the similarity between the name of his home state and the name of the station should ensure that he remembers where the camp is located.

"The next day we show him all over the camp, accompanied by one of our photographers. More correctly, we take him to see everything we want him to share with the Germans. That includes hundreds of tanks lined up ready to cross the Channel, weapons of all kinds including antitank guns, vehicles in profusion, and as many soldiers as possible. The more of our men and weapons that we can convince the Germans will be taking part in the landing in the Pas-de-Calais, the more of their men and weapons they'll move from the real landing site to the fictional one to defend against our mighty onslaught.

"After his visit, we examine each photograph minutely, under a microscope if necessary. If we find something that might reveal the actual location, we either doctor the photograph or, more likely, simply discard it. We'll have plenty of suitable pictures, and we don't want the Krauts even to think that we've altered a photo. In the meantime, we put Hank to work writing a lengthy article about his visit. We warn him that every word he pens will be subject to close military censorship. Then we make any necessary changes to his story. We'll take the greatest care not to let Hank see anything during his visit that we don't want the Germans to know about, so 'censorship' means just adding a few facts and figures regarding the vast scale and power of the invading force that he may have omitted.

"His article appears on the front page of the next day's *Stars and Stripes* under his byline. We even have a photograph of him with a top American general— Patton if we can manage it, otherwise Eisenhower. The story continues inside the newspaper, with more photographs of the camp in 'North Dover.'

"And then we wait. The article will soon get to the *Ausland-SD* (Foreign Security Service), the successor to the *Abwehr*, and the incurably curious SS-General Walter Schellenberg will start asking questions. Why did we publish the story? Why so many photographs? Why did we give the task to a completely unknown reporter like Hank, when we have numerous famous war correspondents in London, including Ernest Hemmingway? And eventually Schellenberg, Hitler's thirty-four-year-old intelligence *wunderkind*, will send messages to his agents in London, instructing them to meet with Hank and obtain more information."

"And do we, in turn, order Hank to stay under cover and stay as far as possible from Nazi agents?" Lieutenant Wallstead asked.

"On the contrary! We encourage him to meet with all and sundry. He'll have a minder of course, in the extremely unlikely event that anyone tries some rough stuff in London, but we allow Hank to speak freely. After all, if we don't want him to inform the Germans about something, we don't show it to him during his visit to the marshalling camp.

"The object of the exercise is to allow Hank to impart fullest details of what he truly believes is our invasion camp in the South East to anyone and everyone who asks. Hank will at all times tell the truth, the whole truth, and nothing but the truth. That's how he was brought up in North Dakota, and a few days in England can't change his deep-seated belief in Truth, Justice, and the American Way."

On hearing the dour, elderly Pankhurst solemnly intoning the catchphrase from *Superman* comic books, the men exchanged surreptitious amused glances. Oblivious to the reactions of her colleagues, Senior Commander Limberg raised her hand.

"Sir, what if someone remembers seeing him in Southampton and asks him about it? That'll blow his story to smithereens."

"That's a good point—let's think about it. The chances of that happening are slim, but it's certainly possible. For safety, during his visit we'll keep him as far from soldiers as possible, and concentrate on vehicles—tanks, jeeps, armored cars and the like. We'll also show him weapons of all sorts, including field artillery. And howitzers, of course; every American artillery regiment has thirty-six howitzers."

"But won't he get suspicious if he doesn't see any soldiers?" Carlyle asked.

"Of course he has to see troops, and in huge numbers. But other than a few generals who'll know to keep their mouths tightly shut, he mustn't meet any soldiers face to face. For example, we can arrange for thousands and thousands of men to form up on the far side of a huge parade ground, and Hank will see them from a significant distance away. We'll accompany him during his visit, and we'll take steps to ensure that he doesn't meet anyone else. We'll think up a credible explanation for that when the time comes.

"Any other questions?"

CHAPTER SIXTEEN

Ausland-SD *Headquarters, Berlin*
Thursday, March 23rd, 1944

"Donndorf," SS-General Walter Schellenberg said, "as you well know, a month ago *Herr* Hitler abolished the *Abwehr* and assigned all its functions to the *Ausland-SD* (Foreign Security Service). He cashiered Admiral Canaris, and you became my aide. What you may not have heard is that he has placed Admiral Canaris under house arrest. I leave it to you to ponder why the *Führer* has taken this action.

"Now, returning to business, I've had another chat with SS-Major Bernhard Krüger. His counterfeiters have produced a first draft of one sheet of the map, the one that includes Calais. Krüger assures me that they understand the basic rule: the map must never ever contradict what the Allies can see from the air. He gave them the correct sheet plus up-to-date aerial reconnaissance photographs, and a list of changes for them to make. Here's the correct map, this is the doctored map for us to check, and these are the latest photographs.

"You can see that the Atlantic Wall corresponds exactly to what we've built so far; the dashed lines show what we're still going to construct. It's identical on both maps. But look here in the area around Calais. Can you see in the doctored map that they've removed a lot of the artillery defenses? This building over here on the real map, the key shows that it's a fortified artillery battery, the one there, do you see it? Now look at the forgery. They've turned it into a barracks. Brilliant, aren't they? Take a moment to compare the two maps. In reality, the Calais district is heavily fortified, of course, but the counterfeiters have cleverly made it look as if even a relatively small invasion force could easily establish a beachhead in that area.

"Krüger tells me that, if we approve this draft, they'll start working on the final version right away. Do you know, Krüger's a funny chap. For example, as you know, the SS control all the concentration camps, and they've issued a rule: every prisoner is to be addressed by the number tattooed on his or her forearm, never by name. Krüger, however, not only addresses every one of his forgers by name, he calls them *Herr* Goldschmidt or *Herr* Levin. And he speaks to them with such respect. But at the same time, when prisoners have needed medical attention, he's had them shot. For fear his secret might get out, he's quite open about the fact that he won't allow his prisoners out of the area of the two barracks and he won't allow anyone from outside, such as a nurse or a doctor, to enter. Such kindness mixed with such cruelty.

"Oh well, what else would you expect from an SS-officer?" said SS-General Schellenberg.

***

The headmaster of Stragham College beamed effulgently. "Mr. Carlyle, of course we're absolutely delighted to help the war effort in any way we can. Mr. Longstreet, our distinguished senior Classics master, is one of our most outstanding pedagogues, but the school will somehow have to manage without him for a few days while he puts his outstanding brain to work for the good of our country."

You'll manage just fine without him, Carlyle thought. *They're already celebrating in the Masters' Common Room. And in all the classrooms.*

"Ah, here's the man of the moment! On behalf of us all, Mr. Longstreet, I wish you good luck and Godspeed as you go off to fight the Hun."

Hector was about to say something nasty to the headmaster in reply when he caught sight of Carlyle and remembered the scene in the safehouse more than three months earlier. He caught himself in time and instead thanked the headmaster politely. He and Carlyle then left, stopping at Mrs. Bunting's house to allow the elderly teacher to pack a suitcase.

Johnson was waiting for them in the library. The schoolmaster seemed delighted; he rubbed his hands together and smiled. "Excellent! Let's get started. What do you want me to do this time?"

"We need another crossword, please." Carlyle said. "It has to have the following words in the top line of the grid: **SCOTLAND** and **NORWAY**. That's eight letters plus six letters, plus a black square between them. That makes fifteen squares in total. Would that work? I believe that all the standard grids are fifteen by fifteen."

"Yes, that's true. And Grid Number 4 has two words of the correct lengths in the top line. That should work well," Hector replied.

"The next part is harder, we think. All crossword grids are symmetric, so the bottom line of the grid contains a six-letter word followed by an eight-letter word. Can you manage to compose a puzzle with the answer **CLIFFS** for 25-across and **BOULOGNE** for 26-across?"

"When you say that this is more difficult, I assume that's because 14-down would then need to be a nine-letter word ending in the letter I where it intersects with **CLIFFS**?"

"Yes, indeed," Carlyle answered, amazed that Longstreet could visualize all the details of the puzzle.

"But as you well know, Mr. Carlyle, the nominative and vocative plurals of all second declension nouns in Latin end with the letter I. And many of those words have been incorporated into English. I'm thinking about words like **CALCULUS** with plural **CALCULI**."

"Yes, but **CALCULI** is only seven letters long, and we need nine. Up to now we've come up empty handed."

"Have you considered Latin phrases commonly used in English, like **ANNO DOMINI**? No, that's no use at all, that's ten letters. I'm starting to see the problem.

Just a minute, I've got it. How about **HOMUNCULI**, the plural of **HOMUNCULUS**, meaning a little man?"

"But isn't the word **HOMUNCULUS** somewhat obscure?" Johnson said doubtfully. "The only place I've seen it used is in writings by alchemists."

"And it's in Laurence Sterne's eighteenth century humorous novel, *The Life and Opinions of Tristram Shandy, Gentleman*," Carlyle added mischievously, knowing full well that Longstreet abhorred all novels.

"I agree that **HOMUNCULI** is somewhat unusual," Longstreet remarked. "But that's actually a good thing. You both know that I almost never include such words as answers in my puzzles; that means that the Germans will notice it. Of course, they'll also notice that it's a Latin word, one of the three signposts I'll insert into the puzzle. The other two, place names outside Britain, are obviously **BOULOGNE** and **NORWAY**. Yes, I believe I can put together a crossword that incorporates your four words. Give me a few days, and I'll see what I can do."

"It's Thursday at noon, Mr. Longstreet," Carlyle said. "I'm afraid that you have only until Saturday afternoon at two o'clock, or at most three. Then we have to rush your clues to Manchester for typesetting. We'll leave you alone now. I'll arrange to have your meals sent in here, so you can compose undisturbed."

***

As they left the room, closing the door behind them, Johnson turned to Carlyle. "Even though we all agreed on it yesterday, I'm beginning to have second thoughts about our crossword."

"What's wrong with it?"

"It's hardly subtle, is it? I mean to say, Scotland is juxtaposed with Norway, the White Cliffs of Dover are set opposite Boulogne. We might as well have dropped one of Marks's dumb homing pigeons over Germany with the message something like, 'Dear Mr. Hitler, we've got two armies. One's in Scotland, opposite Norway, and we're going to invade Norway with it. And the other one's in Dover, across from Boulogne, and we wanted to let you know that the soldiers in Kent are headed for that French city.'"

"I think you're exaggerating a little," Carlyle replied. "It's not quite as obvious as you claim. For example, it takes a few mental steps to go from the answer **CLIFFS** to the city of Dover. We're English, and for us the White Cliffs of Dover are part of our culture. But the crossword is intended for German consumption, and I doubt that they'll immediately jump to the conclusion that **CLIFFS** equals Dover. It should take them at least a minute or two to work it out.

"And in any case, who cares if it's obvious? They sent that man in stage makeup to instruct our friend Hector to find out where we're invading. Longstreet's done even better than that; he's told them where our armies are located as well. The Germans are going to give him a medal."

CHAPTER SEVENTEEN

Lille, France
Thursday, April 20th, 1944

Pierre-Auguste Amblève was in the back garden of his house in an outer suburb of Lille attending to his homing pigeons when he heard a peremptory banging on his front door.

"I'm coming," he shouted.

After checking that all the cages were securely fastened, Pierre-Auguste made his way to the front door and opened it. Standing outside was a *Gestapo* officer in a long double-breasted black leather coat. Behind him stood two French policemen trying to look solemn.

"You are Pierre-Auguste Amblève?"

"Yes, I am."

"Papers, please."

The "please" was a formality. Amblève reached into his shirt pocket and handed over his French identity papers.

"You are a member of the *Fédération Nationale des Sociétés Colombophiles de France?*"

"Yes, I am."

"And what exactly is that organization?"

"It's the French national organization for pigeon fanciers."

"What is your membership number?"

"I'm 8652."

"And that number appears on the bands of all your homing pigeons?"

"Yes, of course."

"And if we find a pigeon with a band on its leg that bears the label beginning FNSCF 8652, followed by the number of the bird, it's yours?"

"Certainly."

"No one else can use that identification?"

"No, they can't."

"Pierre-Auguste Amblève, you're under arrest for treason and crimes against the state. Come with us."

They bundled Pierre-Auguste into a police van. He soon found himself in an interrogation room in *Gestapo* headquarters in Lille. On the table in front of him was a metal cage containing a pigeon. He noticed that the newspaper lining the bottom of the birdcage was in German.

"Amblève, two days ago that pigeon flew into a loft in Bremen. The owner noticed a small container attached to its leg. He put the pigeon into that cage and brought the bird straight to the *Gestapo*. We opened the container and found a message inside written in code, a simple substitution code that a child could break. The message read: GERMAN TROOP TRAIN CALAIS 23 APRIL 2200 HOURS. The message was in French, Amblève.

"The message was unsigned. But the pigeon, like every homing pigeon, bore a band. And the band begins 'FNSCF 8652'—and you've told us that the only person who could use that identification is you, Amblève."

Up to then, Pierre-Auguste was more puzzled than frightened. He realized that someone had made a mistake. He had heard that arguing with the *Gestapo* was a particularly bad idea. So he'd calmly climbed into the back of the police van, certain in his own mind that the matter would soon be sorted out and he could return to his beloved birds. But when the *Gestapo* officer informed him that his unique identification appeared on the band, he became utterly terrified.

"*Monsieur*," he replied, "I don't understand. Look at that pigeon, look at its long neck. That's an English Carrier pigeon. We don't have birds like that in France; it's a separate breed, a separate species. That's definitely not my pigeon."

"Aha! You admit to having a foreign pigeon, one belonging to an enemy country."

"No, *monsieur*, I admit nothing of the kind. And in any event, if someone had given me a British racing pigeon and I released it, it would fly to Britain, not to Bremen."

"But it has your band on it. It's your pigeon, bearing a code message for the enemy."

"May I examine the bird?"

"You may not open the cage. But look at it by all means."

Pierre-Auguste looked through the bars at the metal band on the bird's leg. He examined the bird from all sides.

"*Monsieur*," he said excitedly, "that is not my band."

"Liar! You've told us repeatedly that band is definitely your band."

"No, *monsieur*. Look at the number. My number is, as I told you, 8652. The number on the bird is 8562."

"What? Let me see that bird."

The *Gestapo* officer reached clumsily into the cage and grabbed the pigeon. Pierre-Auguste winced.

"You," the agent ordered the nearest policeman. "Write this down carefully: FNSCF 8562. Then 235."

He shoved the bird back into the cage, trying to ignore the deposit the terrified pigeon had left on the table.

"So tell me, Amblève, whose bird is that?"

"*Monsieur*, I don't have the faintest idea. It has to be a member of the *Fédération Nationale des Sociétés Colombophiles de France*, but I don't know everyone's membership number. I assume that you traced this bird to me by contacting the headquarters of the FNSCF here in Lille. I assume that they can help you."

"In the *Gestapo* we assume nothing. You, lock him up in a cell. And you, fetch someone to clean up the table."

The agent marched out of the interrogation room.

***

"*Monsieur* Lacasse, when I came to your house earlier this morning you gave me the name and address of one of your members. I have another number. I need you to assist me again."

"Certainly, *monsieur*. What is the number?"

"The new number is 8562."

"Isn't that the number you gave me this morning?"

"No. This morning I gave you 8652. This one is 8562."

The secretary of the *Fédération Nationale des Sociétés Colombophiles de France* immediately realized what had happened. Terrified that the *Gestapo* officer might see his smirk, he turned around quickly and went to fetch the membership records from the next room.

"Yes, here it is. Member number 8562 is the late Colonel René Leman, formerly of 202 rue de Rechèvres, Chartres."

"After a member dies, do you assign his number to someone else?"

"Never. That could lead to untold confusion."

"*Monsieur* Lacasse, is it possible that the widow or children of Colonel Leman are currently using that number I gave you?"

"I've never heard of anything like that happening, *monsieur*."

"When did he die?" the agent asked.

The secretary consulted his records. "In 1928. That's the year after the founding of the FNSCF."

"And the life of a homing pigeon is how many years?"

"They can live for up to twenty years, *monsieur*."

"Does that include an English Carrier?"

"An English Carrier?"

"Yes. I understand that it's a separate breed."

"*Monsieur*, if you are in possession of an English Carrier, I can assure you that no French pigeon fancier ever put a band bearing his number on such a bird, let alone a member of the *Fédération Nationale des Sociétés Colombophiles de France*. That would be a national disgrace. The English Carrier is a disgusting creature with a long neck like a giraffe."

He paused for a few seconds and then turned to the *Gestapo* officer with a puzzled look. "*Monsieur*, did you ask me about an English Carrier just after you asked about the lifetime of a homing pigeon?"

"Yes, I did. Why?"

"Because an English Carrier isn't a homing pigeon."

"What is it then?"

"It's a show pigeon. The English breed them and display them at pigeon shows, and only the good Lord knows why they do that. A homing pigeon is a breed known as a Racing Homer, descended from eight different pigeon breeds."

"But the pigeon I have is definitely an English Carrier, and we found a small container attached to its leg containing a secret message."

"*Monsieur*, someone is playing a practical joke on you."

"Someone is playing a practical joke on the *Gestapo*? Do you understand what you're saying?"

"Yes, certainly. But fastening a message container onto the leg of an English Carrier would be like putting a saddle on the back of a cow—you can do it, but it's not much use to anyone. Whoever played the joke was careful to identify the pigeon as belonging to a colonel who died about fifteen years ago. And—"

The secretary's last word went unheard as the *Gestapo* officer stormed out of the house.

***

"Donndorf, we now have a new task. We have to investigate a practical joke that someone has played on the *Gestapo*."

"SS-General, can't they investigate their own practical jokes? I thought that they're in charge of internal security, while we in the *Ausland-SD* are responsible for foreign military intelligence, especially foreign espionage."

"Yes, Donndorf, we are. And that's why SS-General Heinrich Müller, the head of the *Gestapo*, asked me to look into this. It seems that the practical joke, if that's what it is, involves an English Carrier, a breed of pigeon that interests only the British; apparently you won't find any on this side of the Channel. And the message carried by the pigeon involves a possible raid on Calais in two nights' time. That means that the *Oberkommando der Wehrmacht* (Supreme Command of the Armed Forces) is involved in this, too. Here's the file. Look through it and give me your opinion."

Donndorf read through the file. Then he read the entire file a second time, this time examining the photograph of the English Carrier in its cage more closely than before. Finally, he responded.

"SS-General, what we're supposed to think is that some French Resistance leader trained in codes has used a British homing pigeon to try to send a message to London regarding a troop train passing through Calais at ten o'clock on Sunday night. But the bird ended up in a loft in Bremen.

"In reality, the code is essentially a non-code. It's a simple substitution code used in children's games. They didn't even arrange the symbols in groups of five; instead, you can tell the length of each word. And they didn't encode any of the digits.

"Now the homing pigeon. It's British, yes, but it isn't a homing pigeon at all. And either someone placed the bird in that loft in Bremen when the owner was out, or they released it a short distance away and it flew to the nearest loft it could find. And in all probability, it's the only English Carrier pigeon on the European continent; how they got it into Germany is a big mystery.

"And no troop train is scheduled to pass through Calais on Sunday night; in fact, there'll be no military rail traffic at all in the whole region. Three local trains will take workers home after their late shifts, and that's it.

"In conclusion, SS-General, this is clearly a trick of some kind. My best guess—and I stress that it's only a guess—is that the British are targeting one or more locations that night, and not necessarily at ten o'clock. They want us to move as many mobile anti-aircraft units as possible into Calais leaving the real target or targets relatively undefended."

"Plausible, Donndorf. But you're well aware that your conclusion has a weakness."

"Yes, SS-General. As I mentioned, no military trains are scheduled anywhere in northern France on Sunday night."

"Correct."

"But the British may have another target elsewhere in France in mind, perhaps the tank depots to the north of Paris or even the Atlantic Wall."

"I'm tending toward advising the Supreme Command to put all forces on high alert on Sunday night," Schellenberg said. "But in the absence of a clear target, I cannot make a case for moving any military equipment around."

***

At ten o'clock on Sunday night, a squadron of Avro Lancasters bombed German military targets in and around Calais. The Lindemann battery at Sangatte received a disproportionate share of hits, as did the heavy artillery battery at Cap Gris-Nez. Only one bomber was hit, but it managed to limp back over the Channel with two of its four engines out of action. Eventually it landed safely in a potato field not far from Hastings. The planes spared railway stations and other areas where their bombs might have killed or wounded French civilians.

***

"Well, Donndorf, the British managed to fool us this time, didn't they?"

"Did they, SS-General? Some might say that we fooled ourselves."

"Possibly. But what were they hoping to achieve?" Schellenberg asked. "If we'd believed them, we would've fortified Calais and shot down all their bombers."

"Right. Which is why I don't think that the British government was involved."

"What are you saying, Donndorf?"

"Just suppose that we have a German sympathizer in the Royal Air Force. Let's give him a name—let's call him agent MATT."

"Why MATT?"

"After one of our most successful spies in the previous World War, Mata Hari."

"Tell me more about agent MATT."

"Certainly, SS-General. Agent MATT goes on bombing missions against his will, but he has no choice; if he were to nail his true colors to the mast, the British would lock him up as an enemy sympathizer and then he couldn't help us at all. Then he learns that the Royal Air Force is going to attack Calais last night. So he decides to execute a plan that he's been working on for months."

"Go on."

"All his friends know that he's a pigeon enthusiast and that he loves English Carriers, a breed that we on the continent abhor. He tells his fellow aircrew that he's going to play a practical joke on us by dropping an English Carrier pigeon on Germany. He's constructed some sort of parachute-based device that lets the pigeon slowly descend in a cage. When it hits the ground, the cage opens and the pigeon flies out, heading for the nearest loft. He's put French identification on the bird, but no one else who's involved with his scheme is sufficiently knowledgeable regarding pigeons to realize what the FNSCF on the band on its leg means.

"What he doesn't tell his friends is that the pigeon carries a message. He's smart enough to know that we'd ignore a message written in English—that would obviously be disinformation. Instead, he 'encodes' his message in simple French. That way, he can pretend that it comes from a French Resistance group. He drops his pigeon over a large population center while he's on a bombing mission over Germany earlier last week. He and his mates are probably still laughing at the 'joke' they've played on us.

"And that might also explain the simplicity of the code. Agent MATT probably has involved the aircraft mechanics; one of them may have smuggled the bird aboard the plane while he was preparing it for the air strike on Bremen. But the message container must have been empty at the time; the risk of someone finding a piece of paper inside it would be too great. Also, they search the pockets of aircrew before they board their planes, in case they're inadvertently carrying something that would aid us if we capture them. Consequently, agent MATT must have written the message while he was on a plane en route to Germany and he inserted it into the container just before releasing the bird. And the code therefore has to be an extremely simple one."

"I think you're right, Donndorf. A German sympathizer in the Royal Air Force would explain everything. We need to keep a lookout for his pigeons. Only this time we don't want the *Gestapo* to tell the whole world about it. From now on, they need to bring all foreign pigeons straight to us."

***

"Well, Marks, it seems that your friend General Appleby isn't quite as stupid as I'd thought. Among other things, he's used to perfection his ties with Felix Lacasse, the Secretary of the *Fédération Nationale des Sociétés Colombophiles de France*. I assume that before the war he obtained a complete list of the members of FNSCF, especially all the deceased ones."

"Yes, certainly, sir."

"To put the rest of you in the picture: through his work with the pigeon association, Lacasse has established links with a Resistance group in Lille. General Appleby arranged for someone in the group to approach Lacasse to find out what the *Gestapo* was going to do about the bird and the message. They radioed the Free French in London, who told us. And we then informed Bomber Command that the raid could proceed."

"But sir," Chulmleigh asked, "what if the *Ausland-SD* had got involved in the affair? After all, they might have advised the German High Command that we were about to raid Calais, resulting in a huge build-up of anti-aircraft weapons around the port area."

"I didn't see it that way. As you know, the *Gestapo* and the *Ausland-SD* almost never cooperate. In fact, it's going to take a lot of pigeons before SS-General Heinrich Müller, the head of the *Gestapo*, is going to admit that he needs to call in the *Ausland-SD* people. I simply cannot see Müller asking Schellenberg and his crew to investigate a childish practical joke involving a silly-looking bird that someone played on the *Gestapo*."

CHAPTER EIGHTEEN

MI5 Headquarters, London
Monday, May 1st, 1944

" **G**entlemen, Hank is finally on his way to London to write our article for *The Stars and Stripes.*"

The pronouncement triggered smiles all around the table as Air Commodore Pankhurst consulted a file. "Amazingly enough, I managed to get a few of his details correct. His name is actually Cameron Ramstad and he was born and grew up in Minto, in the state of North Dakota, population 630 at the last census."

Their grins broadened.

"He finished high school in June 1940 and went to the University of North Dakota—yes, it seems that they do have a university there. It says here that he 'majored in English Literature'; I think that means that English Literature is the subject that he read at university. He completed his degree in December 1943 and immediately joined *The Stars and Stripes* as a reporter. He must be quite intelligent to be able to complete a four-year degree in only three and a half years.

"It's not clear from this why he isn't in the military; my best guess is that it has something to do with their conscription regulations, which I don't claim to understand. Maybe he's a conscientious objector? Anyhow, General Eisenhower's team understood just what we needed; nothing in his file indicates that the man has ever traveled outside North Dakota. Ignorance is bliss, as Thomas Gray said in his poem, 'Ode on a Distant Prospect of Eton College.'

"They've transferred Ramstad to London; they've organized a room for him at The Dorchester. That's the hotel where Eisenhower lives. I think that billeting Ramstad there is a good idea; the Nazi agents who'll come to The Dorchester to meet with him will conclude that Ramstad is an important person, despite his youth and civilian status.

"As soon as he arrives in London we're going to take him to 'Dover.' The troop train leaves Waterloo Station sometime after midnight; the military authorities will tell us exactly when. We'll get Ramstad aboard at the very last minute, and all the blinds in the train will be drawn; I'm confident that no one will see him. It'll be a slow trip, of course—we're moving a whole army to the South Coast and all the rail lines are busy—so I expect we'll arrive at dawn. I suggest we try to get as much sleep as possible on the train.

"The destination sign is ready for installation on the platform at the station nearest the camp. It's just north of the city of Southampton, of course, but we'll explain that it's a suburban station of Dover. We'll wait in the compartment until all the troops have left, because they're serving us our breakfast there."

"Sir, what do we tell him when he asks why we're not eating in the officers' mess at the camp?" Chulmleigh asked.

"Easy. We tell him that the Southern Railway food is far superior to what he'd get in the mess," Pankhurst replied.

"Sir," Marks asked, with an innocent expression on his face, "I know that most Americans are gullible and that our boy has led a simple life in some godforsaken corner of North Dakota, but won't your claim regarding the excellence of the food on British trains be a little hard for him to swallow?"

"Marks, any more puns like that and I'll have you transferred to Dover. Or Southampton. Or both. Now, where was I? Oh, yes, breakfast in the compartment. After we've eaten, we'll escort him to the camp where General Brandon will meet him and show him what we've told the general we want Ramstad to see, no more and no less. Brandon has his own photographer and the general has told him exactly what to photograph and how to photograph it. More importantly, Brandon has given him precise instructions regarding what not to photograph.

"Lunch will be sandwiches to be eaten wherever we find ourselves at lunch time. When we've shown him everything on our list, we'll take him to the officers' mess where he'll spend the afternoon and evening talking to a bunch of generals—the mess will be off-limits to everyone else. And then, when it's dark, we'll escort him back to the platform to ride back to London in an otherwise empty train that's returning to Waterloo Station for more troops. That seems to cover everything."

At that point, they heard a hesitant knock.

"Come!"

The door opened and a woman entered. She wore an odd uniform: a khaki skirt worn with the shirt, tie, and olive drab jacket of a male American officer. Stranger still, her uniform bore no symbols of rank, but the green armband on her left biceps bore the letter "C."

"Can I help you?" The air commodore was polite but curt.

"Yes, sir. I'm looking for Air Commodore Pankhurst."

"My office is Room 43, on the first floor."

"Your aide, Captain Nicholas, said I should report to you here."

"Can't you see that we're having a meeting?"

"Yes, sir, but Captain Nicholas said that you were waiting for me."

"Waiting for you? Don't be absurd. Why should we be waiting for you?"

"I understood that you'd requested them to transfer me from the States. I'm Cameron Ramstad, war correspondent for *The Stars and Stripes*. I arrived in London early this morning."

The resulting silence was deafening. As almost always, Pankhurst was the first to recover.

"I'm really sorry, Ramstad, but nothing in this file here says that you're a woman. I was expecting a man."

"At least six other female war correspondents are currently here in London, sir, including Martha Gellhorn, Ernest Hemmingway's current wife, and Mary Welsh, his current mistress."

"You seem to be remarkably well informed for someone who's only just arrived here," Pankhurst said.

"I'm an unashamed Anglophile, sir. At college I studied Victorian literature, and I've read every book about your country that I could lay my hands on."

"I see. Well, welcome to Britain, I'm sure you'll enjoy your sojourn here. Please take that empty seat on the other side of the table. Let me introduce you to everyone."

Cameron Ramstad made a point of shaking hands with each of the eight members of the team in turn. Then she looked expectantly at Pankhurst.

"I'm very glad you're here," he said. "I'd like you to visit a marshalling camp and write up what you see. The camp is near Dover, in the South East, but you mustn't mention the location of the camp, of course."

"Can I say that it's in Kent?" she asked.

Trying to hide his surprise at her knowledge of British geography, he replied, "That's up to the military censor. He'll decide whether to allow you to mention the name of the county. We'll travel by troop train, leaving after midnight."

"St. Pancras Station?"

"You don't have to worry about that; we'll pick you up at The Dorchester. But, since you ask, no, it'll be Waterloo."

"That's strange," Cameron said.

"In what way?"

"Well, every novel I've read in which a character travels from London to Dover, he or she leaves from St. Pancras Station. Waterloo Station is for trains to the South West, to Plymouth and Exeter, for example, at least in the books that I've read."

The air commodore tried to cover his confusion by simulating a coughing fit. Then he resumed. "Well, you mustn't believe everything you read in novels. In any event, there's a war on, and the military transport officers certainly know what they're doing. It's going to be a long night, I'm afraid. The South East is clogged with trains taking men and supplies to the marshalling camps. In fact, that's probably why our train leaves from Waterloo—St. Pancras probably doesn't have a spare platform for our train to Dover."

"I'm really looking forward to visiting Dover, sir. Don't you just love Matthew Arnold's marvelous lyric poem, 'Dover Beach'? It's short, yes, but most powerful. And what about those glorious opening lines:

> *The sea is calm to-night.*
> *The tide is full, the moon lies fair*
> *Upon the straits; on the French coast the light*
> *Gleams and is gone; the cliffs of England stand,*
> *Glimmering and vast, out in the tranquil bay.*

"I just can't wait to see the White Cliffs of Dover, 'glimmering and vast.' And Charles Dickens mentions Dover in a number of his novels, especially David Copperfield. I'm sure you remember that David

Copperfield ran away to Dover to be with his Aunt Betsey Trotwood."

"Yes, well, er, that was what Dickens wrote. But I'm sorry to have to tell you that we're not going into Dover itself. As you can imagine, a huge camp like the one you're about to visit has to be located outside the city. Our train will stop at a suburban station. We'll stay in our compartment while they bring us breakfast—the food on British trains is far superior to what we'd get in the officers' mess, of course."

"Really, sir? Then things certainly have changed since the days of Charles Dickens. Near the beginning of Chapter Three of his collection of short stories, *Mugby Junction*, the boy says, 'I am the boy at what is called the Refreshment Room at Mugby Junction, and what's proudest boast is that it never yet refreshed a mortal being.'"

"Yes, yes, I vaguely seem to remember that. Well, after breakfast we'll take you to the invasion camp. You'll be met by the camp commander, General Brandon—"

"I'm extremely pleased that the military authorities have promoted the colonel to the rank of general," Ramstad interrupted with a smile.

"I beg your pardon?"

"I was just making a joke, Air Commodore. Colonel Brandon is the hero of Jane Austen's *Sense and Sensibility*, as I'm sure you know."

"Yes, of course. Well, Hank, I mean Ramstad, now that you know your next assignment, I suggest that you return to The Dorchester. Captain Nicholas will organize a taxi for you. I'll let you know what time tonight we'll pick you up for our trip to Dover. We'll give you more details of your assignment in the train on the way to Dover. Good day to you!"

The door closed behind Cameron Ramstad. The air commodore seemed to have aged ten years. His body sagged, and he stared emptily at the center of the table. Without looking up, in a broken, hollow voice he asked his team, "What do I do now?"

"Actually, sir," Major Tupman said, "I think that the Yanks have been extremely clever. All we need to do is to ensure that Cameron Ramstad never finds out that she's about to visit Southampton. If we can achieve that, she'll turn out to be a highly credible member of the Operation FORTITUDE team. For example, I think we all know a certain Portuguese diplomat, their First Secretary, who's undoubtedly in the pay of the *Ausland-SD*. Dom Tristão Pereira frequently flies to Lisbon, ostensibly to have discussions on a variety of different issues with his government. But our people have followed him, and the discussions he has in Lisbon almost invariably occur inside the German Embassy in that city."

Tupman paused briefly, then continued. "After the article is published, Dom Tristão will certainly receive instructions from Berlin to meet with Ramstad. He'll encounter a young woman with an open face who looks most attractive in an American war correspondent's uniform. When he tries to ask her a question, he'll be engulfed by a torrent of Victorian literature, both poetry and prose. I have no doubt that, amid endless quotations from the works of William Makepeace Thackeray and George Elliot, he'll hear all the details of the camp from her own lips, exactly as she wrote them in her article—after all, she clearly has a superb memory and excellent recall. He won't possibly be able to trip her up, and he'll fly to Lisbon and assure the contingent of *Ausland-SD* officers lurking in Portugal that we have a vast army sitting outside Dover ready to pulverize the Nazi defenders of the Pas-de-Calais. As Alfred Lord Tennyson put it in the last line of 'Ulysses,' truly an immortal poem, 'To strive, to seek, to find, and not to yield.'"

The quotation from Queen Victoria's Poet Laureate for forty-two years had an unexpected effect on Air Marshall Pankhurst. Instantly resuming his customary demeanor, he turned to the Royal Marine and said, "Tupman, one of your many sterling qualities is your ability to get to the heart of a problem and solve it quickly. You rarely misunderstand a situation. But in this instance I'm afraid you've blundered rather badly. My concern is not the credibility of the young woman. On the contrary, I agree with everything you've said; sending Cameron Ramstad to help us was indeed a masterstroke on the part of the Americans.

"My question, 'What do I do now?' referred to the fact that I am about to be trapped in a railway carriage for several hours with an otherwise delightful young person who cannot keep her mouth shut.

"And while on that subject, Tupman," Pankhurst added, shifting smoothly into his low, calm voice that portended imminent danger, "if you or, come to that, if anyone else seated around this table ever dares to quote from the works of a Victorian writer, be it poetry or prose or even a play or a Gilbert and Sullivan operetta, I will personally see to it that he, or she for that matter, is immediately locked up in Broadmoor Hospital for the Criminally Insane for the duration of the war. Only someone who is totally deranged would dare to emulate That Woman in my presence. Am I making myself crystal clear to each and every one of you?"

Eight firm nods followed.

"Good. Now, how do we solve the problem?"

Lieutenant Wallstead slowly raised his hand. "Sir, at an earlier meeting I thought you decided that you, Carlyle, and Limberg would accompany Hank on the trip to Dover. I realize that space is at a premium in troop trains, but you're surely going to be seated in a first-class carriage, which is unlikely to be full. I suggest that you arrange for two compartments, one at each end of the carriage. When you board the train, you seat yourself next to Ramstad, and Limberg sits opposite. Carlyle disappears. Then, when the train has left Waterloo Station, Carlyle enters and whispers something in your ear. You look suitably grave. You turn to the war correspondent and say something like, 'You'll have to excuse me for a minute, Ramstad— something important has just come up. I'll be back in a jiffy.' Then you go into the compartment at the other end of the train and sleep soundly until the conductor wakes you for breakfast."

***

"Are you here to tell us about another bombshell?" one of the Bloxham twins asked Bridget. Like everyone else in the Internment Camp, she could not distinguish between the two of them.

"Fortunately not. I simply want to update the three of you. I've just come back from Major Froschtümpel. While solving Hector's latest effort I quickly noticed the classical signpost; the clue he came up with was **Little Latin men hum; uncoil (9)**. Quite clever really—'uncoil' is part of the anagram as well as the instruction to the solver to rearrange the letters of **hum uncoil** yielding **HOMUNCULI**.

"And then I found something even more interesting. On the top line, 1-across and 2-across read **SCOTLAND** and **NORWAY**, respectively. And the bottom line was **CLIFFS**—that was 25-across— and **BOULOGNE** for 26-across."

"Well, that all seems extremely clear to me," the same twin said. "We have an army in Scotland waiting to invade Norway, and another in Dover about to land in Boulogne."

"Why Boulogne?" Sir Lucius asked.

"It's a port," the other Bloxham twin replied, "a fishing port, the biggest one in all of France. I believe that they specialize in catching herrings. Lucius, old chap, some regions of France have no harbors to speak of, like Normandy. Consequently, we couldn't possibly land in that region. But the Pas-de-Calais has a variety of excellent ports, including Boulogne, which is about twenty miles from Calais in a southwesterly direction."

"Well," Lucius Featherstone said, "that makes everything considerably less clear to me. You've informed me that Boulogne would make an excellent target, but I understood that everything that Hector tells us is fictional. In other words, we have no idea where the invasion will take place, but it's certainly not going to be Boulogne."

"Maybe," Bridget said, "just maybe, our people are playing a rather clever game. Suppose that they've somehow let the Germans know that Hector Longstreet is a true-blue Englishman who's trying to fool them. Then they'll know not to believe a word he says. In particular, the Germans will then be fully aware that Boulogne is merely a feint. So they wouldn't need to fortify it; that port is one place where we'll never invade."

"And then we invade Boulogne," said the first Bloxham. "Brilliant!"

"But what do I do now?" Bridget asked.

"I don't understand all the ins and outs," Sir Lucius Featherstone said. "But it seems to me that you need to play a straight bat."

"Meaning what exactly?"

"It's a cricketing term."

"We didn't play cricket at my school," Bridget said.

"Of course you didn't, my dear," Sir Lucius said. "Cricket is played at boys' schools, and you're not a boy. I was using the phrase figuratively. What I meant was that you should act in a straightforward manner. Don't try to work out what the spies and secret agents are up to. On Mondays, solve Longstreet's puzzle, and if Hector has inserted military information, don't tell Froschtümpel; come and tell us about it. And if it should happen that the infernally cunning major hands you a completed grid with a secret message embedded in it, go ahead and compose a set of clues for him—and inform us right away.

"In short, Miss Hawkesbury," Sir Lucius said, "stop worrying, don't try to be clever, and just do your job. Or as Sir Henry Newbolt put it in his immortal poem, 'Vitaï Lampada,' in my opinion the greatest poem ever written, 'Play up! play up! and play the game!'"

"Just ignore him, Miss Hawkesbury," one of the twins said, "he's back on his cricket wicket."

CHAPTER NINETEEN

MI5 Headquarters, London
Wednesday, May 3rd, 1944

"Well, gentlemen," Air Commodore said, "I thought that our visit to 'Dover' went extremely smoothly, with the exception of one unfortunate incident that I'll come to later. Miss Ramstad saw exactly what we wanted her to see in the way of weapons and vehicles and the like. She saw thousands of troops, but all from a safe distance. And the only people she encountered face-to-face were Carlyle, Limberg, and me, plus a dozen American generals—and no one else.

"Now, I'd forewarned the Americans that Ramstad has memorized virtually every book by a Victorian novelist, dramatist, or playwright. I also told them I was bringing with me several cases of eighteen-year old Lochervan whisky, 'the crowning glory of the whisky maker's art,' and reminded them that whisky is an excellent painkiller. I arranged for the mess stewards to keep the various generals' glasses full at all times.

"The problem arose when Ramstad finally came to the end of her description of all the Victorian novels that mention Dover, all the Victorian poems about Dover, and all the Victorian plays that have scenes set in Dover. We were blessed with a lengthy silence. Then General Brandon, who really should've know better, decided to chip in with his tuppence worth. The bloody man can't hold his liquor.

"'Miss Ramstad,' he said, slurring his words, 'did you know that Act IV, Scene 3 of Shakespeare's *King Lear* takes place in the French camp near Dover?'

"'And Scenes 4 and 7, as well,' Ramstad replied. 'And Scene 6 is set in fields near Dover. And what about Act V? Scenes 1 and 3 are at the British camp near Dover and Scene 2 takes place between the two camps.'

"And then she said to Brandon, 'Since you clearly love *King Lear* as much as I do, why don't we all perform the play here and now in the mess? You and your colleagues can read the male parts and I'll play Cordelia, Regan and Goneril.' And she shouted to a mess steward to bring some copies of the complete works of Shakespeare.

"I rushed outside after the steward and I told him that he was to come back after about five minutes and explain most apologetically to General Brandon that someone had taken the only copy of Shakespeare from the camp library. The steward came back at the right time and recited his lines quite convincingly. To which General Brandon replied, 'Not to worry, I have a copy in my quarters.'"

"What did you do, sir?" Johnson asked.

"I looked at my watch, and said something like, 'Merciful heavens, we've got a train to catch.' We then hurriedly said our goodbyes, and the driver rushed us to the station. We waited on the freezing platform for nearly two hours for the train to arrive. But the torments of Hades would have been preferable to amateur dramatics with an all-star cast of inebriated American generals.

"Ramstad is working on her article, and the proofs of the photographs should be ready for our inspection by the end of this meeting. I can't wait to see the story in Friday's *Stars and Stripes*. And I look forward to being present at the court-martial of General Brandon on a capital charge of conduct unbecoming of an officer, followed by his execution by the most painful means possible—listening to Cameron Ramstad recite Victorian poetry."

The Air Commodore's remark triggered a burst of heartfelt laughter. Then Lieutenant Wallstead put up his hand.

"Yes?"

"Sir, I've just thought of a possible problem. You told us that all the military personnel saw Ramstad from a distance, with the exception of various generals who can be trusted to say nothing."

"Yes. And?"

"What about the mess stewards, sir?"

The air commodore's face fell.

"And sir," Limberg added, "what about the stewards on the train who served her breakfast, as well as other members of the staff of the train that took her to Southampton? And the train staff on the return journey back to London?"

***

"What do you think of the article?" Pankhurst asked later that day. "Can we pass it on to the next committee for vetting?"

"It looks fine to me, sir," Major Tupman said. "One comment, though. It doesn't state where Cameron Ramstad is staying."

"Yes, that's deliberate. We don't want every American soldier in London coming to The Dorchester to ask Miss Ramstad for a date. On the other hand, anyone who really needs to meet with her, like a certain Portuguese diplomat, can telephone the United States Army Public Relations Office in London and obtain her address. Any other comments?"

***

"SS-General, three nights ago the British bombed Berlin."

"Yes, Donndorf. With the Allied bombardment of transport and communications targets in France night after night, we were all hoping that they'd forgotten about Berlin. But the bombing seems to have restarted. We lost hundreds of people. Fortunately, the fires had difficulty crossing our wide boulevards, but tens of thousands of Berliners are nevertheless homeless. We shot down fifteen of their bombers and eight of their fighter planes. They shot down thirty-one of our fighters. But the real problem is that they'll soon replace the fifteen bombers, the eight fighters, and their aircrews—we cannot."

Donndorf nodded grimly to acknowledge that he had understood. He then returned to what he had been saying.

"SS-General, the morning after the raid, a pigeon fancier in the western suburb of Tegel found an English Carrier in his loft."

"Why did it take such a long time for us to learn about it? We've instructed the police and the *Gestapo* to rush any strange pigeons to us."

"SS-General, one of the targets of the air raid was the training area for flak troops in Tegel. The suburb was badly bombed. Pigeons were understandably of lower priority."

"Yes, of course. I understand now. What did they find fastened to the pigeon?"

"An identification band on its leg, ostensibly from a member of the *Fédération Nationale des Sociétés Colombophiles de France*. Our people contacted Felix Lacasse, the Secretary of the society, in Lille. It's the same sort of story as before: the FNSCF member, a highly respected senior civil servant who lived in Marseilles, died several years ago."

"Just a minute," Schellenberg said. "How did agent MATT get hold of the membership list?"

"It seems that when you release a homing pigeon, even a highly trained one that's never strayed before, it can sometimes turn up in a strange loft, hundreds of miles from home. Before the war, in a spirit of mutual cooperation, pigeon fanciers widely circulated information that might assist in returning lost birds to their owners. When someone found a pigeon that didn't belong in their loft, they consulted the relevant membership list and informed the owner, who then made arrangements to retrieve it. That means it isn't at all surprising that someone in Britain has a pre-war copy of the FNSCF list, including the membership numbers of dead members."

"And did they find a message attached to the English Carrier?"

"Yes, they did. Again it was in French, and again it was in the same substitution code. He replaced every instance of the letter A by the letter J, and so on. It's really childish."

"And what was the message?" the SS-General asked.

"FIRST UNITED STATES ARMY GROUP IN KENT TO INVADE BOULOGNE."

"What?"

"Yes, SS-General. Agent MATT seems to have access to top-secret information."

"Information that ties in with what Longstreet is telling us."

"Actually, SS-General, Longstreet is more precise. He used the answer CLIFFS in his latest crossword to inform us that the invasion force will sail from the port of Dover, whereas the pigeon man merely specified Kent, which is quite a large county with several good ports."

"But agent MATT has found out about FUSAG. Anyhow, it appears that Britain has a number of

German sympathizers whom they trust sufficiently to tell them military secrets. I thought that the British were more careful than that."

"SS-General, as you know, I studied at Heidelberg University. But I spent one semester at the London School of Economics. One of the many useful things I learned is that the British leadership places virtually unlimited faith in their fellow members of the aristocracy. Two students in my class were out-and-out communists. But because one was the son of a viscount and the other was an earl, everyone assumed that they weren't even socialists. Instead, they were 'poseurs' or 'they were going through a phase.' If agent MATT went to one of the top British schools, like Eton or Harrow, no one would even dream of questioning his loyalty."

"But what about Forbes Penthwick, the leader of the British National Socialist Party? He's the son of a marquess, the second-highest rank in the British peerage. Nevertheless, they interned him in 1940."

"SS-General, he tried to overthrow the elected government and replace it with a fascist state. He went a bit too far, even for an aristocrat. But provided that agent MATT doesn't air his pro-Nazi opinions outside the fellow-thinkers in his social circle, no one will suspect a thing."

SS-General Schellenberg stared out the window for nearly a full minute. Then he turned and looked straight at his aide.

"Donndorf, both you and I have extremely suspicious minds. Are you thinking what I'm thinking?"

"You mean that the various pieces of information regarding Boulogne as the invasion target are in reality components of a clever British disinformation campaign?"

"Of course."

"Well, SS-General, Longstreet came to our embassy in London in mid-1938. I find it difficult to believe that MI5 sent him to us to establish a communications channel, via crossword puzzles no less, in the anticipation of a possible war that wouldn't be declared for another year. And despite my many suspicions regarding agent PICKFORD that I've repeatedly raised with you, the one thing that's overwhelmingly in his favor is that he gave us the blueprints of the Muir bombsight way back in mid-1937. MI5 was so totally disorganized in those days, so unprepared for the forthcoming war, that it's hard to conceive of their officers being able to set up a trusted conduit from London to Berlin at that time; they simply didn't have the skills or the manpower to achieve such a thing."

"I agree on both counts. Longstreet and PICKFORD cannot conceivably be British plants, and for that reason we probably should trust the information they send us. Of course, it's always possible that MI5 have cottoned on to their activities and, consequently, Longstreet and PICKFORD are unwittingly sending us disinformation. But I am firmly of the opinion that they believe that whatever they send us is factually correct. Neither of them is trying to deliberately mislead us."

"Yes, indeed, SS-General. But what about agent MATT?"

"What about him?"

"Unlike Longstreet and PICKFORD, he's only just appeared on the scene. He doesn't have a history that goes back to well before the war started. And the circumstances are really weird: English Carrier pigeons, a trivial substitution code, and messages in French. It's all terribly bizarre."

"No more bizarre, perhaps, than an elderly schoolteacher of Latin and Greek turning up at our embassy with a proposal to hide messages in crosswords. And we've agreed to trust Longstreet."

"That's true, SS-General. The whole situation is typically British: odd-looking pigeons that have no homing instincts, and turning coding into a game. Perhaps we're looking at agent MATT the wrong way."

"Meaning what?"

"Meaning that the circumstances are so incredibly unlikely that he must be genuine. Even the British, masters of unconventionality and idiosyncratic quirks, couldn't have dreamed up a disinformation scenario that's so outlandish and, quite frankly, so ludicrous. If I'd written a spy thriller and included anything as hard to believe as English Carrier pigeons turning up mysteriously in German lofts, any sane editor would have rejected the book on the spot. And yet the arrival of those pigeons actually happened. And not just once but twice. SS-General, I think we have no alternative. We have to believe that agent MATT is for real."

CHAPTER TWENTY

MI5 Headquarters, London
Wednesday, May 3rd, 1944

"Well, Marks, it seems that one of your pigeons actually found its way into a Berlin loft."

"We were extremely lucky, sir. The plan was for the aircrew on one of the planes leading the air raid to release ten birds over Hanover on their way to Berlin. But because the flak around Minden was much heavier than usual, they had to turn north for some miles before heading once more towards Berlin, and they bypassed Hanover. The first city they encountered was Berlin itself. As a result, they dropped the pigeons as soon as they found themselves flying over a major suburb, which happened to be Tegel.

"But Tegel turned out to be the target of some of the other planes taking part in the raid. As a result, the cardboard cages glided slowly to the ground, they opened, the pigeons flew out—and the next wave of Lancasters bombed them. As I said, sir, it was just luck that one of the pigeons managed to survive and make its way to a loft."

"And what with the bomb damage we managed to inflict on Tegel, it took two days for the bird to end up in the hands of the *Ausland-SD*," Pankhurst said.

"Did you say '*Ausland-SD*,' sir?" Tupman asked.

"Yes, I did. We've been lucky with that, too. *Monsieur* Lacasse in Lille, the Secretary of the Pigeon Fanciers Association, told his contact in the French Resistance that this time it was someone from the *Ausland-SD* who contacted him regarding the band on the pigeon's leg. He was adamant on that point. I'm pleased to report that I was wrong; the pigeon plot has attracted the attention of SS-General Schellenberg and his merry men far sooner than I'd thought."

"That means that now we have three conduits for disinformation," Wallstead said. "We've got agent PICKFORD and his team, Hector Longstreet, and now the pigeons."

"Plus all the double agents, of course," Harkness added.

"But don't we have to consider a possible danger?" Limberg asked. "If we overwhelm the *Ausland-SD* with a wide variety of different messages from their agents in Britain, all saying that the invasion will be in the Pas-de-Calais, probably in Boulogne, won't the Germans get suspicious? After all, it's one thing for sources to be consistent. It's quite another to receive a whole host of reports from your many agents, each of them containing exactly the same supposedly top-secret information."

"That's a really good point, Limberg. I think I need to meet with the Double-Cross people. We can't have all the double agents telling Germany the site of the invasion. After all, how many of them would have access to that information? For the sake of credibility, some of those who claim to have found out the location have to get it wrong."

"And what about the PICKFORD subagents, sir?" Johnson asked. "Some of them report to PICKFORD along the lines that they played bridge at the Army and Navy Club and during a hand they overheard Rear Admiral Plunkett say something about a forthcoming naval maneuver. Perhaps we can create gossip of that kind to implant a small amount of doubt regarding the Pas-de-Calais as the target—until we get closer to the actual invasion, of course."

"And what about Southern Norway, sir?" Carlyle inquired. "We seem to have stopped providing information about our forthcoming assault in that region."

***

"Yes, sir," said Miss Ermintrude Harrington, the headmaster's secretary. "I understand. The car will be here at Stragham College in ten minutes' time to pick him up. I'll tell Mr. Longstreet right away."

She rushed from her desk to his classroom, threw open the door without knocking, and announced dramatically, "Mr. Longstreet, your country needs you!"

Hector Longstreet was standing in front of the blackboard explaining Latin deponent verbs to a class of totally disinterested thirteen-year old boys. Without as much as looking in her direction, he said calmly, "Please go away, Miss Harrington. Now, boys, here's an example. *Loqui* is passive in form but active in meaning. Paullson, what does *loqui* mean?"

"But Mr. Longstreet, the government—"

"Paullson, do you know what *loqui* means?"

"No, sir."

"Mr. Longstreet, they phoned and they said—"

"Paullson, the English adjective 'loquacious' describes someone who talks too much. Do you know of anyone currently in this room, Paullson, whom you might describe as loquacious? Someone, perhaps, who is standing by the door chattering away while I'm trying to teach you about deponent verbs? Anyone, Paullson?"

The boy, wise beyond his years, kept his mouth tightly shut.

"Well, Paullson, now that you know the meaning of the word 'loquacious,' would you care to hazard a guess at the meaning of the word *loqui*?"

Miss Harrington disappeared, the door slammed shut, and the lesson continued.

"Paullson, I believe we were discussing the deponent verb *loqui*. Look over here. I've written the English word loquacious and under it the Latin word *loqui*. What do you think *loqui* means? Could it possibly mean 'to speak' or 'to talk'?"

"I don't know, sir."

"Paullson, you miserable excuse for a human being, do you know anything at all? You were quite unable to discern who the loquacious person in the room was, and now you seem to have no idea—"

This time the headmaster flung the door open. "Ah, Mr. Longstreet. Wonderful news—they need you again! Here, let me help you remove your gown and then escort you to the front door of the school to await the arrival of the car, which will be here shortly. Boys, you will sit in absolute silence and study your Latin textbooks until I return to continue the lesson, which seems to be on deponent verbs. How fascinating! I'll be back shortly."

The two men left the classroom. As they exited from the school building a car drew up. After a stop at Mrs. Bunting's house to allow the schoolmaster to pack a suitcase, the chauffeur drove Hector to the safehouse. Johnson and Carlyle were waiting in the library.

"Mr. Longstreet," Carlyle asked, "we need your cruciverbalist skills once more. Could you construct a puzzle that includes the word HARDANGERFJORD?"

"That's fourteen letters. Grid Number 11 has two thirteen-letter words: 1-down and 10-down, but we have room to extend both to fourteen letters. I should have no problem in coming up with an adequate puzzle. On the other hand, it's a good thing that it's only Wednesday. That gives me three full days to compose a set of clues."

"Why," Johnson asked, "should it take you longer than usual?"

"The word HARDANGERFJORD has fourteen letters, including the letter J. I'm probably going to have to work day and night to come up with a suitable clue. It seems to me that an anagram is the only possibility. But it's going to take me until after lunch on Saturday to come up with something like Jumping frog jarred hand in Southern Norway (14).

"And now, I ask you to leave me to my labors. I'll take my meals in here, starting with lunch right now, so that I can compose without interruption. And the staff need reminding that the 1929 Château Margaux is one of my particular favorites."

Johnson hurried Carlyle into the park-like garden and pointed wordlessly in the direction of the electrified fence. Even though he was on the point of exploding with rage, Johnson managed to control himself until they were fully seventy-five yards from the house before he erupted.

"It took that arrogant bastard just a few seconds to work out that frog jarred hand is an anagram of HARDANGERFJORD. How does he do it? And without pencil and paper—or in his case, pen and paper. He worked the whole thing out in his head. And he even managed to come up with clever wordplay. The clue needs to contain something to tell the solver to rearrange the letters of frog jarred hand. And what does he use? Jumping. Everyone knows that frogs jump, so it's a perfectly natural word to use and it fits in beautifully.

"He's probably the smartest person I've ever met—and unquestionably the most unpleasant. And now he's taking a three-day holiday at the government's expense."

"Actually, Johnson, I think we're getting a real bargain here. For the cost of three days' worth of unrationed food and a few bottles of the finest vintage claret that Château Margaux has produced this century, he'll tie up at least a hundred thousand of Hitler's troops and over two hundred tanks in the vicinity of Bergen—more than a thousand miles away from the beaches of Normandy. And the students and staff of Stragham College will have three days without their beloved Mr. Chips."

CHAPTER TWENTY-ONE

Ausland-SD Headquarters, Berlin
Saturday, May 6th, 1944

"Donndorf, have you seen yesterday's *Stars and Stripes?*"

"Yes, indeed, SS-General. The front-page article on that marshalling camp in the South East of England is most puzzling."

"I agree. It's probably the longest article they've published in that newspaper in several months. In addition to the detailed story, it includes lots of photographs. But why did they give the task to someone called Cameron Ramstad?"

"SS-General, I read about her in that brief write-up that they included. It seems that she finished university less than six months ago. She's freshly arrived in Britain. The Allies have Ernest Hemingway as their top military correspondent, but they gave this plum job to her. And we can't explain it away by saying that they wanted the story to have a woman's perspective; there's nothing even remotely feminine in the entire article. And they've got at least six top female war correspondents in London, including two of Hemingway's wives or mistresses or concubines or whatever. And with all that firepower, they assigned this major journalistic task to a raw beginner named Cameron Ramstad."

"What's your theory, Donndorf?"

"I think we first need to answer another question: why did they want the story to appear in the first place? Everyone knows that the Allies are preparing to invade Europe. Our agents in London tell us that the streets are packed with soldiers wearing the widest variety of different uniforms, and many of the larger provincial cities, especially ports like Liverpool and Glasgow, are also teeming with military men from all over the world. The Allies have to organize those soldiers in such a way that vast numbers can embark on ships and then invade Europe en masse. To that end, they've set up these marshalling camps close to ports on the South Coast of England to enable them to easily move thousands of men across the Channel to a nearby harbor in a few hours.

"It's now certain that the marshalling camps are in two main areas. In the north, in Scotland, they're assembling the British Fourth Army, or BFA. Our agents have infiltrated the area to obtain as much information as possible. We've discovered that the soldiers have been issued with booklets containing useful phrases in Norwegian. Also, there's a village called Inveraray on the West Coast where they've trained tens of thousands of men in amphibious-landing techniques. They've been practicing landing maneuvers in Loch Fyne, a seawater loch; a fjord and a sea loch are essentially the same thing. One of the

PICKFORD subagents is in the Army Catering Corps and is responsible for ordering the food for the training center. As a result, we have an accurate picture of the size of the army that's going to invade a Norwegian fjord from Scotland: ninety-five thousand men."

"Yes, Donndorf, but what's your point?"

"SS-General, not a word about the British Fourth Army has appeared in *The Stars and Stripes*. And yet they included this huge report on the camp in the South East."

"But Donndorf, *The Stars and Stripes* is an American newspaper for American troops. Why would they publish a story about the British Fourth Army?"

"With all due respect, SS-General, the current issue alone contains two articles on the British Eighth Army in Italy."

A long silence followed. Then Schellenberg spoke.

"I see what you mean, Donndorf. What you're saying is that the Allies ordered the article to appear in their military newspaper to unambiguously inform us that they've constructed a large embarkation camp somewhere in Kent. Now why would they do that? Don't they realize that we've known every detail about those camps for months now?"

"SS-General, the British aren't stupid. They've got nearly a hundred thousand men in Scotland and about a hundred and fifty thousand in the South East—they can't possibly keep that information secret. They have to be aware that we know about the BFA in Scotland and FUSAG in Kent. They've tried to be clever.

Wherever possible they've located those camps in wooded areas to make it harder for us to estimate troop concentrations from aerial photographs. They've blocked off the roads in the vicinity of the camps to all civilian traffic. The embarkation camps are now sealed; they're not granting passes to the soldiers.

"Perhaps they don't realize that we know the actual numbers of troops in each area, but the people in MI5 couldn't possibly think for one minute that we're unaware of the two areas of embarkation camps, both rapidly filling with troops. Even if they're stupid enough not to realize that we have *Ausland-SD* spies all over Britain, they see our planes flying over South East England taking reconnaissance photographs, trees or no trees.

"That tells us, SS-General, that the British know that we know about FUSAG in Kent. Why would they organize for a rookie reporter to come to England to publicize an embarkation camp in the South East?"

"Why, Donndorf?"

"Because the camp that Cameron Ramstad saw isn't in the South East. It's somewhere else."

"Are you out of your mind?"

"SS-General, let's suppose just for the sake of argument that the Allies have a third army assembling in secret somewhere in Britain. We know beyond all doubt that FUSAG will invade the Pas-de-Calais and BFA will head for somewhere in Southern Norway. Our forces will be waiting in full force in both locations and we'll crush them. But what if the Allies have yet another army?"

"How come we don't know about it yet?"

"SS-General, perhaps the British have been smarter than we think. They've set up two armies and done nothing to prevent us finding out about them. Our many agents in Britain have provided us with a huge array of different sorts of information. We know about their weapons, landing craft, food, ammunition, chaplains, waterproof gear, and field hospitals. Fuel is a big issue; our spies have been on the lookout for new oil storage depots. We've received reports about morale, increases in radio traffic, and even fights in the bars near the camps before they sealed them a few days ago. We know about the gifts from American servicemen seeking the favors of the local lasses; we've learned how many of those women are now sporting nylon stockings. We even know how many of their younger brothers and sisters have been bribed with chewing gum and chocolate bars. We've seen aerial photographs of the warships that are going to bombard the shore just before the invasion starts and the landing craft and barges they're going to use to transport the troops to the beaches. We know all about their airfields and how many planes they have. Our agents have informed us in detail about the paratroopers who are going to land just before the sea-borne invasion starts, as well as the commando raids that are on the schedule.

"In short, SS-General, we probably know as much about the enemy's armies as the Allies do. In particular, they've split their forces into two in the hope that at least one will be able to successfully establish a beachhead from which the invasion can spread. In response, we've divided our forces into two to be able to defend against assaults both in the Pas-de-Calais and Southern Norway. However, as I suggested, just suppose they've been exceedingly clever and divided their forces into *three* armies. They've let us find out everything we could possibly learn about two of their armies, FUSAG and BFA. They have no reason to keep anything under wraps; the two corresponding invasion sites, the Pas-de-Calais and Southern Norway, are obvious. But what if they have a third site that they've kept totally secret? The two armies that we know about will invade Europe and we'll throw everything we have against them. And once all our forces are committed to their respective battlefields, the third army will cross the seas unopposed and that will be the end of the Third *Reich*."

Schellenberg looked at his aide in horror. "Donndorf, do you really believe what you're saying?"

"It explains everything. A third area of totally secret embarkation camps must exist. But some information has apparently leaked. It clearly hasn't reached any of our agents yet, but the Allies are terrified that we'll soon find out about their deception. To protect their secret, they send a rookie reporter, someone who's just arrived in Britain, to visit the third army and write a story for *The Stars and Stripes*. She's young, she's ignorant, and most of all she's never been to England. So it was easy to convince her that the camp that she was visiting is in the South East. The numerous photographs that accompanied the story are all pretty generic; she could've been virtually anywhere other than a hilly area."

"You may be right. And if you are, we're going to have to interrogate her and find out what she really saw, as opposed to what they told her she saw."

CHAPTER TWENTY-TWO

MI5 Headquarters, London
Monday, May 8th, 1944

C ameron brought the engraved dinner invitation card to the morning meeting to ask the air commodore what she should do. The printed parts of the card were hard for her to decipher, because the engraver had used an ornate form of round hand, an English style of handwriting essentially unchanged from the seventeenth century. But the name of the guest and the date and time of the dinner were even less legible, because the calligrapher who had written them on the card had employed an even more excessively florid round hand, with flourishes and ornaments in every conceivable place.

"Someone delivered it by hand to The Dorchester early this morning and a bellboy brought it up to my room. I've spent nearly half an hour trying to read it," she said. "I think that the letters at the bottom read 'R.S.V.P.' but they're really tiny and surrounded by numerous twirls and spirals."

"Let me have a look at it," Pankhurst said. "Too many calligraphers these days pride themselves on their ability to write beautiful documents in round hand that no one can read. And that's apart from the fact that that sort of calligraphy went out of fashion about two hundred years ago. In fact, I can't think of a single novel set in Victorian times that mentions round hand. Ramstad, can you?"

For once Cameron was silent. Then she shook her head. "No, sir, I can't think of one either."

"There you are then," the air commodore said. Suddenly he recalled that Sir Joseph Porter's first song in *H.M.S. Pinafore* contains the line, "And I copied all the letters in a big round hand." Terrified that the American war correspondent would remember that and set them all singing Gilbert and Sullivan operettas, he flashed a warning look in the direction of Captain Marks who, from the expression on his face, had clearly thought of the song at the same time as his superior officer.

Pankhurst rushed on. "Anyhow, His Excellency João Maria da Silva e Gama, the Portuguese Ambassador to the Court of St. James, and Mrs. da Silva e Gama have invited you 'and a guest' to dinner at the Embassy on Saturday night at eight. Obviously, they read your excellent article over the weekend, and I have no doubt whatsoever that the First Secretary, Dom Tristão Pereira, wants to ask you all about it."

"Is there a reason why I shouldn't accept?"

"On the contrary. We were hoping that Dom Tristão would want to talk to you about your visit to Dover. You can answer all his questions freely, other than telling him that you were in Dover. Say 'Kent,' instead, just as you did in your article."

"That's fine, sir. And who will be my guest that evening?"

"What I think they'll arrange is a dinner for six: the Ambassador and his wife; the First Secretary and his wife, Dona Guilhermina; and you and your guest. As you obviously know from innumerable Victorian novels, after you've all finished the dessert the Ambassador's wife will try to get your attention. Then she'll signal that she's about to leave the dining room. The youngest male at the table will walk to the door and open it and hold it open during the departure of the ladies to the drawing room for coffee; the other gentlemen will stand as you and the other two ladies leave the room.

"My guess is that, when the ladies rise, Dom Tristão will find some reason to escort you to another room to give him the opportunity to ask you questions in private. That tells me that your guest needs to be someone who can make conversation with the Ambassador while they pass the port clockwise from the one to the other, ensuring that the decanter doesn't touch the table as it moves around."

"How can you pass a port decanter clockwise when only two men are left at the table?"

"That's a very good question, my dear. I suggest that you ask the Ambassador when the gentlemen rejoin the ladies in the drawing room. Now, let's return to the issue of your guest. I think we need someone who's familiar with Portugal. I know a Royal Air Force officer who'd be the very person. He was our air attaché in Lisbon before the war. And he's unmarried, so he can certainly accompany you to the dinner without the slightest breach of etiquette. His name is Group Captain Sir Willoughby Teynham.

"Johnson, you know the drill. Here's the invitation. Write out something appropriate that Ramstad can copy on Dorchester writing-paper in her neatest handwriting. And show her what to write on the envelope. Ramstad, don't worry, they're used to people who are unfamiliar with the finer points of social behavior. Just do your best. Then call a pageboy and ask him to hand-deliver it to the Embassy; it can't be more than half a mile from the hotel. Tip him a pound."

When Cameron had left, Carlyle turned to the air commodore. "Sir," he asked, "I'm a little surprised that you didn't send me, or even Limberg, to accompany Ramstad to the dinner. After all, we were with her in 'Dover' and we could've supported or supplemented some of her statements."

"Who knows the answer to that one?"

Limberg's hand shot up. "General Eisenhower has forbidden anyone who knows any details of Operation OVERLORD to leave Britain, and the Embassy of the Republic of Portugal is foreign soil."

"Correct. Actually, I can think of another reason, too. But I devoutly hope that I'm totally wrong."

***

"Donndorf, we've had another message from Hector Longstreet. Sunday's puzzle contained the word **HARDANGERFJORD**. The only thing we haven't yet learned from him is where Eisenhower is going to direct his feints."

"SS-General, I'm suspicious of all this."

"But Donndorf, I thought we agreed that Longstreet is genuinely on our side."

"I have no doubt about that. None at all. But I'm starting to wonder if the British are feeding him false information."

'Why do you say that?"

"SS-General, think about the type of information we usually get. Some months ago, one of our agents sent a radio message informing us that he went to get a suit made, and the tailor told our man that he's going to have to wait several months because the tailor and his assistants are snowed under with making officers' uniforms. And from that we deduced that a troop build-up was starting in Britain.

"A month ago, WILKINS MICAWBER—he's one of agent PICKFORD's most reliable subagents—recently went by train to visit his mother in Plymouth. He commented how empty the whole area was. From that, the members of my group were able to infer that no Allied troop build-up has occurred in that part of the West of England. Now, the *Führer* has been wondering if the Allies plan to invade Bordeaux. If that were the case, the whole region surrounding the major naval base at Plymouth would be a hive of activity. As a result, we were able to reassure *Herr* Hitler that Eisenhower was planning, at most, a minor feint toward Bordeaux.

"Our agents provide us with snippets of information, such as an item of gossip overheard at a game of poker at Brooks's Club in St. James Street regarding the transfer of a general to the Fourth British Army headquarters in Edinburgh Castle, a remark an inebriated spectator made at a football game between soldiers from Canada and South Africa about having to eat whale meat, or an incautious article in a newspaper describing what was probably an act of sabotage at a factory. We discard items of dubious validity and piece the rest together to try to determine where the Allies are going to invade. Sometimes the information is a little more specific, such as the widening of a road to a probable embarkation port, or even a new large sign directing traffic to that port. But what we receive is never in black and white—we always need to interpret and make deductions.

"And then we have Longstreet and his cryptic crossword clues. First he informs us about a raid on Rouen that doesn't take place. Yes, total cloud cover blanketed the whole of Normandy for three successive nights, so that doesn't tell us anything either way. In response, we asked him for information about the forthcoming invasion and he told us that the Allies have an army in Scotland that's going to invade Norway and another one in Dover heading for Boulogne. In other words, suddenly, out of nowhere, we're given detailed precise information in response to our query. And as if that wasn't enough, now he tells us that the enemy's exact target in Norway is Hardangerfjord.

"Here's how I see it, SS-General. We now have nearly eighty agents in Britain sending us information on a regular basis. As I said, most of their material consists of items that require processing of some kind. Even when they give us precise information, it's usually incomplete. You'll remember that last month one of our agents managed to find out the exact number of Spitfire aircraft produced during the previous week at the Castle Bromwich Aircraft Factory in Birmingham. But he couldn't tell us how many were Mark IX and how many Mark XVI, and he was unable to come up with any other figures. Yes, he has an informant in the factory, but that was all the information he was able to obtain from her. In contrast, this man Longstreet tells us where the two invasion armies are located and precisely where they're headed. It's just too good to be true. The only explanation that makes any sense to me is that the British are feeding him disinformation via his former pupil on the Imperial General Staff."

"Donndorf," Schellenberg replied, "I think that you're overlooking a few facts. You were somewhat disingenuous when you informed me that Longstreet 'told us' where the Allies are going to invade. He did no such thing. Instead, he composed cryptic crosswords in which he deeply embedded the information for us. Without Bridget Hawkesbury in Civilian Internment Camp Ilag VIII in Tost, we wouldn't have learned anything from his puzzles. And furthermore, if it weren't for Major Froschtümpel's clever stratagem, she'd never have unknowingly helped us the way she has. Let me put it even more bluntly: how could Longstreet have known in 1938, a year before we interned Miss Hawkesbury, that we'd have a British cryptic crossword expert in a camp in Upper Silesia solving his puzzles and willingly handing over the solutions to us?

"And another thing. I agree with you that our other agents are sending us fragments, whereas Longstreet is providing us with information of the highest quality, albeit hidden in cryptic crosswords. But perhaps you're overlooking the fact that everything that Longstreet communicated to us we've already deduced, to a greater or lesser extent, from information from other agents. That is to say, we've learned nothing new from what he's told us.

"You were in the *Abwehr* for several years before it became part of *Ausland-SD*. You and your colleagues have been receiving information from Britain since before the war started. You told me that your team carefully analyzed everything that the *Abwehr* agents sent to you and then decided whom you could trust and which agents were less reliable. You tested each new shred of data that you received against what you already knew or thought you knew. And Longstreet's information, superb in quality though it is, merely confirms what you'd already concluded. To take your earlier example, the *Führer* wondered if the Allies are going to invade Bordeaux and you and your group told him no. You based your conclusion in part on the report from subagent WILKINS MICAWBER. Now we learn from the crossword puzzles something we already knew, that Bordeaux is not the real target. Yes, Longstreet's information supersedes thousands of messages we've received—but only because what he's told us is fully consistent with all those many earlier reports.

"And one final remark, Donndorf. Let's just suppose you're correct, and that the material that Longstreet has sent us is actually disinformation provided by the British. That would also mean that everything that our agents in Britain have sent us for the last five years is also disinformation. A week ago, Major Hässler suggested that all our agents in Britain, without exception, were in fact double agents under the control of MI5. Twenty-four hours later he was on the Eastern Front. And in the highly unlikely event that you don't understand why, allow me to spell it out for you. If Major Hässler were correct, that would mean that hundreds of former *Abwehr* officers, now *Ausland-SD* officers, including yourself, have been consistently fooled for years. And no one is ever going to admit to that. Not even you, Donndorf, not even you.

"And while I'm on the subject, may I remind you that the information we're getting via those pigeons from the man we've decided to call agent MATT is as precise as Longstreet's and is equally consistent with what we already know. Accordingly, before you suggest that the British are feeding disinformation to Hector Longstreet and agent MATT, my advice to you is to think extremely carefully about the consequences of what you're about to say."

CHAPTER TWENTY-THREE

The Dorchester, London
Saturday, May 13th 1944

"Miss Ramstad, please," the group captain said to the receptionist. She picked up a telephone and dialed Cameron's room.

"She'll be down shortly, sir."

Sir Willoughby Teynham saw a group of women emerge from an elevator. He looked for someone in a glamorous evening gown with appropriate jewelry, not realizing that American women correspondents wore their uniform day and night. Cameron, in turn, was unaware that the Royal Air Force had suspended the wearing of mess dress for the duration of the war. Eventually the man wearing blue-grey Royal Air Force war service dress located the woman in the uniform of a "gal correspondent."

"The reason I arranged to meet you at seven," he said, "was because I wanted us to have a drink and get acquainted before the car arrives at about a quarter to eight. Harry Craddock, one of the world's great barmen, invented the 'Dorchester of London' cocktail here and he still serves it at the Dorchester Bar. It's through that archway."

"What's in it?" she asked a little nervously.

"That's hush-hush. Unless you have the very highest security clearance, I can't possibly tell you. On the other hand, half of London knows the secret recipe, so I suppose I could share it with you in the strictest confidence: dry gin, rum, and forbidden fruit liqueur."

"What on earth is forbidden fruit liqueur?"

"It's made from pomelos, something similar to grapefruit."

"That sounds a little too exotic for me. Would you be terribly insulted if I had a pink gin?"

"Not at all. In fact, I think I'll join you. We have a long night ahead of us."

"Good evening, Harry."

"Good evening, Sir Willoughby. Two Dorchesters, sir?"

"Not tonight, Harry. Two pinkers with plenty of bitters."

"Of course, sir."

Sir Willoughby took the drinks to a table in the center of the room, where a pageboy would easily be able to spot them when the car from the Portuguese Embassy arrived. The group captain had gone straight from a boys' boarding school to the all-male Royal Air Force. As a result, despite many years in the diplomatic corps as an air attaché, he still found it hard to talk to women. Cameron Ramstad did her best to keep the conversation going, but was greatly relieved when she heard a pageboy calling her name.

"Your car is outside, miss."

"Thank you."

"What time do you have?" Sir Willoughby asked him.

"I make it just on half past seven, sir."

"I do, too. Miss Ramstad, the embassy is no more than half a mile from here, and with the fierce petrol rationing, the London traffic is nothing like what it used to be before the war. It shouldn't take much longer than five minutes to drive there. Anyhow, it's better to be early than late. But arriving twenty-five minutes early borders on bad manners."

They followed the boy outside to where the black Rolls-Royce Phantom III was parked in front of the Dorchester. As they neared the vehicle, Sir Willoughby observed, "The car seems to be empty."

Cameron nodded. The pageboy opened the nearside passenger door. As they stepped inside, they realized that two people were seated in front, both fully engaged in looking for something in the glove box; all that the passengers could see were the backs of their identical black coats and chauffeur's caps.

The pageboy now shut the door carefully. Hearing the click, the two men immediately straightened up and greeted their passengers. Almost in unison they politely said, "Good evening, sir. Good evening, madam," but without turning around. Neither of them said another word as the car slid smoothly into Park Lane and soon neared Hyde Park Corner and the Wellington Arch. Sir Willoughby sat back, expecting the chauffeur to take Grosvenor Crescent, the fourth exit from the roundabout, which would lead straight to Belgrave Square. But the driver ignored the turning and instead chose the next exit, Knightsbridge.

"We're early, so you're taking the scenic route, I see," Sir Willoughby remarked.

"Something like that, sir."

But when the chauffeur also ignored the left turn into Wilton Place and continued along Knightsbridge, Sir Willoughby became concerned. "I say, driver, what's your game?"

The man in the passenger seat spun around. He had a handkerchief tied over the lower half of his face and his cap was lowered; all they could see were his eyes. "Please sit back, sir," he said. "I don't want to have to use this." In his hand he held a Webley Mk VI revolver.

Sir Willoughby put a protective arm around Cameron's shoulder to reassure her.

"Sir, you'll notice the absence of door handles and window winders in the passenger compartment. I want you to close the window blind on the left. Slowly now, sir, very slowly. Yes, that's fine. Now, miss, will you do the same for the window blind on the right? Good. Sir, I need you to lower the back blind. That's good. Now both of you sit on your hands. That's right."

As they complied with his final instruction, he vaulted lithely over the walnut burl partition that separated the driver's compartment from the passenger area. He lowered one of the dark red leather jump seats and sat on it.

"And now I'm going to close these blinds between the passenger compartment and the driver. Done.

Please make yourselves comfortable; it won't be too long a ride."

"Who are you, dammit? And what do you want?"

"Please sit back and relax, sir. They'll explain everything when we get there."

***

At ten minutes to eight, the black Rolls-Royce Phantom III from the Portuguese Embassy slid smoothly to a halt in front of the Dorchester.

"Miss Ramstad, please," the driver said to the top-hatted elderly doorman.

"Mate, you picked 'er up not fifteen minutes ago. Is this some kind of joke? If that's wot yer up to, I'm not in the mood. There's a war on, in case you wasn't aware."

"No, no, this is no joke. Are you saying that Miss Ramstad has already left the Dorchester?"

"She and a group captain got into a black Rolls-Royce Phantom III. The car yer driving," he added pointedly.

"Doorman, I give you my word I haven't been here this evening. I've been cleaning and polishing this car in the embassy garage for the last hour. And no, I'm not drunk. Where can I find a phone?"

***

The black car turned into a garage. The driver climbed out. They heard what sounded like him shutting a wooden door of some kind behind them.

Then he opened the passenger door of the Rolls. He, too, was now wearing a handkerchief to hide his features, and they saw a revolver in his hand as well.

"Come here, Miss. Sir, you stay there—don't try anything or I'll shoot the lady. That's right, Miss, stand over here. Now put your hands behind your back. I'm going to slip these handcuffs on you. That's right. Now, walk towards that door at the back of the garage. It's ajar—you just push it open with your shoulder. Now walk along the corridor into the boathouse. That's right. Now stop. I'm going to put this hood over your head."

As the thick fabric hood fell onto her shoulders, she felt a sharp prick in her left biceps. Then just blackness.

***

"Gentlemen," Air Commodore Pankhurst said, "this is Deputy Assistant Commissioner Avery from the Metropolitan Police Service. He's come here this evening to assist us. Every MI5 agent we can spare is combing the streets of greater London. Scotland Yard also has every available man and woman on the job. We've called out the military police, too, as well as the Thames Division, in case they're intending to use a boat to smuggle Ramstad and Teynham on board a U-Boat. Or a flying boat ... a Blohm & Voss BV 138 could get them to Berlin in four or five hours.

"The kidnappers knew that they had no more than twenty minutes before we'd raise the alarm, less if the car from the Portuguese Embassy was early. And they were well aware that we'd immediately set up roadblocks around the city. I'm therefore all but certain that they must be within ten or at most fifteen miles of the Dorchester. If we haven't found them by midnight, we'll widen the search.

"Here's what we know. A Rolls-Royce apparently identical to the one belonging to the Portuguese Embassy picked them up around half past seven. That means that they knew that Ramstad and Teynham were waiting at the Dorchester for the embassy car to pick them up for dinner. Now, who would know that fact?"

He paused, then answered his own question. "The staff at the Portuguese Embassy had to know, of course, including the chauffeur. We have to include the calligrapher who wrote the invitation—he or she probably could've guessed the pick-up time. We don't know whom Ramstad told. She might have informed the hall porter at the Dorchester that she was expecting a car, but that would be far too late for the kidnappers to be able to do anything about it. My guess is that the First Secretary, Dom Tristão Pereira, is behind all this. He's undoubtedly in the pay of the *Ausland-SD*. But he has diplomatic immunity, which means that we can't go out and arrest him."

"We can arrange for our government to declare him *persona non grata*," Carlyle suggested, "and his government will recall him to Lisbon."

"We certainly can," Pankhurst replied. "And if we did, that might result in a huge row with neutral Portugal, a fight we cannot afford. If the daily flights to and from Lisbon were to cease, our flow of intelligence would be gravely affected."

"Air Commodore," the Deputy Assistant Commissioner offered, "we've already put a cordon around the embassy. I think that that's about as far as the government will allow us to go."

"I agree. Now we have to wait—the police are trying to find people who saw the car."

***

Cameron awoke to find herself confined to a heavy metal chair. Thick leather straps pinioned her arms to the armrests; her ankles were fastened to the base of the chair. Two heavy straps across her body held her torso immobile. And her head was in some sort of metal clamp—she could not move it in any direction.

"Good, you're awake," said a deep voice from her left.

She heard footsteps, and a tall man walked into her field of view. He was dressed in the black uniform of an officer in the General SS, with a red swastika armband on his left upper arm. His right eye socket held a frameless monocle with a hole drilled through the glass near the edge. A thin black cord was threaded through the hole and looped around the man's neck. He spoke with a slight German accent.

"Where am I? And who are you?"

"Miss Ramstad, allow me to introduce myself. I am SS-Major von und zu Reckling. And you are in an interrogation room in SS Headquarters in Berlin.

Behind you is Dr. Wilbert Krebaum who has been looking after you for the past few hours."

"Past few hours? How long have I been unconscious?"

"We brought you in the Rolls-Royce to a house on the River Thames—you saw the boathouse. Dr. Krebaum put you to sleep, we loaded you into the back of a boat and took you down the river to a point several miles offshore. A seaplane landed, picked you up, and brought you here to Berlin."

"Why am I here? And why have you tied me up like this?"

"I want to know all about your visit to Kent."

"You can read about it in last Friday's *Stars and Stripes*."

"I have, Miss Ramstad. I congratulate you. It was an excellent story, well researched and well written. But I want to know more. Let's start at the beginning, shall we? A car picked you up from your hotel. Which hotel was that? It's not mentioned in the article."

"What does that matter?"

"Miss Ramstad, as I just told you, I want to know *all* about your visit. Every detail. Every single detail. I must ask you again, which hotel?"

Cameron thought for a minute. As far as she was concerned, they had told her only one secret: the name of the railway station. She decided that she would grudgingly give him all the information he wanted, except that one fact. Then she wondered if he would torture her to learn what he wanted to know.

"Tell me again why you want to know the name of the hotel," she demanded.

"Miss Ramstad, you're in no position to make demands like that. You know the sentence your unfunny comedians use when they imitate us, 'Ve haff vays of making people talk.' Actually, they're quite right; we do have ways of making everyone talk, even you.

"But before I forget, they tell me that you have a really bad habit. It seems that you have the tendency to quote from Victorian literature. Endlessly. I want you to know that I'm not interested in any literature other than German literature, which is, after all, the finest literature in the world. Accordingly, I would suggest that, if you get the urge to spout Victorian poetry or prose, you manage to restrain yourself. Your comedians never say it, but I assure you that 'Ve haff vays of making people shut up, too.' Unpleasant ways. Very unpleasant ways. And now for the third and last time, what is the name of the hotel?"

"The Dorchester."

"There, that wasn't too hard, was it? Next, the car took you to a station. Which station was that?"

Cameron decided that she would tell the truth about everything; after all, they had told her that only one item was secret.

"Waterloo."

"Are you sure about that?"

"Yes, quite sure."

"You took a train to Kent from Waterloo Station?"

"Yes, I did. They told me that the railway system is crammed to capacity with trains taking soldiers to the marshalling camps in the South East. That night, St. Pancras didn't have an available platform for us."

"Are you telling me the truth?"

"Why would I lie to you about a thing like that? We both know that trains for the South East usually leave from St. Pancras. So why would I tell you Waterloo unless it was the truth?"

That answer made sense to the SS-Major, and he decided to go on to his next question.

"You say you boarded the train at Waterloo. What time was that?"

"Somewhere around midnight."

"And did the train leave shortly after that?"

"Yes."

"What did you see from the train window?"

"Nothing."

"What do you mean, 'nothing'?"

"The carriage blinds were down. They told me that the black-out was strict."

"But you could have lifted the blinds if the carriage lights were off."

"I went to sleep almost immediately after the train left Waterloo."

"And when did you wake up?"

"A steward brought me breakfast. He raised the blind—it was daylight. I ate in the compartment. Soon after, they came from the camp to fetch me."

"Who came?"

"A driver with a jeep, and a photographer. They took me to the camp, where General Brandon met me. You can read in the article what I saw, especially hundreds of tanks and armored vehicles lined up. I also saw a field hospital and a medical dispensary, but I didn't mention them in the article, for obvious reasons. I saw thousands of troops marching in formation on the edge of an airfield; I was standing on the balcony of the control tower. No, I didn't see any planes. For lunch, we ate sandwiches in a room at the base of the control tower. They were cheese sandwiches made from English cheddar. The cheese was delicious, but the bread was dry and somewhat stale. And the sandwiches had no pickles or any condiments of any kind, which I considered to be a mistake. How hard would it have been for them to find—"

"Miss Ramstad, let's get back to the military details. After lunch, what did you do?"

"I saw more vehicles of various kinds, especially jeeps. Lots and lots of jeeps. You can see them in the photographs that accompanied my article. Then they took me to the officers' mess where I spent the afternoon talking to various generals. I'd understood that Scotch was in short supply in Great Britain and very expensive, but they seemed to have an unlimited supply of eighteen-year-old Lochervan whisky, which they kept telling me is 'the crowning glory of the whisky maker's art.' We all drank lots and lots of Lochervan. And after dinner, I discovered that General Brandon and I shared a common love of *King Lear*, by the British playwright William Shakespeare."

"You can skip the attempt at humor, Miss Ramstad. I know the play. It's nowhere near as good as any of the plays of Friedrich Schiller, by the way. So, you all performed *King Lear.*"

"No, we didn't. First the steward couldn't find a copy of the play in the camp library. And then, when General Brandon offered the use of his personal copy, Air Commodore Pankhurst hurried us to the station, where we sat for two hours waiting for the train."

"You mentioned Air Commodore Pankhurst and you said that he hurried 'us' to the station. Was the air commodore in the officers' mess? And if that's the case, why?"

Now I've done it, Cameron thought. *Now they'll kidnap Pankhurst and Carlyle and Limberg.* "He brought the whisky."

"Miss Ramstad, Air Commodore Pankhurst is a senior Royal Air Force officer. He's been involved in military intelligence for years, decades perhaps. And you're trying to tell me that he runs a black market in eighteen-year-old Lochervan whisky, 'the crowning glory of the whisky maker's art'?"

"SS-Major, that's the truth. He wasn't in my compartment on the way to the South East—you can ask the steward. The air commodore turned up at the officers' mess at the same time as I did, and he brought with him several cases of Lochervan whisky. And the 'us' is Pankhurst and me. And the reason I didn't mention him up to now was that it didn't seem relevant."

"But the lack of condiments on the cheese sandwiches was relevant?"

"To me it was. I like a good cheese sandwich. And I much prefer Bourbon to Scotch."

"You told me that you and the air commodore sat at the railway station for two hours, in the cold wind, waiting for a train to take you back to London."

"Yes."

"Which railway station was that?"

"It looked like the same one where I had my breakfast, where they picked me up in the jeep."

"Yes, but what was the name on the board?"

"What board?"

"The name board. Every station has to have a name board; how else would passengers know that they've arrived at their station and that they must alight from the train?"

"I don't remember any name board."

"With your photographic memory? I've heard that you can quote thousands of lines of poetry correctly, but you can't remember a name board at a station?"

"Perhaps they took it down for security. I do remember that in June 1940, at the start of the war, a German invasion of England appeared to be inevitable. In the hope of confusing the enemy, the British removed all street signs near the coast. And they removed the railway station signs as well. That must be why I don't remember the sign; they removed it in 1940."

"I don't think that's true, Miss Ramstad. The embarkation camps are new, as are the railway stations they've built for the soldiers to disembark and travel to the camps. For some reason, you're not telling me the name of the station. This is your last chance. If you refuse again, Dr. Krebaum will inject you with a truth serum.

"What is the name of the station?"

"I have no idea."

"Doctor Krebaum, the sodium thiopental."

"Don't you mean sodium pentothal?" Cameron asked.

"Silence!" the SS-major shouted. "You've had your chance to speak. Now shut up until the drug takes effect."

Cameron felt herself lapsing once more into unconsciousness. As she came around, she heard the SS-major repeating, "The name of the station. The name of the station."

She tried to control herself, but she heard herself saying, "North Dover."

"Is that the name of the station? North Dover?"

"Yes."

"North Dover was the station where you had breakfast, and where you boarded the train to return to London?"

"Yes."

Then she felt the prick of yet another needle, and she was senseless once again.

CHAPTER TWENTY-FOUR

MI5 Headquarters, London
Sunday, May 14th, 1944

"Gentlemen, it's five o'clock in the morning. I suggest we get a few hours of sleep and meet here at eleven. No, make that ten o'clock. I've no doubt that the police are working flat-out to find them. Maybe we'll hear some good news then."

***

Cameron woke to find herself lying on the floor. The interrogation room was empty—even the chair was gone. She heard groaning coming through the door to the next room. She was extremely stiff. Her head ached worse than any hangover she could remember, but somehow she managed to get to her feet. A wave of dizziness almost caused her to fall, but she willed herself to stay upright. She walked slowly toward the door, her arms outstretched to aid her balance.

She gingerly tried the handle, fully expecting it to be locked. To her surprise, the door moved. Taking care to open it just a crack, she peeped through the gap into the next room.

She saw what looked like the entrance hall of a suburban English house. Lying on a Wilton carpet in the middle of the room was Sir Willoughby Teynham. He was gagged; his arms and legs were tied with ropes. Ignoring him, she tiptoed to the window and looked outside. It was broad daylight. She saw two British policemen walking along the sidewalk away from the house. She ran to the door, flung it open, and shouted, "Police, help! We've been kidnapped!"

***

"SS-General Schellenberg," SS-Major Krüger said, "here's the map of the Atlantic Wall, as requested— the Jews have finished it. As you can see, it consists of fifty-six separate sheets. I've had our people check the map against aerial photographs, and they found no inconsistencies. Of course, you and I know that only one of the Lindemann Batteries actually exists. But it's impossible for the Allies to tell that from the air."

"What about the Frenchmen working as forced laborers? What if they somehow manage to tell their friends, who tell the French Resistance, who tell London?"

"What are the slave laborers going to tell their friends," SS-Major Krüger replied, "even assuming they find some way to communicate with them? They haven't seen the map, so they have no idea that a building that they've constructed is supposed to be a Lindemann Battery or, rather, the way a real Lindemann Battery looks from an airplane."

"And I assume that the same applies to all the other buildings that, according to the map, house artillery of various sorts."

"Yes, of course."

"What about the minefields?" Schellenberg asked. "According to your map, we've laid mines all over the place, especially in Northern France. Why, if this map is even remotely accurate, we must've laid millions of mines on the beaches."

"Surprisingly enough, SS-General, the mines are real. As I think you know, it's impossible for us to make large naval guns and install them in France at this time, but mines are another matter. Yes, all the minefields are exactly as indicated on the map, and for good reason. Suppose that, when the map falls into their hands, the Allies wonder if it's pure disinformation. They may decide to test its accuracy and stage a feint somewhere. And the first thing they'll encounter, wherever they decide to attack, will be underwater mines. When they find that the initial defenses are precisely as shown on the map, they're pretty sure to believe that the rest of what we've depicted is correct, too."

Schellenberg did not want to contradict Krüger, but the SS-General looked somewhat skeptical. Then he said, "But any raid, no matter how large or how small, will almost certainly begin with an Allied naval bombardment. According to our map, the nearest

Lindemann Battery will blow their ships to kingdom come. Won't the lack of naval gunnery from our battery make the Allies highly suspicious?"

"Perhaps. Or they may view it as a trap. They may think that we're waiting for a significant number of their soldiers to get ashore, and at that time we'll sink their ships, preventing the men on land from retreating. And then we'll use our fortified gun emplacements to wipe out the enemy on the beaches."

Schellenberg looked even more skeptical.

"SS-Major, suppose that a fleet of Allied warships appears off, say, Dunkirk. They'll start a naval bombardment of the landing beach. But we won't reply. The reason, of course, will be that we don't have any naval guns in the vicinity of Dunkirk that are capable of sinking warships. But will the British and Americans really think that we won't respond because we're waiting for them to land their troops so that we can sink their warships and then counterattack and wipe out all their men?"

For a long while, the SS-Major said nothing. Finally, he spoke.

"SS-General, all that I'm prepared to say is that someone believes that, and that person has ordered us to ensure that this map falls into Allied hands. I believe that it is in everyone's best interests to obey this order."

CHAPTER TWENTY-FIVE

MI5 Headquarters, London
Monday, May 15th, 1944

"Gentlemen," Pankhurst said, "after intense inquiries, here's what we know and what we don't know—yet. German agents are at work in Britain. First, we have Mr. Blenkenship, the young man with the handlebar moustache and vicious scar, in all probability both false. But is he actually an enemy agent? Or is he just an out-of-work actor wearing white gloves whom someone, possibly Dom Tristão Pereira, paid to deliver the letter? We don't know yet. We're in the process of approaching every theatrical agency in the country.

"Then we have the chauffeur and his accomplice. Both Ramstad and Sir Willoughby are convinced that they're English. Our best guess is that they're two strong-arm men. Someone paid them to do the kidnapping, once more possibly Dom Tristão Pereira. They wore handkerchiefs to disguise their appearances; Ramstad and Teynham could see only their eyes. We put the doorman at the Dorchester to work with photographs of known criminals, the 'Rogues' Gallery' at Scotland Yard, but to no avail; he sees so many people drive up in cars that he cannot recall the faces of either the chauffeur or his accomplice.

"We found the stolen Rolls-Royce in the garage of the house in Kingston-upon-Thames. They'd wiped the car down thoroughly; our men found no prints anywhere. We learned that they took it from Lord Stockdale; because of the petrol rationing he'd stored it in his garage for the last few years and therefore he didn't miss it when it disappeared. The gang removed the door handles and window winders from the passenger compartment. They also installed blinds that, when lowered, ensured that the passengers couldn't see where they were going. They even removed the rear-view mirror, and that meant that the passengers couldn't see the driver's face. Again, we have no leads.

"In fact, they wiped down the whole house and removed everything, including the chair and the syringes. We've learned that the house has been empty since the war started. The owner inherited the house in 1938. He's currently with the Eighth Army, probably in Italy, and we're trying to contact him. But how did the gang find out about it, and how did they gain access? The police are working on that as well.

"Finally, we turn to SS-Major von und zu Reckling and Dr. Wilbert Krebaum. Our best guess is that 'Dr. Wilbert Krebaum' was actually Dom Tristão Pereira and that he was waiting at the house in Kingston-upon-Thames when the kidnappers arrived in the

Rolls-Royce. The First Secretary arrived back at the Portuguese Embassy at about ten o'clock on Sunday morning, telling the policeman standing outside that he and the entire staff of the embassy had been out all night looking for their missing guests. We haven't yet found out how he made his way back to the embassy from the house in Kingston-upon-Thames. Maybe he walked—it's only ten miles. As far as we can determine, he didn't take a taxi. Possibly he took a bus for part of the way. But we cannot do anything about it. He has diplomatic immunity, and that's that. We've arranged to tail him from now on, every time he leaves the embassy, and we'll make sure that he knows that he's being tailed. But that's as far as we can go.

"As for 'SS-Major von und zu Reckling,' he's the real problem. Could he be the same person as Mr. Blenkenship, the man who delivered the letter to Mrs. Bunting? Mrs. Bunting was convinced that Blenkenship is a pilot, probably from the moustache, the scar, and the white gloves. But the SS-major is tall, and men that tall have difficulty fitting into the cockpit of a plane. My best guess is that they're two different men. As I said, Blenkenship, or whatever his real name might be, could well be an English actor. The man playing the role of the SS-Major grilled Cameron Ramstad extremely skillfully—you've all heard what she told us. In my opinion, the *Ausland-SD* sent a professional interrogator to London to find out exactly what Ramstad saw. I gather that they don't have such experts themselves, so they borrowed one from the SS. Do you all agree?"

Pankhurst's acknowledged the nods all around the table.

"I assume that he brought with him the necessary drugs and syringes, and taught Dom Tristão what to do. But another possibility exists. Perhaps Dom Tristão stayed well away from Kingston-upon-Thames, and the *Ausland-SD* sent two men to London, namely the interrogator and the doctor. But whether one or two German agents came here, what we have to find out is: How did they get into Britain, and how did they get out? The answer to both questions is probably a U-boat on a deserted beach. The important thing is that by now they're in all likelihood back in Germany and have told SS-General Schellenberg two important facts. The first is that the marshalling camp that Ramstad observed was in North Dover. The second is that I'm a whisky black marketeer specializing in eighteen-year-old Lochervan whisky, 'the crowning glory of the whisky maker's art.'"

And the air commodore started to laugh. Five of the six military officers had been with him since the outbreak of war, and none of them could recall hearing him laugh out loud before. Out of politeness, they began to laugh along with him, and soon everyone in the room chortled for a few seconds.

Then Harkness put up his hand.

"Yes, Harkness?"

"Sir, why didn't they kill Ramstad and Sir Willoughby?"

"Good question. I've been wondering about that myself. One possible explanation is that the two strong-arm men made it a condition of their employment. Kidnapping two people for less than a day is one thing, but murder is quite another. I think that they told Dom Tristão that if either victim were harmed, they'd go to the police. But I suspect they had a much stronger reason. Does anyone have an idea?"

Tupman raised his hand. "Sir, they must want us to know that they know that Ramstad told them that the marshalling camp she saw was in North Dover, and that the Germans now know for sure that we're going to invade the Pas-de-Calais."

"Quite right. But why do they want us to know that? Yes, Limberg?"

"Today is the fifteenth of May. The invasion has already been postponed once, which means it'll have to be within the next two or three weeks. It's too late to change our plans; if we invade this year, it has to be the Pas-de-Calais, and they've told us that they're waiting for us there. Or we'll have to wait another year, by which time they'll have reinforced the Atlantic Wall along its entire length. As far as the Germans are concerned, they'll win whichever alternative we pick."

"That's excellent news," Chulmleigh said. "They're all ready for us in the Pas-de-Calais, but we're going to invade somewhere else."

***

"Welcome back to Germany, Donndorf! I trust that your trip to London was a great success and that you've found out all about the third army. Tell me everything."

"SS-General, getting to London was easy. When I arrived in Lisbon, the head of the *Ausland-SD* there handed me false identification papers and a refugee visa, both courtesy of the counterfeiters of Operation BERNHARD. I flew from Portela Airport in Lisbon to Whitchurch Airport outside Bristol. When I arrived, the British passport control officers merely glanced at my papers—those forgeries are of the highest quality.

"Waiting outside the airport with a large black car was Dona Guilhermina, the wife of the First Secretary at the Portuguese Embassy in London. I handed her the ampoules we'd hidden in the lining of my attaché case. I didn't have to explain anything to her—she's a registered nurse. She drove me to Kingston-upon-Thames."

"Yes, I was going to ask you about the house."

"En route, she explained that Captain Albrecht Soltmann, the Assistant Military Attaché in London, received orders in 1938 to set up a safehouse in London. She said that she thought that the orders came from the *Abwehr*—now the *Ausland-SD*, of course—but she's not certain about that detail. Anyhow, Soltmann came up with a rather clever way of renting a house that couldn't be traced back to us. One warm day he decided to go to a pub for a pint of beer. Next to him stood a young man in a well-tailored suit. He wore a black armband. Soltmann offered his condolences. The man said that his father had died some two weeks before, leaving him a handsome house in Kingston-upon-Thames, complete with a boathouse. For sentimental reasons, he didn't want to sell the house in which he'd grown up, but it had far too many rooms for a bachelor like himself. The other alternative was to rent it out, but his friends had assured him that the unending responsibilities of a landlord would drive him crazy.

"Captain Soltmann had an idea. He introduced himself under a false name. He said he was a married man with a beautiful mistress, and he wanted to set her up in a comfortable house in London. Discretion was absolutely vital because, if his rich wife found out, she'd divorce him on the spot, leaving him penniless. So Soltmann offered to rent the house at nearly twice the going rate, the rental paid annually in advance into a Swiss bank account that he'd open for the homeowner. This would be a gentlemen's agreement; obviously Soltmann would not sign a lease of any kind. Furthermore, he agreed to pay all property taxes, insurance, and other expenses, and would be responsible for repairs and upkeep.

"The home owner thought that this was an outstanding idea. It would provide him with a large tax-free income while liberating him from any obligations as a landlord. They shook hands on the spot. The first year's rent soon arrived in the Swiss bank account. The funds came from Berlin, but the young man was not to know that. On learning that his tenant had paid the money, the young man handed the keys over to Soltmann.

"With the outbreak of war in September 1939, all our diplomats had to return to Germany immediately. Dom Tristão has been working with us since 1936, and he therefore he knew about the safehouse. He soon realized that the property was a white elephant—we had no possible use for it. On the other hand, he wasn't responsible for the rent, and all he had to do was come to the house about once a month to collect any letters that had accumulated since his last visit, accompanied by a cleaning crew organized by the Croydon Gang. The job of the cleaners wasn't just to dust the mantelpiece. They were instructed to wipe down every square inch, removing any trace of fingerprints. And they did this even if no one had been to the house since the last cleaning.

"SS-General, do you know about the Croydon Gang? Two utterly ruthless brothers, Ernest and Arnold Croydon, run the outfit. We pay them a monthly retainer, also via Switzerland, and they assist Dom Tristão as needed, in addition to the monthly cleaning.

"Consequently, when you instructed Dom Tristão to organize the kidnapping, he called in the Croydons. He arranged for a large sum to be paid into their account and they did the rest. That included setting up the 'interrogation room' complete with metal chair. I understand that the chair is now somewhere at the bottom of the River Thames, together with all the medical equipment that Dona Guilhermina used to such good effect, as well as the SS uniform they organized for me.

"The chauffeur and his colleague were from the Croydon gang, of course, as was Mr. Blenkenship, who delivered the crossword to Hector Longstreet. Anyhow, after Dona Guilhermina had rendered the reporter and the group captain unconscious, the driver called in the cleaners to start sanitizing the entire house, other than the interrogation room, as well as the Rolls-Royce and Dona Guilhermina's car.

"They tied up Sir Willoughby. Dona Guilhermina gave him another dose of the anesthetic, larger than before, and they left him lying on the hall carpet. Not surprisingly, our expert doctors had correctly calculated the dose of whatever it was that knocked Cameron Ramstad out, and she came to her senses in less than half an hour. I proceeded to ask her every detail of her trip to what she claimed was Kent, in South East England. Her answers appeared to be truthful, but she refused to give me the name of the railway station; obviously, the British had told her to keep that piece of information secret. However, she let slip that our old adversary, Air Commodore Archibald Pankhurst, has a business on the side selling top-quality Scotch whisky."

"Are you serious, Donndorf?"

"Oh, yes. I'm quite certain that she was telling the truth about that, too. And I can certainly believe it— you and I know how many German generals are enriching themselves via the war."

Schellenberg nodded.

"But she stubbornly refused to tell us the name of the railway station. I had no choice; I asked 'Doctor Krebaum' to administer the truth serum."

"Did the American reporter see the doctor?"

"No. They hooded Ramstad when they first brought her into the house, and the metal chair was equipped with a clamp that held her head fixed. Her field of vision was severely restricted."

"Fine. Please continue, Donndorf."

"The truth serum worked quickly. When she regained consciousness she immediately told me the name of the station: North Dover."

"Are you sure that she said 'North Dover'?"

"Yes, SS-General. I went over it three times. Then Dona Guilhermina gave her a large dose of the anesthetic to put her to sleep until mid-morning, to give us plenty of time to get away. We untied her from the chair and laid her on the floor. The clean-up crew removed the chair, sanitized the room, and then left.

"I couldn't possibly go back the way I'd come. A refugee returning to Portugal the very next day after he'd arrived would invite all sorts of unwanted questions. And 'Doctor Krebaum' made it clear from the start that she wanted to leave Britain immediately after the interrogation, and permanently; she doesn't have diplomatic immunity. So we put on the police uniforms that the Croydons had provided for us, complete with identification cards. I doubt that they were as good as what the Operation BERNHARD forgers would've produced, but to my untrained eye they seemed excellent.

"We drove to the nearest public telephone, where Dona Guilhermina phoned the embassy to tell them to send a radio message to Lisbon; Lisbon then phoned Berlin to arrange the pick-up time. It certainly would've been unwise if the Portuguese Embassy in London had sent a message directly to Germany. Dona Guilhermina then drove us to Essex in her large black car, a model that the British police use quite widely. As luck would have it, no one stopped us.

"She took us to a deserted beach. There was no need to wipe the car down again, because we were wearing gloves. Soon we heard a flying boat, a Dornier Do 26. She signaled to the pilot with a flashlight, he sent a dinghy for us, and here I am."

"And so you are. By the way, why did you leave the reporter and her escort in the safehouse? Wouldn't it have been better to carry them, unconscious, to a deserted park, say, and leave them there? Why did you give up the safehouse to MI5?"

"SS-General, the Croydon brothers absolutely insisted that we do that. Under no circumstances did they want the police to start a London-wide investigation. Yes, we gave up the safehouse, but we certainly don't need it and have never needed it. By leading the British police to the house in Kingston-upon-Thames, the Scotland Yard investigation is now largely centered on that location. The other condition of the Croydons was that we had to give an undertaking that we wouldn't harm Ramstad or Sir Willoughby in any way."

"For the same reason?"

"Exactly. The brothers and their confederates are doing extremely well out of this war and they don't want the police snooping around any of their numerous lucrative schemes. They've apparently cornered most of the black market in food, cigarettes, and gasoline; their enforcers keep rivals out of the game. The Croydons print counterfeit food, clothing, and gasoline coupons. Initially they didn't want to handle the kidnapping at all, and the only thing that could budge them was the inducement of an extremely large sum of money transferred to their Swiss bank account."

"I understand. And of course you had to adhere strictly to the two conditions Croydon brothers imposed on you. They certainly don't sound like the sort of people you want to cross."

Donndorf grinned.

"Now for the big question," Schellenberg said. "We sent you to England to find out about the third army. But it turns out that Ramstad was in Kent after all. What do you have to say about that?"

"With the greatest respect, SS-General, I'm still strongly of the opinion that she wasn't in Kent, let alone on the platform of North Dover station, because no such station exists."

"What?"

"Yes, SS-General. We've made the most extensive inquiries."

"But the embarkation camps are only a few months old. This would be a new station."

"Certainly, SS-General. But nevertheless, as I said, there just isn't such a station. And the embarkation camp in the article isn't located immediately to the north of Dover. If you check the aerial photographs, you'll see that the terrain all around the city is largely rolling hills; that doesn't fit in with the pictures in *The Stars and Stripes*. The nearest flat land is at least three miles North West of the city, around the village of Temple Ewell. Personally, I wouldn't consider that to be 'North Dover,' but it does form part of the Dover urban area."

"In your opinion, Donndorf, what's going on?"

"I still believe that what I said to you before I left for England is correct. The British sent a rookie reporter in the middle of the night to a camp somewhere in England, and tried to convince her that she was in North Dover. That leaves two questions we have to answer: Where was she in actuality, and why did they send her there?

"The troop train left from Waterloo Station. That's the station for the South West, including cities like Portsmouth and Southampton. But trains bound for Kent, which lies to the South East of London, don't leave from there. And a reporter who's been in England for a while would never swallow the line that the troop train left from Waterloo because all the platforms at St. Pancras were in use."

"But Ramstad did."

"Yes, SS-General. And that's why they chose a beginner to report on the story—she'd believe anything they told her."

"Just a minute, Donndorf, I've thought of something. I think that they set Cameron Ramstad up. They were hoping we might kidnap her and interrogate her under truth drugs. They showed her what they wanted her to see and they told her what they wanted her to believe. Then they instructed her to keep the name of the station secret to ensure that, when we interrogated her, we'd administer sodium thiopental."

"I think you're right, SS-General. They brought her out from America, arranged the visit to the camp, and organized the story in *The Stars and Stripes* for one purpose and one purpose only, and that was to make us believe that a major embarkation camp is situated in the vicinity of Dover when it's actually somewhere else."

"And what's the reason, Donndorf?"

"SS-General, suppose you were General Eisenhower, and you'd decided to invade Boulogne with two hundred thousand men. And—"

"Don't you mean a hundred and fifty thousand, Donndorf?" Schellenberg interrupted.

"No, SS-General, that's the whole point. Eisenhower wants us to think that only a hundred and fifty thousand troops will be involved in the invasion of the Pas-de-Calais. As Voltaire said, 'God is always on the side of the big battalions.' Their extra fifty thousand men will overwhelm our defenses unless we've prepared for them. But Eisenhower has a problem. It's always possible for a good espionage service to estimate the size of an army quite accurately. That's why we collect information on food, water supplies, uniforms, and radio traffic as well as scrutinize aerial photographs of barracks and the like. And how does Eisenhower hide a hundred and fifty thousand men in Kent, directly opposite the Pas-de-Calais? The answer is that he doesn't. He's made no secret of the embarkation camps for a hundred and fifty thousand troops in Kent. We've known about those camps from the time they started to construct them, and the reports we continue to receive make it abundantly clear that about a hundred and fifty thousand troops are indeed preparing to invade France from there."

"I think I see where this is going, Donndorf. But please continue."

"Thank you, SS-General. That leaves an additional fifty thousand troops that Eisenhower doesn't want us to know about. Given that they have to travel by ship to the Pas-de-Calais, and that the train with Cameron aboard left from Waterloo Station—a really bad mistake, by the way—I suspect that the remaining fifty thousand men are in secret embarkation camps near Southampton and Portsmouth."

"Just a minute, Donndorf. How do you hide an embarkation camp, let alone camps for that many troops?"

"You don't. The British have been expecting us to invade since 1940. That's why they've constructed a vast number of camps of all kinds along the entire length of the South Coast of England. Southampton and Portsmouth are huge ports situated only twenty miles apart, and therefore there are many large camps in the vicinity that are at least four or five years old. My guess is that Eisenhower has converted several of the existing camps into embarkation camps, making as few external changes as possible. As a result, neither our spies on the ground nor in the sky have detected anything. We'll have to get our agents into that area to tell us what's actually happening."

"Donndorf, send out a message to all our agents in Britain. As a matter of urgency, we need to find out everything we can about troops in the South of

England outside of Kent, and especially in Hampshire."

"Certainly, SS-General. By the way, I forgot to mention one minor item to you. I've learned that, since December 1943, all the payments we've made to the Croydon brothers' account in Switzerland have been in those counterfeit British banknotes printed in Sachsenhausen. That includes the exorbitant sum we had to give them for organizing the kidnapping. I believe that you probably need to know that, if we lose the war, the members of the Croydon gang will undoubtedly come to Germany and kill every single surviving member of the *Ausland-SD*."

***

"Sir Lucius," Bridget Hawkesbury said, "Hector has sent more information—or rather, disinformation. At least I hope it's disinformation."

"Do you want me to summon the twins?"

"No, I don't think you need to do that; you can pass the information on to them when you next see them. Yesterday's puzzle from Hector included **HARDANGERFJORD**, together with a classical reference, **ZEUS**. The clue was **Greek god turns canal upside down (4).**"

"Ah, I see it. Hector is referring to the Suez Canal. If you reverse the letters of 'Suez,' that is, if you turn the canal upside down, you get **ZEUS**, the King of the Greek gods."

"Precisely."

"In other words, first he told the Germans about the Pas-de-Calais and Norway. Then he homed in on Boulogne and now Hardangerfjord. I suppose in his next puzzle he'll tell us when the invasion is finally going to take place. Personally, I can't wait. I'm totally sick of living here in Upper Silesia. But at least it's better than Lower Silesia."

CHAPTER TWENTY-SIX

MI5 Headquarters, London
Wednesday, May 17th, 1944

"Gentlemen, it seems that I've committed a major blunder," Pankhurst said. "I sent Ramstad to Southampton to convince the Germans that our phantom army in Kent is real. From the avalanche of messages from the *Ausland-SD* to their agents in Britain in the last two days, it now seems incontrovertible that we needn't have brought her to Britain to write that article—we've successfully fooled the Nazis all along. For the past five months, they've fervently believed that our nonexistent forces in Kent are going to invade Boulogne, which is exactly what we wanted them to think.

"However, something that Cameron Ramstad said, possibly under the influence of sodium pentothal, has now alerted them to a military build-up of fifty thousand men in Hampshire that they didn't know about before."

"But sir," Limberg asked, "how could they possibly have been unaware of our forces in that county? I know that we're weakening the *Luftwaffe* day by day, but their planes still overfly the entire length of the South Coast of England, from Land's End to Margate. They must have seen our military might in Hampshire."

"As I understand it, Limberg, they've always been aware of our ability to defend the South Coast against attack, including naval bases, air defenses, and army posts. As a result, the presence of Allied forces in that part of Britain hasn't revealed any secrets to the Nazis. But now they strongly suspect that we have a large embarkation base in Hampshire. If they think that we're going to use those men against the Pas-de-Calais then fine; they'll shift more troops to that area, making Normandy even more vulnerable. But if they suspect that we're going to use our forces in Hampshire to invade, say, the Normandy beaches— which is exactly what we're going to do—then it's going to lead to disaster.

"How can we convince them that our sole target in France is Boulogne? And how do we explain that the embarkation base featured in *The Stars and Stripes* isn't where Ramstad said it was? And finally, why do we even have an embarkation base that far from Kent in the first place? Any ideas?"

"Sir," Wallstead asked, "how many men do they think we have in Kent?"

"About a hundred and fifty thousand. Why?"

"Well, sir, as you know, we train our troops in sea assault techniques at Inveraray on Loch Fyne. Two or three months ago, a group of about thirty young officers based there had a brilliant idea. They equipped themselves with jeeps and radio sets and drove around the loch for a few days, pretending to be commanding officers of large groups of soldiers who were training for a major amphibious landing. The Germans picked up their radio transmissions and concluded, as the officers wanted them to do, that these regiments and battle groups couldn't possibly be ready for the invasion of Europe before September 1944; we still had to solve numerous problems that arose when trying to organizing the movements of many thousands of men. Also, as you just said, the Germans think that we have about a hundred and fifty thousand men in Kent waiting to invade the Pas-de-Calais, plus fifty thousand more in Hampshire."

"Correct on both counts, Wallstead."

"Well, sir, now we should combine these two pieces of disinformation. We need to tell them that based on what we learned on Loch Fyne we're unable to organize more than five thousand men to leave a port on a given day and land successfully in France. It's just too complex an undertaking to successfully coordinate the landing craft, the naval vessels providing support fire, and the aircraft bombing the enemy gun emplacements. And we can't cope with more than a total of fifty thousand soldiers on one day from all ports combined. The answer has been to set aside a number of ports in Kent and Hampshire to send the men to the Pas-de-Calais over four days."

"Wallstead, the Germans aren't fools. They know that the simultaneous onslaught of two hundred thousand men might be able to overcome the opposition in Boulogne, but four smaller waves of fifty thousand each would be wiped out."

"Sir," Limberg said, "disinformation is most successful when the recipient already firmly believes what you're telling him. The Germans are certain that we're headed for Boulogne, which means that anything we tell them that reinforces their conviction will fall on willing ears.

"In fact, sir, far from committing a blunder I believe that you've made a major positive contribution. The Germans will soon believe that our invasion force will be one third larger and they'll therefore have to move more troops into the Pas-de-Calais area, away from Normandy."

"I hope you're right about that, Limberg. But we still don't have a reason why we arranged for Ramstad to write that article."

Squadron Leader Harkness spoke up. "That's not a problem, sir. We've been keeping the fifty thousand men in Hampshire a secret. But then we arrested a German spy carrying information about an embarkation camp near Southampton. We couldn't determine whether the enemy agent managed to get any information to Berlin. So, just in case, we arranged for Ramstad to write an article about the Southampton camp and locate it in Kent. Only an inexperienced reporter newly arrived in England would fall for that."

"Let me think about all that and then discuss it with the powers that be. If they agree to your ideas, how are we going to inform the Germans? Agent PICKFORD has a few subagents on the South Coast, including a waiter in Portsmouth—I think that might work. None of the double agents are currently in Hampshire and, with the travel ban in coastal areas, it's going to be hard to come up with a convincing story for them. As for Hector Longstreet, this sort of information can't be incorporated in the answers to a crossword puzzle. Any other suggestions?"

"What about my pigeons, sir?" Captain Marks asked. "We've still got lots and lots of them. I think you could write one or two sentences that would explain the situation to the *Ausland-SD*, in that silly French code, of course."

"Actually, Marks, that's a good idea. I'll pass it on later today. Anything else we need to know?"

Carlyle raised his hand. "Sir, as you know, I'm a liaison officer with the French Resistance movements in Normandy. A month or two ago, General Charles de Gaulle, the head of the Free French, summoned one of their senior leaders, Clément de Ville, to London for consultations. He's planning to return to France next week to make sure that the various Resistance Groups are going to rise up just before we invade and destroy the Germans' communications networks, especially the rail links. We're sending him back to France in a Lysander. We think he'll be safest if we ask the group headed by François in Saint-Auban-sûr-Lot to receive him."

CHAPTER TWENTY-SEVEN

Ausland-SD Headquarters, Berlin
Thursday, May 18th, 1944

"Well, Donndorf," SS-General Schellenberg said, "we've found another pigeon. This one was in a loft in Oberhausen and presumably Agent MATT dropped it off en route to last night's raid on Essen or, more correctly, what's left of Essen, which isn't too much. And you'll be most interested to learn about the message."

"Which was what, SS-General?"

"PRIMARY TARGETS BOULOGNE AND BOKNAFJORD."

"Boknafjord? Where's that?"

"If it makes you feel any better, Donndorf, I had no idea either. It turns out to be the next major fjord to the south of Hardangerfjord; the openings into the North Sea of the two adjacent fjords are about forty miles apart. The city of Stavanger lies on the southern shore of the Boknafjord."

"SS-General, this message means that either they've slightly changed their plans or, more likely, the

Allies are going to split their forces into two. That reinforces my belief that this is no diversionary tactic. The Allies are planning a major assault in the vicinity of Stavanger."

"I agree, Donndorf. But I'm still not happy that Longstreet has informed us about only the Hardangerfjord, whereas agent MATT told us that the primary target is the Boknafjord."

"Unless, SS-General, they're getting their information from two independent sources. Longstreet has a former pupil on the Imperial General Staff. What if agent MATT is, say, Polish? We know that Poles have been flying with the Royal Air Force since the fall of Poland in 1939. Could he be obtaining his information from the Polish government-in-exile?"

"It's possible. But would a Pole have access to English Carrier pigeons?"

"Probably not. Was it one of those birds again?"

"Yes. It was the same story all over again. The owner of the loft found the bird the morning after an air raid. The note was in French, in the same code as before."

"And the alleged owner of the bird, SS-General?"

"Actually, this was very interesting. The bird belonged to one Heinrich Müller."

"You mean the head of the *Gestapo*?"

"Not exactly, Donndorf. Yes, the owner had the same name as the *Gestapo* chief. But the pigeon fancier in question died in 1929. Previous to that he was a professor of surgery at Strasbourg University. Once again agent MATT chose as putative bird owner a reputable professional man who's been dead for fifteen years or more."

"SS-General, it appears that agent MATT has access to the complete list of the members of the National Federation of French Pigeon Fancier Societies. He could have chosen any of hundreds of names, perhaps thousands. But he selected Heinrich Müller. I have no idea why."

"Nor do I, Donndorf. But there has to be a reason."

***

"Good news, Marks," Air Commodore Pankhurst said. "Last light we received a brief message from the Resistance group in Lille. One of your twenty pigeons turned up in a loft in Oberhausen. Now please tell the others why you decided to label the leg band with the number of a deceased member of FNCSF named Heinrich Müller."

"Yes, sir. Well, I was looking through the membership list that General Appleby lent me, and I saw the name. And what came to mind was Limberg's Seven Bridges of Königsberg problem. She told us that it's unsolvable. That gave me an idea. I realized that I could waste a lot of the time of senior *Ausland-SD* officers by giving them an unsolvable problem to solve, particularly with the invasion looming."

"Marks, are you saying that the only reason you arranged for the owner of the pigeon to have the same name as the *Gestapo* chief was to get people at the *Ausland-SD* to wonder why you did that, instead of spending their valuable time trying to work out where we're going to invade?" Chulmleigh asked.

"Exactly! And I'm pretty sure that it's working."

"Let's hope you're right," Pankhurst said. "Now, gentlemen, we need to move on to a different topic. You'll remember that we've given the *Ausland-SD* two adjacent lodgement locations in South Norway. We decided to do that for two reasons. We wanted to give them something to think about, like Marks and his latest dead pigeon fancier, one Heinrich Müller. But more importantly, the Germans are likely to get suspicious if every piece of information they receive regarding our invasion targets is identical."

"But, sir," Harkness said, "aren't they also likely to get suspicious if they get different information from two otherwise impeccable sources?"

"Not if the two targets are right next to one another, like Hardangerfjord and Boknafjord."

"With respect, sir, I'm not sure I fully agree with that. One possibility is the Germans will come to the conclusion that Longstreet and Marks are getting their information from two different high-level sources. But they might instead come to a different inference."

"And what's that?"

"They may conclude that one of the two informants is right and the other is wrong. But they won't be able to tell which is which without undertaking a detailed re-examination of everything they've received from both agents, which is the last thing we want."

"Why?"

"Because one of the agents doesn't exist—Marks, I think you know just what I mean by that. And the other agent, Hector Longstreet, is a most unlikely friend of the Nazis. If they arrange for someone here in Britain to talk to his former pupils, they'll quickly start to realize that he's as loyal a British subject as you'll get."

"I see what you mean, Harkness. What do you suggest we do?"

"We need to communicate with the *Ausland-SD*. But Longstreet is essentially limited to sending one-word messages. And how can he include the word **BOKNAFJORD** in a puzzle? I doubt if one person in a hundred in this country has even heard of it. Including the name of the fjord in a crossword in *The Sunday Intelligencer* would result in all sorts of unfortunate questions being asked. I think that it would be a serious mistake to get Longstreet involved here.

"On the other hand," Harkness continued, "not too many of Marks's pigeons have reached their intended destinations. Correct me if I'm wrong, Marks, but I believe you've dropped pigeons over Germany on four occasions. The first time all twenty of them disappeared, but we were lucky the next three tries; one of each set of twenty birds got through on each occasion. My concern is we have to resolve this issue, but an approach that has only a 3.75 percent success rate just isn't good enough."

"What do you think we should do, Harkness?"

"I suggest that we use a PICKFORD subagent in Scotland to inform the *Ausland-SD* that the 'British Fourth Army' assault of Southern Norway will consist of two thrusts: Force A, consisting of Canadian divisions, will invade via the Boknafjord; and the British divisions of Force B will advance along the Hardangerfjord."

"Fine. That should solve the problem. Now, what's happened to our idea of dropping a senior officer killed in a motor accident into the hands of that French Resistance group?"

"I'm sorry, sir," Johnson said, "but the Operation FORTITUDE people vetoed the idea. The minor reason was that it seems that general officers and field officers don't get killed in road accidents—they have drivers to keep them off the streets if they're under the weather."

"You mean if they're drunk, don't you?"

"Possibly, sir."

An irritated Air Commodore Pankhurst made a noise that sounded something like "P'tcha!" Then he went on. "And the major reason?"

"Too risky, sir. It's just too similar to Operation MINCEMEAT."

"You mean the one where Colonel Digby-Smith was sentenced to five years in prison for saying too much?"

Johnson took the hint.

***

"Well, Donndorf, the *Führer* is delighted with your analysis of the situation in Southern Norway. I've just been to see him to present your findings. He was particularly taken by the fact that the two different pieces of information came from three independent sources. He knew all about the PICKFORD subagents, of course, but I had to explain to him that SARAH GAMP was a Dickens character. Once he'd realized that our subagent in Edinburgh is a woman who works in a bar located right by Edinburgh Castle, the headquarters of the British Fourth Army, it all went smoothly. The Allied plan seems clear: British troops intend to advance up the Hardangerfjord, Canadians along the Boknafjord."

"And did you explain to him about Hector Longstreet and the cryptic puzzles?"

"Of course," SS-General Schellenberg replied. "When it comes to an item of military intelligence, *Herr* Hitler always makes up his own mind as to its reliability. So I went through the full story. He seemed fascinated by the idea of using a crossword as a way to communicate secretly in wartime."

"And the pigeons, SS-General?"

"From his experiences in the trenches of the First World War he was familiar with the use of homing pigeons. Of course, he'd never heard of an English Carrier pigeon, but he quickly caught onto the significance of a pigeon that won't return home. He wondered why a British spy would drop a pigeon over Germany with a message in a French code when it suddenly came to me: Agent MATT is a Canadian."

"A Canadian, SS-General?"

"Yes. That would explain why he knew about the plan for Canadian troops to invade along the Boknafjord, and also the messages in French. The vast majority of Englishmen are monolingual, and if they've learned another language at school, it's probably Latin. But most Canadians have at least a rudimentary knowledge of French, and French is the only official language in the province of Quebec."

"But would a Canadian be a pigeon fancier?"

"Many Canadians emigrated from Britain. That means that it's certainly possible."

"And the British connection would explain the interest in English Carrier pigeons?"

"Precisely, Donndorf."

CHAPTER TWENTY-EIGHT

Saint-Auban-sûr-Lot, France
Tuesday, May 30th, 1944

"Bless me, Father, for I have sinned. It has been a week since my last confession."

"François," Father Patrice said as patiently as he could manage, "how many times do I have to tell you that you say those words only if you come here for confession? Remember, when I summon you to the confessional booth to give you the latest orders from our German friends, you just say 'Good morning, Father Patrice,' or something like that."

"Good morning, Father Patrice."

The priest rolled his eyes. "François, it's nine o'clock at night."

"But you just said that I should say 'Good morning, Father Patrice.' I assumed it was some sort of code."

Father Patrice rolled his eyes again, this time so far into his head that for a moment the elderly priest worried if he would able to roll them back again.

"Never mind. Just listen to what I have to tell you."

"Yes, Father."

"Do you remember the ambush that Jean-Michel and Armand set up three years ago?"

"An ambush? Not exactly, Father."

"They hung a wire between two trees on the main road and painted it black. A motorcycle dispatch rider came by. The wire knocked him off the motorcycle, which careened into a tree, killing the guard in the sidecar. Do you remember now?"

"Yes, that was the night that the Germans found Jean-Michel and Armand with the radio. They shot them on the spot."

"Yes, François, and from then on you were in charge of the Resistance group—under my orders, of course. Well, tomorrow night you're going to set up a similar ambush."

"In the same place, Father?"

"No! Very definitely not in the same place. You know the large wheat field that's next to the main road?"

"Of course."

"Now, imagine that you're walking along the main road toward the village. The wheat field is on which side?"

"On the left, Father."

"Exactly. Now, you keep walking along the road, past the end of the wheat field. What do you see next?"

"You see a huge oak in front of you. It's the beginning of the forest. The road swings sharply to the right, and then equally sharply to the left again to avoid that old tree."

"And then?"

"As the road straightens out you come to two other massive oak trees, one on either side of the main road."

"Correct. Now, in the shed where we keep our supplies you'll find a long wire."

"No, there isn't, Father. I was in the shed earlier today."

"François, tomorrow evening at nine o'clock you *will* find a wire in the shed, together with two pots of black matte paint, two brushes, a pair of linesman's pliers, six flashlights, and a yardstick. Do you understand?"

"I think I do."

"You will go to the shed with two of the others, and you will bring the wire, the paint, the brushes, the pliers, the flashlights, and the yardstick to the two trees. Tell the rest of the group to meet you at the trees at half past nine."

"But what if the Germans spot us?"

"First, you'll walk through the forest. You know the path to take—it's the one from the shed to the oak trees. And second, no Germans will be in that area tomorrow night."

"Why not, Father?"

"Because I'm telling you that. Do you understand?"

"Yes, Father."

"Now, when you get to the two trees, you'll measure up exactly six feet from the ground and then fasten the wire at precisely that height."

"But the wire will sag in the middle."

"Yes, you're quite right. Once you've fastened the wire firmly between the oaks, measure the height of the lowest point of the wire above the road. It's supposed to be four and a half feet. You may have to adjust the wire on the trees to get the height just right. Do you understand?"

"Yes, Father."

"Then you order two members of your group to paint the wire black. One starts at one end, one at the other end."

"Can I ask Madeleine to work from the one end and Alphonse from the other?"

Exercising extreme self-control, Father Patrice somehow managed to stay calm. "Francois, you can ask anyone you wish to do the painting. Do you understand?"

"Yes, Father."

"You take all your equipment—paint, brushes, yard stick, pliers, everything—and you conceal the items behind a big tree well away from the road. Then you and your group hide and wait. At about eleven o'clock a motorcycle dispatch rider will come along the highway in the direction of the village. He'll have to slow down for the two bends, but he won't see the wire because you've painted it black. The booby trap will knock him off his machine, and he'll be killed. Just as before."

"What about the guard in the sidecar?"

"No sidecar, no guard. Just the driver."

"Then I grab the dispatch case and bring it to you?"

"No! Absolutely not! This is a very special messenger with a very special message. The dispatch case won't be in either of the panniers."

"Where will it be, Father?"

"It will be fastened around his body."

"So I tear it off his body and bring it to you?"

"No! And no again! As I just told you, this is a very special messenger with a very special message. The dispatch case will be sealed, of course. But the straps of the dispatch case will also be sealed. If you remove the dispatch case from the body, you'll break the seals. And under no circumstances are you to break the seals. Repeat after me: I must not break the seals under any circumstances. If I do, I will go straight to Hell—no absolution will be possible."

"I must not break the seals under any circumstances. If I do, I will go straight to Hell—no absolution will be possible. I understand, Father."

"For the sake of your immortal soul, I hope that's true. Now, what do you do with the body of the dead motorcycle dispatch rider?"

"I don't break the seals."

"Correct. And without breaking the seals, you and the members of your group will carefully carry the body a few yards beyond the edge of the wheat field and lay it on the ground, amongst the young wheat, where no one can see it. Then you take the pliers and remove the wire from the trees, pick up the motorcycle, and hide the wire and motorcycle behind the same tree where you hid all the equipment."

"And the pliers?"

"Yes, the pliers, too."

"I understand, Father."

"Good. Now, at about midnight, a British Lysander plane is scheduled to land in the wheat field. The moon will be full in five days' time, and the pilot therefore shouldn't have any trouble finding the target zone. What did you do the last time a Lysander came?"

"We hid in the wheat field, and we used flashlights to make a letter T. Three of us stood in a row at the far end making the top of the letter, and one stood in the middle of the letter and the fifth one was at the base of the T and we shone our flashlights directly at the plane. The Lysander landed near the middle of the T."

"But what about the wind?"

"The wind, Father?"

"Yes, the wind. The plane has to land into the wind. That means that first you have to determine which way the wind is blowing, and then you must arrange the T in such a way that the plane lands into the wind. Do you understand?"

"Yes, Father."

"Now, when the plane lands, you must carry the body of the dead dispatch rider up to the plane. This may confuse the pilot. After all, he's been told to deliver a Resistance leader to Saint-Auban-sûr-Lot; the pilot won't know anything about the dead dispatch rider. First, you welcome the leader back to

France. Then you show the pilot the seals and you impress on him how vitally important it is for him to take the body back to London with the seals unbroken. Do you understand?"

"I think I do, Father."

"When the Lysander has taken off again, you return to the tree where you hid everything. You take the wire, the paint, the brushes, the pliers and the motorcycle, and you hide them."

"What about the yardstick?"

"Yes, yes, the yardstick, too."

"And the flashlights?"

"François, you have to hide everything."

"Do we hide all the items in the old well behind the flour mill?"

"No, they know about that. You must take the motorcycle apart and hide the various bits and pieces in different places. Then, even if they find, say, a motorcycle tire, they won't realize that the rest of the components of the motorcycle are hidden all over the village and the surrounding countryside. And you distribute the other stuff in the same way. That will confuse the Germans if they find one item somewhere. And you absolutely have to send the Resistance leader to me at my house. Do you understand?"

"Yes, Father."

"Repeat everything from the beginning."

It took three complete repetitions before Father Patrice was satisfied that François understood everything that he had to do. Reluctantly he dismissed the "head" of the Resistance group.

CHAPTER TWENTY-NINE

Saint-Auban-sûr-Lot, France
Wednesday, May 31st, 1944

"This is truly excellent wire, François," Gérard said. "Where did you get it? Oh, wait, I can see a label on this side. It's pretty dark in here—the window of the shed is absolutely filthy—but I think I can make it out: Drahtzug Dalheim Aktiengeselschaft. Wow! You've managed to get hold of a reel of top quality German wire. How did you do it?"

François had to think quickly, not his strongest suit. "Gérard, ask me no questions and I'll tell you no lies."

"I understand. You've found a way to get what we need from the German camp at the T-junction at the end of the main road. Well done, François!"

"Gérard, you carry the bale of wire that you admire so much. Blanche, take the two paintbrushes, the pliers, and the six flashlights—use some of those hessian bags lying against the far wall. I'll carry the cans of paint and the yardstick.

"Now remember: Not a word as we walk through the trees. German soldiers are everywhere, and sound travels at night, especially in the stillness of the forest. The watchword is absolute silence. Do you understand?"

Blanche and Gérard nodded.

"No whispering, no muttering, nothing. We walk from here along the path to the two trees on the corner of the large wheat field in total silence. What are those monks called who never say anything?"

"You mean the Trappists?" Blanche asked.

"Yes, that's it. We're going to walk along the path through the forest like three Trappist monks."

The members of the Resistance group walked slowly along the path through the trees, taking the greatest care not to step on dry branches or anything else that might make a noise. François was well aware that no troops were in the vicinity, but he played along. Eventually they reached the two trees, where they found the other three members of the group waiting.

"Any problems?" François asked quietly.

Sylvain gave a Gallic shrug, simultaneously raising his shoulders, sticking his lower lip out, raising his eyebrows, and holding out his hands with the palms upwards. Madeleine and Alphonse simply shook their heads.

"Good. Let's get to work."

François was not particularly intelligent, but he had one attribute that made him the ideal front man for Father Patrice: once François eventually understood all the aspects of a task, he was fully capable of ensuring that his group could successfully carry it out to completion. Accordingly, they soon had the wire strung in place, with its lowest point exactly four and half feet above the surface of the road. It gleamed in the bright moonlight, despite the heavy foliage overhead. Madeleine and Alphonse gave the wire a coat of the black matte paint, taking care to cover the entire shiny metal surface. When the painting was complete, they hid all their equipment behind a large tree, well away from the road.

Now François called the group together. "In about an hour," he said, "a German dispatch rider will approach from that direction on his motorcycle. He's carrying a message that we have to ensure gets to London. A plane will land in the wheat field behind us. We'll guide it down with flashlights as before.

"The vital thing is that the document the driver is carrying is top secret. It's in a sealed leather case, and the case is fastened to the dispatch rider's body with more seals. Do not break the seals. That's the most important aspect of this operation. I repeat, do not break the seals.

"We'll carry the body of the German soldier to the Lysander and load it aboard after the passenger has climbed down. I cannot stress too highly that when we carry the body from the road to hide it in the wheat field while we wait for the plane to arrive we have to be careful not to break any of the seals. When the plane has landed and we carry the body to the Lysander, watch out for the seals. And as we load it into the plane, be careful with the seals. Is everyone clear on what's going to happen next?"

The other five nodded. Then the six members of the group moved away from the main road and hid behind trees and bushes.

At seven minutes to eleven they heard the motorcycle approaching. François was the only member of the group who had been present at the earlier ambush. The sound of the approaching vehicle brought back memories of Jean-Michel and Armand and the role he had played in their deaths at the hands of the German occupiers, but he put those thoughts out of his mind as he tried to catch sight of the driver through the undergrowth.

Within a few seconds he heard a cry as the dispatch rider's chest smashed into the wire at thirty miles an hour, throwing him onto the road and killing him instantly. They all rushed forward, with François shouting, "The seals! Remember the seals!"

All six of them helped to carry the corpse of the dispatch rider to the wheat field. They carefully laid it down on the ground. The growing wheat was not tall enough to shield the body from view, but they had no alternative. Next, they returned to the site of the ambush to clean it up. Gérard wheeled the motorcycle from where it had fallen onto the road and hid it behind the same large tree as before. Then he returned to the group with the pliers. They unfastened the wire from the two trees and coiled it as best they could—the black paint was still wet in a few spots— and placed it next to the motorcycle and the other items. Finally, they each picked up a flashlight and headed for the wheat field.

"Alphonse, which way is the wind blowing?"

Alphonse pulled an immature ear off the nearest wheat plant and let it drop.

"Directly toward the road."

"Fine. Alphonse, I want you to stand here where I'm standing. Gérard, you go about twenty yards to my right and Blanche the same distance to my left. The three of you make the top of the T. Next, Sylvain, you walk about fifty yards forward—you're the middle of the letter. And Madeleine, you're the base, so walk about a hundred yards from here. I'll stand by the body. After the plane lands, I want all of you to run to where I'll be standing and help me carry the body carefully to the Lysander. It's essential that nothing happens to the seals. All clear?"

The members of the group took their places. Close to midnight they heard the whine of a Bristol Mercury XX engine. They all switched on their flashlights and scanned the night sky to try and locate the plane painted matte black, the same color as the paint on the wire they had used to bring down the motorcyclist. Finally, they saw it and pointed their lights directly at the Lysander. The pilot landed the plane neatly in the middle of the field. After catching sight of a man climbing out of the rear cockpit and down the fixed ladder on the port side, Gérard raced toward François, and the others soon followed. The pilot turned his plane around, ready to taxi back to the far side of the wheat field, make another one-hundred-and-eighty-degree turn, and take off into the wind.

Rigor mortis had not yet started to set in, and the six members of the group therefore had no difficulty in ferrying the body to the Westland Lysander Mk III. As they approached the ladder, the pilot shouted, "Hey, what's going on?"

François spoke no English, but he immediately understood from the pilot's tone of voice that he was unhappy with the situation. Without letting go of the body, he turned his head toward the man who had just climbed down from the plane and said in French, "Welcome to France! Please tell the pilot that he has to take this dispatch rider to Britain without breaking any of the seals. He's carrying a vitally important message."

Clément de Ville turned to the pilot and translated. The pilot shrugged, then said, "Go ahead. But I have to take off immediately."

The group lifted the body into the rear cockpit. As they shifted the corpse to fit in the seat, they heard François mutter under his breath, "If I break the seals, I'll go straight to Hell—no absolution will be possible." They took no notice.

They stood back from the plane and waved to the pilot. He smiled, waved, and headed for the far side of the field. Within a few minutes he was back in the air, en route to England.

François turned to Clément de Ville, kissed him on each cheek, and once again welcomed him to France.

"Come with us back to the village. Father Patrice says that you are to stay at his house."

"Father Patrice?"

"Yes. He's the parish priest."

"But what does he have to do with anything? Aren't you the leader of this group?"

"Of course I am, but we respect Father Patrice and—"

"That means you discussed this whole operation with Father Patrice. Why?"

"Well, as I just said, we all respect Father Patrice and—"

"I don't," Blanche spoke up. "He's a collaborator. That night when the Germans took Jean-Michel and Armand and killed them, some people whispered that Father Patrice was behind the whole thing, but the faithful of his flock tried to hush everything up. And François, now I understand what you muttered when we levered the dead soldier into the plane and why you said it. Your words were, 'If I break the seals, I'll go straight to Hell—no absolution will be possible.' And you said that because that's what Father Patrice told you."

"I said nothing of the kind."

"Yes, you did," several voices chorused.

"And that means," Blanche continued, "that Father Patrice is behind this entire enterprise, and that in turn means that this is a German trick. We have to warn the British right away."

"Just a minute," Clément said. "François, why did you discuss this operation, including my arrival here this evening, with Father Patrice?"

François said nothing.

"Unless you give me a good reason, I have to assume that you're working for *les Boches* (the Germans)."

François could not think of anything to say. Clément took a revolver out of the pocket of his jacket and shot François twice in the head.

A voice shouted out a command in German. Dozens of soldiers armed with Schmeisser machine pistols poured out of the forest into the wheat field. The Resistance members turned to flee, only to see more soldiers rising from the undergrowth at the edge of the other side of the large field. Within a minute, all five remaining members of the Saint-Auban-sûr-Lot Resistance group were under arrest, together with Clément de Ville. After checking them for weapons, the soldiers marched them to the main road, where a police van drew up and took them to *Gestapo* headquarters in Rouen.

***

The chair behind the desk in the office of the commandant of the German base located at the T-junction at the end of the main road was empty. Two men sat on the other side. One wore a priest's cassock. The other was tall, with a frameless monocle in his right eye socket.

"Colonel Donndorf, what's going to happen now?" Father Patrice asked.

"First I need to know who was involved in the operation. Until you spoke to François last night, did you share any information with anyone?"

"Of course not, Colonel. Everything was handled over the telephone between you and me. Then I called François in and instructed him. What a tragedy! The man was as great a friend of Germany as I am. I had visions of François achieving wonderful things after we've won this war. But it was not to be. 'How unsearchable are His judgments and how inscrutable His ways!'"

"Yes, indeed, Father. Now, after you spoke to François, how did you arrange to get the wire and the paint and the other items on the list into the shed?"

"I asked Gaston, the taxi driver in our village, to drive me here; I told him that a soldier at the base had been badly hurt in an accident and they'd called me in to administer the last rites. I informed Gaston that I had no idea how long I'd be, and I'd telephone him when I wanted to return to the village. Of course, the real reason was that I didn't want him to see me leaving the base carrying those items, and I certainly couldn't ask him to take me to the shed where the group keeps its equipment. So when I had everything we needed, I asked my escort, Captain Jakobi, to arrange transportation. He was kind enough to take me in his staff car. Then I walked from the shed back to my house."

"And no one saw you entering the shed with those items or leaving it empty handed?"

"No. The shed is on the edge of the woods well outside the village, and Captain Jakobi and I looked around carefully before he dropped me off there."

"Are you absolutely certain that, other than you, the only Frenchmen and Frenchwomen who knew about the operation are the six people we arrested tonight on the wheat field?"

"Yes."

Colonel Donndorf pressed a button under the desk. The door opened and four armed soldiers entered.

"Father Patrice, this operation has to stay top secret. No one is ever to know that we've penetrated the French Resistance. I'm sure you'll understand that that means we're going to have to execute every French citizen who knows the truth behind the ambush. I'm afraid that includes you."

CHAPTER THIRTY

Royal Air Force Station Tempsford,
Bedfordshire, England
Thursday, June 1st, 1944

"Sir, did you know that you have the body of a dead German soldier in your rear cockpit?"

"Is that a fact, Sergeant Hoskins? Just give me a second to unfasten my seat belt, turn around, and take a look. Good heavens, man, you're quite right—someone's gone and put a Kraut corpse in my plane! I wonder who could have done that? Was it there when I took off earlier tonight?"

"I don't think so, sir. If I recollect correctly, I believe you had a French gentleman seated in the back."

"Did I really, Sergeant? Well, someone seems to have swapped my live Frenchman for a dead German. Do you have any idea whodunit?"

"No, sir, I don't."

"Well, what should we do about it, Sergeant? That German soldier looks very dead to me."

"Perhaps I should call an ambulance, sir?"

"What a brilliant idea, Sergeant Hoskins. And after you've done that, you might want to lubricate the automatic slat and flap system. It seemed a little stiff when I came in to land."

"That was probably caused by the big stiff in your rear cockpit, sir."

***

"Gentlemen," the air commodore said, "We've received a document with apparently perfect provenance. Sir Austin Sheppard, the eminent pathologist, told me this afternoon that he's found nothing up to now that could make him doubt that the body is that of a German motorcyclist named Wilhelm Weierstrass who died when he hit a wire stretched across the road. The fact that our pilot picked up the corpse not far from where the same Resistance group killed another motorcycle dispatch rider with a wire in 1941 reinforces what Sir Austin said.

"Regarding the matter of the sealing wax, some of the seals were cracked, understandably, but none were broken. The Germans used straps to fasten the messenger's satchel to his body, and they placed seals where the straps crossed. The satchel itself had two locks, both sealed. And the document inside was sealed in an envelope.

"As you know, inside was a detailed map of the Atlantic Wall and all its fortifications. In particular, it shows that the area in Normandy where we intend to invade is heavily defended. If the document is genuine, then the landings on the beaches of Normandy will be an unbridled bloodbath."

"If the provenance is that good, sir," Limberg asked, "why do you even consider the possibility that the document is disinformation?"

"For three reasons. First, this morning our people studied the map—all fifty-six sheets of it. They computed how much steel would be required for the various fortifications. And according to their calculations, the howitzers and naval guns and other artillery alone would require about twice as much steel as we think Germany has produced since construction of the Wall began."

"But, sir," Harkness said, "we don't know for sure how much steel Germany has actually produced—it's only an estimate. Also, some of the fortifications may be imaginary, but some may well be real. In particular, we don't know anything about the buildings and artillery in the Normandy beach sector. The map may well be perfectly accurate in that part of France."

"Quite correct," Pankhurst replied.

"My second reason for doubting this map," he continued, "is that the people whom we think were responsible for ambushing the dispatch rider have disappeared—all of them. We transmitted a radio message to a nearby Resistance group to send someone to get further information to help us decide about the reliability of the map. In a village like Saint-Auban-sûr-Lot it's almost impossible to keep a secret. All the inhabitants know—or think they know—who the members of the local Resistance group are. It seems that every one of those people has disappeared, as has Father Patrice, the parish priest. In addition, the plane that brought the body of the German dispatch rider to Britain was actually on a mission to return a senior Resistance leader to France, and Clément de Ville has disappeared, too. He hasn't turned up at any of the places on his itinerary."

"And that could mean," Tupman suggested, "that after the plane took off with Weierstrass, the dead motorcyclist, German troops converged on the party. My cousin told me that the Germans have built a major camp close to the village."

He paused, then added, "But that wouldn't explain why Father Patrice has disappeared as well."

"Why not?" Wallstead asked. "Perhaps he's part of the Resistance, too."

"On the contrary, my cousin told me that many of the villagers view the local priest as a collaborator. If the Germans arrested the villagers responsible for killing the dispatch rider, the last person they'd take would be Father Patrice."

"But the villagers may be wrong," Johnson said. "Perhaps his pro-German attitude is just a cover."

"Perhaps," Tupman replied. But it was clear from the look on his face that he remained to be convinced.

"My third reason," Pankhurst resumed, "is that the provenance is not merely good, it's too good. Who ever heard of three levels of seals? Sealed envelopes are not that unusual; we do that quite often when we don't want a messenger to be tempted to take a peek at the document he's carrying. And on occasion we've sealed the locks of satchels and attaché cases, and we've seen the enemy do that, too.

It's not as common as a sealed envelope, of course, but it happens with documents of the highest level of secrecy. But neither I, nor anyone else I've discussed this with, has ever heard of sealing the container to the messenger."

"But sir," Carlyle said, "doesn't every King's Messenger have to chain the diplomatic bag that he's carrying to his wrist?"

"Certainly," the air commodore replied, "but chaining is one thing, sealing is quite another. After all, you can unlock a lock and fasten the chain to someone else's wrist. But it's extremely hard—but not totally impossible—to break a seal and then reseal it in an undetectable way."

He looked around at the members of his team. No one said anything.

"Finally," he said, "it's just too close to the operation that Colonel Digby-Smith outlined to Limberg. Actually, Limberg now has the same security clearance as the rest of you, which means that we can talk about Operation MINCEMEAT. Near Huelva in Spain, we floated ashore the body of a Welshman who'd died after ingesting rat poison. The only reason the Spaniards didn't realize that he hadn't actually drowned is that Roman Catholics are generally opposed to post mortems and, as a result, the corpse was never properly examined. We'd looped a leather-covered chain around the belt of the trench coat worn by the dead man and fastened it to an attaché case containing letters.

"The body was supposed to be that of a mythical Major Martin who'd drifted ashore when his parachute failed to open properly after a plane crash. We constructed a cover identity and placed identification cards as well as a splendid collection of personal possessions in the pockets of the battledress that the corpse wore.

"The ruse was a total success. The Germans read the letters and interpreted them the way we'd intended. And they now 'knew' that we'd be invading Greece and Sardinia but not Sicily, whereas the converse was true.

"Now look at the case of Wilhelm Weierstrass. Sir Austin performed a meticulous post mortem. He has no doubt at all as to how the man died. He was riding a motorcycle when his chest collided with a stationary horizontal wire, probably spanning the road between two trees.

"Also, in all likelihood the soldier's identification papers are one hundred percent genuine, and it certainly seems that the body belongs to a *Wehrmacht* soldier named Wilhelm Weierstrass. We spent months assembling the personal possessions of 'Major Martin' and writing and rewriting the letters he was carrying, but our experts tell me that what they found in the dispatch rider's uniform is just what you'd expect to find in the pockets of a German soldier stationed in France. We slaved away for weeks and weeks to create a persona that seemed natural, but in the case of Weierstrass everything we've found on his body seems instinctively genuine and nothing essential seems to be missing.

"Now, we'd never even think of achieving perfect provenance by taking a British Army officer up in an airplane, flying off the coast of Spain and throwing him out of the door with a deliberately defective parachute. But the Nazis would have no scruples about sending an innocent dispatch rider to his death at the hands of the French Resistance to ensure that we received the Atlantic Wall map in such a way that we simply couldn't question its provenance.

"Finally, contrary to what Colonel Digby-Smith told you that night in the mess, Limberg, we hadn't placed any plans in Major Martin's briefcase. Instead, it contained three letters from which the Germans deduced our intentions regarding the next step in our conquest of Europe. But Wilhelm Weierstrass was carrying a top-secret map of the Atlantic Wall. There's nothing for us to infer.

"The 'Haversack Ruse' dates from the First World War and more specifically, the Sinai and Palestine Campaign in October 1917. A British soldier named Arthur Neate rode up to the Ottoman Turk line near Gaza. Not surprisingly, a few of the enemy fired at him. He pretended to be shot and wounded. As he galloped away, he let a bloodstained haversack fall to the ground; earlier he'd stained it with blood. Inside his haversack were fictional plans for an attack on Gaza, together with a collection of carefully assembled personal effects, just as we did for Major Martin. General Allenby took the deception further by ordering his radio operators to send out messages ordering the troops to search for the 'missing' haversack. On one occasion, Allenby's staff prepared a set of daily orders that included sending a patrol to thoroughly search the area where the haversack had been 'lost.' They then wrapped a sandwich in those daily orders and left it near the Turkish line. As soon as he was sure that the Turks had taken the bait, Allenby assaulted Beersheba instead of Gaza. Understandably, the Turks thought the attack was just a feint. At twilight, the Australian Fourth Light Horse Brigade staged a four-mile charge, the last and the greatest cavalry charge in history. As a consequence of the Haversack Ruse, Allenby took Beersheba and went on to conquer Jerusalem and the whole of Palestine.

"But with Wilhelm Weierstrass, the Germans have reduced the Haversack Ruse to the simplest possible format. They've presented us with a map sealed in an attaché case fastened to a dead dispatch rider. If the map is genuine, we dare not invade Normandy. It's as easy and straightforward as that."

CHAPTER THIRTY-ONE

MI5 Headquarters, London
Friday, June 2nd, 1944

"Gentlemen," Air Commodore Pankhurst said, "Last night I attended another meeting with General Eisenhower and his senior staff. Again it lasted more than two hours, but the situation hasn't changed one iota. No one is prepared to state categorically that the map is genuine—on the contrary—but none of the experts have been able to find fault with it. We've done another round of air reconnaissance of the Normandy landing beaches as well as many other regions of France; we don't want the Germans to learn the area we're really interested in. No one has yet found a contradiction between any of the photographs and the fortifications shown on the map. However, a camera in a plane can't help us to see what's inside the various buildings.

"Towards the end of the meeting, Ike said almost exactly what he said at the previous meeting, namely, that if the map is accurate, we're going to lose about two hundred thousand men on the ground and in the naval vessels and the landing craft. It'll set the end of the war back by at least one year, more likely two. On the other hand, if the map is disinformation, then landing on the five Normandy beaches is the best alternative for winning the war quickly. But can we take that chance?

"I said that I'd noted that the best and brightest Allied minds had been unable to determine whether the Normandy portion of the Atlantic Wall map is genuine. I suggested that the members of my team look at the entire map and see if they might come up with anything. So, gentlemen, they handed a copy to me, all fifty-six sheets. On each of the large tables in the next room they've laid out seven sheets of the German map and copies of the best maps we have of the areas covered by those sheets. You have four hours. Go!"

The six military officers headed for the next room, closely followed by Johnson and Carlyle. They each chose a table at random and started comparing a sheet of the map of the Atlantic Wall with the corresponding map that the air commodore had found for them. He joined them a few minutes later with a pile of files. He went over to an empty desk, sat down and proceeded to work through the material he had brought in his usual methodical way.

The room was silent for about fifteen minutes. Then Squadron Leader Halstead shouted out, "And I thought that the Germans were so punctilious!"

Everyone looked at him. "Yes, Halstead?"

"Sir, when I was a boy, we used to spend two weeks every summer in a tiny village on the west coast of Brittany called Sainte-Anne-la-Palud. The chief attraction was the endless white sandy beach. The hotel where we stayed is at one end of the beach, together with four or five houses. And a chapel about half a mile inland plays a major role in the religious life of the Breton people. They make annual pilgrimages to the church."

"And?"

"Well, sir, the second sheet of the German map in my pile shows Sainte-Anne-la-Palud. But the Germans have made a mistake. Instead of Palud, P-A-L-U-D, they've written P-O-S-U-L. They've got the second, third, and fifth—"

Before Halstead could complete his sentence, the invariably calm and unemotional Captain Marks had jumped to his feet, knocking over the high stool on which he had been sitting. He ran to Halstead's table, shouting, "Show me! Show me!"

Taken aback by this totally uncharacteristic behavior, the others stared at him.

"What is it, Marks?" the air commodore asked cautiously, concerned that the captain in the Royal Medical Corps was exhibiting the first signs of a nervous breakdown.

"Sir, that's not a mistake. That's a deliberate name change by the person who made this map."

"Is that the case?"

"Yes, sir. The word *posul* is Hebrew for 'disqualified' or 'defective,' and is often used to describe a document that is invalid."

"But, Marks, why would Hebrew have a word for a disqualified or defective or invalid document?"

"Because, sir, we read the Bible aloud in our synagogues from a handwritten Hebrew scroll made of parchment."

"You mean the *Torah*?" the air commodore asked, revealing once more his extensive general knowledge.

"Yes, sir, that's what we call it. A specially trained scribe writes it with a quill pen. And if someone sees the slightest error, be it a missing letter or even a misshapen letter, the scroll is declared to be *posul* and is unfit for use until an expert scribe can correct the Hebrew text."

"Just a minute, Marks. Why would the Germans get a Jew to forge a map for them? They consider your people to be subhuman, and certainly unfit for something as important as creating a map that will have a critical effect on the outcome of the war."

"It's a question of security, sir. If a team of Germans had constructed the map, the danger always exists that someone might say something to someone else and soon the news that the map is actually German disinformation would reach our ears. We know that the Nazis are using slave labor in their concentration camps. They've set up a team of Jews to create this map. And when the task was complete, I've no doubt that they killed every last one of them."

"But why would Jews cooperate in such work? Why would they help the Germans?"

"Sir, suppose you were standing in a Nazi extermination camp, with gas chambers in front of you and crematorium chimneys billowing smoke and ashes into the air from the burned bodies of thousands of murdered human beings. If you were given the choice of immediate death or the possibility of living a little longer by drawing a map, which would you choose?"

A lengthy silence ensued. Then Pankhurst spoke again.

"Marks, why did the Jewish engraver change the spelling?"

"Well, sir, he wanted us to know that the map is a Nazi deceptive trick. But he had to do it subtly. If the Germans had the slightest suspicion that he was trying to tell us the truth, they'd kill him on the spot. But more importantly, they'd replace him with someone else who might not be brave enough to take the risk of informing us that the map is disinformation."

"Marks, you're saying that the map is a deliberate attempt to mislead us, and we can safely invade the Normandy beaches right now. But what if you're wrong and Halstead is right? What if a German drew the map? What if he was extremely tired when he got to Sainte-Anne-la-Palud and he copied a few letters incorrectly? Are you that certain that you're prepared to risk the lives of two hundred thousand men on the basis of what might just be a spelling mistake? As Sigmund Freud put it, sometimes a cigar is just a cigar."

Marks said nothing for a long while. Then he said, "Sir, despite the Germans' reputation for accuracy, Hallstead found a mistake. Why don't we keep looking and see if we find another one?"

"Are you suggesting that this Jewish map engraver deliberately inserted another wrong name?"

"I'm not claiming anything like that, sir. All I'm saying is that we should keep looking. You said we have four hours, which means that we have about three and a half hours left."

"All right, Marks, I take your point. Everyone get back to work. Just sing out if you see anything even slightly suspicious."

They inspected the maps for another half hour. None of the eight members of the team noticed anything unusual. Then Pankhurst announced that they all needed a tea break, and they trooped behind him to the canteen. They all felt a definite tension in the air as they sat at a large table and drank their tea. Marks sensed that his colleagues could not decide whether he had come up with a breakthrough discovery or whether the stress of the past five years of ceaseless wartime intelligence work had caught up with him. In the canteen, as in any other public place, they were invariably scrupulously careful to restrict their conversation to inconsequential small talk. But now they could not stop thinking about the elephant in the room. After a few half-hearted attempts at conversation, the entire team lapsed into silence.

"Gentlemen, duty calls," the air commodore announced, and they went back downstairs.

Soon after they resumed work, Halstead shouted out again. "Sir, I think I've found something else here that's odd. On the map of France you gave me, I can see this *commune* called Saint-André-Treize-Voies. I reckon the township is about forty miles from the coast, according to the scale of the map. But on the same sheet of the German map that had that other

312

mistake on it, the *commune* has shifted westward almost to the Atlantic Wall."

"Marks, go and have a look. Walk, man, you don't have to run."

Halstead placed the forefinger of his left hand on the British map to show Marks the position of the township. Then, using the point of his pencil, he indicated where the *commune* appeared on the German map of the Atlantic Wall. Marks studied the two maps for a brief moment and then looked up. He could hardly speak from excitement, "Sir, look here. On the map you gave us, the name of the township is Saint-André-Treize-Voies. That's Saint Andrew of the Thirteen Routes. But look at the German map. Instead of 'T-R-E-I-Z-E' he's written 'T-R-E-I-F' and—"

Limberg chimed in and was even more animated than Marks. "Sir, I grew up in an assimilated Jewish home. My father changed our last name from 'Bloomberg.' Almost no one knows that I'm Jewish, not even my closest friends. But despite my almost total lack of Jewish knowledge, I know that *'treif'* is a Yiddish word meaning 'unfit for consumption' or 'unclean'—it's the opposite of *'kosher.'* And that means—"

Air Commodore Archibald Pankhurst reached his hand out. "Give me those maps," he ordered. "I'm off to see General Eisenhower."

CHAPTER THIRTY-TWO

MI5 Headquarters, London
Tuesday, June 6th, 1944

"Gentlemen," Air Commodore Archibald Pankhurst said gloomily, "the invasion of Europe has begun, but we have to do much more. Yes, we've helped in every way we could to contribute to the operation to convince the Germans that a major sea-borne invasion of Boulogne is underway. Last night, the Royal Air Force destroyed radar stations in many places along the French coast. In addition to bombing every installation that might provide information to the Nazis regarding the Normandy beach area, we've tried to wipe out the stations that cover Boulogne.

"We've also dropped dummy paratroopers over the area surrounding Boulogne. It's going to be a while before the Germans realize that they aren't the real thing, and every additional hour we can keep Hitler from sending his tanks into Normandy can mean the difference between success and failure on the landing beaches as our men try to defend their beachheads."

"What about 'window,' sir?" Johnson asked.

"If you're referring to small thin pieces of aluminium cut to half the wavelength of German radar receivers, the current word is 'chaff.' You really need to keep up to date with the latest technical jargon, Johnson."

The MI5 agent immediately realized that, despite his calm outward appearance, the Air Commodore was a bundle of nerves.

"Sorry, sir. I meant to say, what about chaff?"

"Yes, we've dropped piles of it over Boulogne and in the surrounding areas, including over the sea. It should appear on what's left of the German radar systems as a continuous blip, and fool them into believing that we're attacking Boulogne in force. We're hoping that they'll interpret the offshore chaff as a major naval task force. And if that doesn't work, we've also sent out a few small ships towing blimps. Those barrage balloons should dupe the Germans into concluding that we've got battleships and cruisers out there and that we're trying to protect our fleet against their aircraft; our apparent hope is that their planes will be destroyed when they collide with the metal cables that tether the blimps. And other small ships are towing radar-reflecting balloons to make the Germans think that we have a really large fleet off Boulogne. Finally, we have a few patrol boats in the area emitting smoke screens, with radar operators sending out signals all the time and hordes of radio operators chattering continuously. In short, we're trying to deceive the Germans into believing that we've placed a huge sea-borne task force off the coast of Boulogne—when it doesn't exist. Our fleet is nowhere near there; the warships are protecting the Normandy landing beaches."

"Do you think that all this will work, sir?" Major Tupman asked. "I'm really worried that Hitler will bring his tanks to bear. As I understand the German order of battle, they've deployed both the Second Panzer Division and the One Hundred and Sixteenth Panzer Division near Boulogne. We have to ensure that they stay in that area as long as possible."

"Well, Tupman, that's what this meeting is all about. One step we've already taken is that agent PICKFORD sent out a message today stating categorically that the invasion of Normandy is a diversion. He's never deliberately sent incorrect information before, so we can only hope that his controller in Berlin will inform Hitler that he needs to defend Boulogne against the real onslaught. But what about tomorrow? And Thursday? How are we going to persuade the Nazis to continue to believe that we have two hundred thousand men waiting in Kent and Hampshire to invade the Pas-de-Calais?"

"Sir," Marks said, "I don't think that my pigeons would work. For one thing, I doubt if we have any spare planes available to drop them over Germany. And, as Harkness pointed out about three weeks ago, the probability of success is too small for something as important as this."

"What should we do? Anyone?"

Carlyle raised his hand. "What about Hector Longstreet? I could go over to Stragham College and pick him up. We'll get him to compose a puzzle that would inform the Germans that two hundred thousand men are poised to invade Boulogne in forty days' time."

"Why forty days?"

"Well, sir, we've been sending disinformation to the Germans telling them that forty-five days after the first feint attack we're invading Boulogne in full force."

"And what words would go in the puzzle?"

"We obviously have to have **BOULOGNE**, sir," Carlyle said. "And I suggest we include **QUARANTINE**."

"You've lost me," Wallstead said.

"Sunday is in five days' time. The invasion of Boulogne is supposed to take place forty-five days from today, or forty days after Sunday. The word 'quarantine' comes from the Latin *quadraginta* meaning 'forty'—when a ship from a country with the plague arrived off Venice, the Venetians kept the vessel in isolation for forty days, and—"

"But we have a problem," Harkness interjected. "The word **TWOHUNDREDTHOUSAND** is eighteen letters long."

"True," Limberg replied, "but we could have **TWOHUNDRED** as the answer to one clue with **THOUSAND** near it in the grid."

"And what about including **KENT**?" Lieutenant Commander Chulmleigh asked.

"Aren't we being a little too ambitious?" Pankhurst asked.

"Not necessarily, sir," Limberg said. "Let's tell Hector what we want in the puzzle and see what he can do for us. If he can't find a way, no one can."

"That makes good sense. Carlyle, off you go. Fetch Longstreet and take him to the safe house."

***

When Carlyle reached Stragham College, he went to Miss Harrington's office. The room was empty, but the connecting door to the headmaster's study was open. Carlyle knocked gently, and the headmaster called out, "Who is it?"

"Headmaster, it's Carlyle."

"Come in, come in! Miss Harrington has gone to the post office in the village. I assume you're here to take our senior Classics master? Let's go and fetch him."

The door of the classroom was open. "Mr. Longstreet, your country needs you once again!"

Carlyle looked at the boys. He expected to see relief on their faces, but much to his surprise, everywhere he observed a look of limitless admiration. In spite of everything, Longstreet had become the school hero. Then he realized why: Hector Longstreet was the only person at Stragham College who was involved in the war effort because all males between eighteen and fifty-one-years-old were subject to conscription. Furthermore, here was a man well past retirement age who was still serving his country.

"Boys, I'll be back in a minute to resume Mr. Longstreet's lesson. In the meantime, you will show your respect for his dedication to our winning this war by studying your Greek textbooks until I return."

The two men led Longstreet toward the front door of the school. As he passed Miss Harrington's office, Hector gave a little gasp and crumpled to the ground.

The two men grabbed him before his head could hit the floor. They lifted his surprisingly light body, carried him into the office, and sat him down on the school secretary's chair. His face was ashen, his skin clammy.

"I'm going to call an ambulance," the headmaster said.

"No!" Carlyle replied. "It has to be a military ambulance. Let me handle this. You look after Mr. Longstreet."

"Why a military ambulance?"

"I'll tell you later."

He reached across to the telephone and made a quick call. "They're on the way. Now, sir, I need to take you into my confidence. At noon today, the BBC will announce that the invasion of Europe has begun. Mr. Longstreet has played a vital role in that operation, to such a great extent that, if news of his collapse were to reach Germany, tens of thousands of men may die unnecessarily. Accordingly, I need you to give me your word that you won't tell anyone that Mr. Longstreet is ill."

"But why?"

"Headmaster, this is more than just a matter of national security. As I just told you, tens of thousands of lives are at stake here. Do you give me your solemn word that you will mention to no one at all that Mr. Longstreet is ill?"

"Yes, of course."

"And what are you going to say if somebody asks you about the military ambulance that's about to arrive at the school?"

"What do you want me to say?"

"Tell them that, with the invasion, we needed to rush Mr. Longstreet to headquarters without delay, and that a military ambulance was the quickest way to achieve this."

"Yes, I'll say that. Where will you take him?"

"To a military hospital, to make quite sure that no one mentions that he's ill."

"Can we come and visit him?"

"I'm afraid not. But as soon as he recovers, we'll move him to a civilian nursing home where I'm sure he'll welcome your coming to see him."

They siren grew louder as the ambulance drew up on the driveway. The headmaster ran to open the front door, and Carlyle took a good look at the schoolmaster. His condition appeared to have worsened. Now his eyes were rolled back.

Two stretcher-bearers entered the office. They expertly lifted Longstreet onto the gurney and carried him to the ambulance. Carlyle and the headmaster followed a few yards behind. The ambulance crew closed the back door of the vehicle and raced away down the drive with the siren blaring again.

The two men returned to the office. "Carlyle, what I'm asking you is probably a military secret, but why is it so important that no one learns that Longstreet is ill?"

"Headmaster, you're quite right. It *is* a secret, a top secret in fact. But perhaps I can give you an analogy. Suppose that one of our leaders has recorded a radio address to be broadcast to the German people, urging them to lay down their arms in the light of our invasion today. But suppose further that that person falls seriously ill before we can broadcast the address. If the Germans knew about our leader's illness, wouldn't you agree that a lot of the power of the address would be lost?"

"Yes, I suppose that's true."

"Well, a similar situation applies to Longstreet's illness, only it's much more important. As I said, if the Nazis were to find out, the result would be untold loss of life. That means that I'm going to hold you to your solemn word—you are to say nothing to anyone about Hector Longstreet's condition."

***

"And that's the situation, sir," Carlyle said. "The doctors aren't yet sure what the problem is, but as soon as they've determined the cause of Longstreet's collapse and his prognosis, they'll let you know."

"But why did you instruct the headmaster not to say anything about Longstreet's condition?"

"As I was helping him to the chair, it suddenly occurred to me that all is not lost."

"Oh?"

"Yes, sir. I believe that Limberg can construct Longstreet's crossword puzzle for this Sunday."

Everyone turned to her.

"Maybe I can, but only with your help. How many of you are cryptic crossword aficionados?"

Eight hands were raised.

"And who considers himself to be a puzzle expert?"

This time she saw only seven hands. But after looking around the table, the modest air commodore slowly raised his hand, too.

"As I told you a while ago," she said, "I haven't composed a puzzle since before the war, and I'm certainly not another Hector Longstreet, but I'll do my best—with your assistance. It's not going to be easy to copy his marvelous style, but it might help if we had some of his previous puzzles."

"I'll send someone to Mrs. Bunting's house in Upper Stragham to collect his files," Pankhurst said. "In the worst case, we'll just use some of his old clues. I've never been in favor of plagiarism—it's nothing short of intellectual theft—but with this many lives at stake, I'm prepared to make an exception.

"But what about the headmaster?" he continued. "Can he be trusted to keep his mouth shut? Do we need to take him into custody until next Saturday afternoon when we've delivered the puzzle to the printers?"

"I don't think we have to," Carlyle said. "In retrospect, perhaps I was unduly cautious when I told him not to let on that Longstreet is so sick. After all, how could the Germans possibly find out about Longstreet?"

"And more to the point," Squadron Leader Harkness added, "why on earth would it even occur to them to check up on the schoolmaster?"

CHAPTER THIRTY-THREE

Civilian Internment Camp Ilag VIII,
Tost, Upper Silesia, Germany
Monday, June 12th, 1944

"Sir Lucius, I have some good news—I think. It's from Hector Longstreet—I think."

"What on earth do you mean, Miss Hawkesbury?"

"I've just come from Major Froschtümpel's office. He gave me the latest puzzle from *The Sunday Intelligencer.*"

"You mean Longstreet's puzzle?"

"Yes and no."

"I'm afraid you've totally lost me, Miss Hawkesbury."

"Sir Lucius, I don't know how to explain it. In fact, I don't even pretend to understand what's happened. As always, the puzzle appeared under the name Ramirez, Longstreet's *nom de plume*. A few of the clues were vintage Longstreet, in every sense. I recognized them; they were taken from some of his old puzzles. He's never done that before. It was almost as if

Hector just couldn't be bothered to come up with fresh clues, or perhaps he's too old or too tired."

"Or too ill?"

"Possibly. But the rest of the clues I can only describe as Longstreet imitations, and in some cases pretty poor imitations at that. And the crossword has no overall style. The puzzle appeared to have been composed by a committee. I'm sure you remember the old joke: a camel is a horse put together by a committee. Well, yesterday's puzzle was distinctly camel-like."

"And was a message hidden in the grid?"

"Oh, yes. And I'm not sure if that's good news or bad. Hector—or the committee—informed the Nazis that two hundred thousand troops currently stationed in Kent will invade Boulogne in thirty-nine days' time."

"Merciful heavens! If the people who composed that puzzle are German agents, then there's going to be an unholy massacre."

***

"Donndorf, I don't believe a word of this," SS-General Schellenberg said. "Someone is selling us a bill of goods. It's all just too obvious."

"But SS-General, the information was hidden deep in the puzzle. If it weren't for Bridget Hawkesbury at Civilian Internment Camp Ilag VIII, we wouldn't have been able to decode the message that Longstreet sent us. Because that's what his crossword was: an encrypted communication. And furthermore, everything we've received from him fits in precisely with what we've learned from our other sources in Britain. If you're right, that would mean the British have been fooling the entire *Abwehr* for more than five years. And that's not possible."

"Is that so, Donndorf? Do you remember what the *Führer* said when he disbanded the *Abwehr*? He described the organization as a total failure, peopled with incompetents. And I agree with that assessment. As far as I'm concerned, the fact that you came to me with this crossword as if it were pure gold puts you in the same dismal category as your inept colleagues.

"This puzzle is British disinformation. But before I take it to *Herr* Hitler, I need you to contact the Croydon Gang in London. They need to talk to Longstreet and find out exactly what's going on."

***

"Mrs. Bunting?" the middle-aged man in the beautifully tailored suit asked in his high-class accent.

"Yes?"

"May I please see Mr. Longstreet?"

"I'm afraid he's not here, sir."

"May I ask where I could find him?"

"I'm not too sure, sir."

"As you can see from this letter, I'm from MI5, the Security Service. It's most important that I speak to him as soon as humanly possible."

"Please come inside in, sir, and sit down. Now that I know who you are, I can tell you that Mr. Longstreet is away helping the government."

"Helping the government? What do you mean? Isn't he a schoolmaster?"

"Yes, he is, but every so often the government sends a car for him and he goes away for a few days."

"Do you have any idea what he does when he's away?"

"Well, sir, since you're from the Security Service, I can tell you. It has something to do with the crossword puzzles he sets."

"Crossword puzzles? Are you serious?"

"Oh, yes, sir."

"Well, how do you know that? Did he tell you?"

"Oh, no, sir. Mr. Longstreet never says a word about his work for the government. But whenever he leaves, a van comes here and they take away all the folders containing the crosswords he's composed in the past. And then, just before he returns to Stragham a few days later, they come back and replace everything exactly where it was."

"But surely the government doesn't need crossword puzzles? Don't you think they're making use of his word skills to break German codes or something like that?"

"No, sir," Mrs. Bunting said, "it's definitely crosswords. He always comes back on a Saturday evening, and his puzzle is published the next morning in *The Sunday Intelligencer*."

"But it's Tuesday morning. Did he come back on Saturday evening?"

"Well, now that you ask, sir, not this time. And he's been away since last Tuesday—he's never worked that long for the government. And I'll tell you something else, sir. They pick him up at the school and bring him back here to pack a suitcase. But this time they took him straight to wherever they take him and then they came to get all his things for him. It's most odd."

"Do you have the dates when he's been away working for the government?"

"Yes, sir, I do. It doesn't seem right to charge him for his meals on the days when he's not here, so I mark it all on my calendar. Let me get it for you—it's in the kitchen. I won't be a minute."

Mrs. Bunting handed the calendar to her visitor.

"May I copy down these dates?"

"Certainly."

"Thank you, Mrs. Bunting. And now, if I could please see his room?"

"Of course, sir. I'll show you up. Kindly follow me upstairs."

She opened the door and invited her visitor to enter.

"It's completely empty!" he said.

"Yes, sir. As I told you, on Tuesday they came to collect his things. In the past, they just took his old crosswords. He has folders filled with the puzzles that he's composed over the years. The government people took it all away last Tuesday, like before. But they also took everything else. They even took his typewriter. Isn't that odd? Wouldn't you think that the government has more than enough typewriters?"

"What about financial records? And correspondence from the newspaper? What about all the letters from the many admirers of his wonderful puzzles?"

"He never keeps any letters, sir; he says it's against his principles. And his sole financial record is his savings book from the bank. He usually keeps it in the folder with the latest puzzles, and that's gone, too. As you can see, the room is empty."

"I need to find him, Mrs. Bunting."

"Have you tried the school?"

"Stragham College? Yes, I went there first. The school secretary told me that he was on leave, so I came here."

"Yes," Mrs. Bunting said, "that's what the government people told the school to say when Mr. Longstreet is working for them. My instructions are to tell people 'he's not here,' just as I did when you arrived."

"Does he have any family? Perhaps I could contact his children and locate him that way."

"As far as I know, he has no family at all. He's lived here for more than twenty years, ever since he came to the school, and he's never mentioned any family to me."

"Friends, then?"

"I don't know of any, sir. Mr. Longstreet has just one interest in life, and that's his crossword puzzles."

***

"Well, Donndorf, what do you say now? Just before each of the puzzles with secret messages appeared in *The Sunday Intelligencer*, Longstreet was

329

away from Stragham 'working for the government.' He returned home on the Saturday evening, when the crossword was in the hands of the printers, ready for publication. Those puzzles that Bridget Hawkesbury solved for us contain pure disinformation. And now Longstreet has disappeared off the face of the earth, and we can't find out anything more."

"SS-General, I really don't know what to say."

"Because there's nothing you can say. The British have completely fooled you and your hopelessly incompetent colleagues for years. The attack on Normandy a week ago wasn't a feint—it was the real thing. But we haven't brought any reinforcements into the area to defeat the Allies. Instead, we're waiting patiently for the invasion of Boulogne to start in just over a month's time, an invasion that's never going to happen. I'm off to see the *Fuhrer*."

"Just a minute, SS-General. You've just said the British have fooled the *Abwehr* for years. That may well be the case. But if you're right, they've also fooled the *Führer*. Are you quite sure you want to go and tell him that? You know the penalty for treachery: they hang you, naked, with a piano wire around your neck, suspended from a meat hook, while movie cameras roll, and they send your family and close friends to a concentration camp. And the worst form of treachery imaginable is telling the *Führer* that he's wrong. Actually, that's the second worst. The very worst kind is proving to him that not only is he wrong beyond all possible doubt, but that he's persisted in his folly."

CHAPTER THIRTY-FOUR

MI5 Headquarters, London
Monday, July 31st, 1944

"Gentlemen," Air Commodore Pankhurst said, "the objective of Operation BODYGUARD was to mislead Hitler with regard to both the time and the place of the invasion. More specifically, General Eisenhower charged us with ensuring that Hitler would wait at least fourteen days before deciding to order his Fifteenth Army to go from the Pas-de-Calais to the Normandy landing beaches, some two hundred miles away.

"I'm delighted to report that Hitler finally ordered his Fifteenth Army into battle fully forty-five days after D-day. Operation BODYGUARD has been a great success up to now. I would like to thank each of you for your many contributions.

"Now, as a consequence of Hitler finally realizing that the Allies aren't going to invade Boulogne after all, we're about to get a visitor."

They heard a soft knock on the door. "Ah, speak of the devil. Come!"

The door opened, and Hector Longstreet shuffled in. Everyone in the room, including Pankhurst, instantly sprang to their feet. Limberg rushed to the door, took the elderly man's arm and slowly escorted him to the empty chair at the foot of the table. Once he was seated, everyone else followed suit.

"I believe you know Carlyle and Johnson, but allow me to introduce the other members of my team."

Longstreet nodded to each uniformed officer in turn.

"Mr. Longstreet," Pankhurst said, "I'm delighted to see you again. I believe that you have a few things to tell us."

"Yes, indeed. I'll start at the beginning. Nearly two months ago I woke up and found myself in a bed in a military hospital. The medics quickly came to the conclusion that the problem was my ticker. But they aren't heart specialists, so they decided to call in the right sort of doctors. The answer that the consultants came up with wasn't too reassuring. It seems that my heart could give out at any time—or I could live for a little while yet. They do have a word for my condition, but because it's longer than fifteen letters, I wasn't terribly interested in hearing it."

Everyone around the table grinned.

"They told me to get my strength back and to take life easy. My teaching career is over, I'm afraid. Instead, I'm supposed to do nothing all day—as if I could. At the very least, I intend to compose more crossword puzzles. That battle-axe of a matron in her stiffly starched white uniform wouldn't allow me to engage in cruciverbalism. She claimed it put too much strain on my heart. As far as she was concerned, I had to lie back in bed and relax. What a load of poppycock!

"What did cause my heart considerable strain was when Air Commodore Pankhurst was kind enough to visit me and showed me the crossword puzzle that you composed together. He explained the circumstances behind your creation. I certainly applaud your efforts, but may I respectfully remind you of the proverb *usus est magister optimus*. Mr. Carlyle, would you care to construe?"

"Sir, would you accept the idiomatic translation 'practice makes perfect'?"

"I certainly would. At the same time, I stress that your country should be proud of the effort that you put in and grateful that the Germans fell for the ruse. But with the shiny exception of Miss Limberg, whose clues really weren't too bad, I would suggest that the rest of you might perhaps think about exercising your God-given talents in a different direction. A totally different direction."

It was starting to become apparent to everyone that his illness and, more particularly, his future prognosis, had changed Hector Longstreet. The sadistic streak was gone, replaced by a sardonic sense of humor. His obnoxious smirk had also disappeared. Now he had a shy smile that invited the listener to share with him his newly found pleasure in life and in living. The phrase "death-bed conversion" crossed more than one mind.

"After a week," Longstreet went on, "the doctors told me that they could do no more for me, and it was time to go home. However, they'd received the strictest order that, for my protection, I had to remain in that military hospital, which was located inside a closely guarded army base. Air Commodore, I believe I have you to thank for keeping me alive. I strongly suspect that you issued that order once you learned about Mrs. Bunting's visitor who claimed to be from the Security Service. Am I warm?"

"Yes, indeed. Something made Mrs. Bunting contact us, and we immediately realized that the Nazis wanted to interrogate you in connection with your crosswords. Your landlady, through no fault of her own, had let slip certain facts about your government work. We had to ensure that you were safe, and the best way to do that seemed to be to keep you in the hospital."

With a broad smile on his face, Pankhurst continued. "Of course, Mr. Longstreet, we were very worried. No, we weren't concerned that something might happen to you. Our real anxiety was that imprisoning you in a hospital bed for possibly some weeks would result in nervous breakdowns, if not suicide attempts, on the part of many of the poor nurses whose duties included keeping you between the sheets. Surprisingly, that's not what happened.

"That 'battle-axe of a matron' told me that you spent every minute of every day going from bed to bed, helping the injured soldiers, consoling them, hearing their tales of what happened to them in Normandy and, on one memorable occasion, even though you're not a Roman Catholic, assisting a chaplain to give the last rites. Yes, you did drive the nurses up the wall, but only because they kept telling you to go back to bed and look after your own health, whereas you insisted that the young men's morale was far more important.

"Gentlemen, while the battle was raging across the Channel in Normandy, a no-holds-barred, far more vicious and unforgiving fight was storming in that hospital. It was an Amazonomachy, a battle between a horde of relentless female warriors on the one hand and our Mr. Longstreet on the other. And Mr. Longstreet won, day after day. To mark that triumph, together with your cruciverbalist defeat of the Nazi *Reich*, tomorrow you will go to Buckingham Palace where the King will honor you with the British Empire Medal, awarded 'in recognition of meritorious civil or military service.'"

Hector Longstreet beamed with genuine pleasure. "It takes a lot to leave me speechless," he said, "but that last remark of yours certainly did the trick."

He went on. "I intend to spend what time is left to me—be it days, weeks, or possibly a month or two—composing crosswords. Yesterday your people returned me to Mrs. Bunting, and I have to say that it's good to be home again. I celebrated by resuming my career as a cruciverbalist."

He took an envelope out of an inside pocket of his suit. Placing the envelope on the table, he announced, "This contains my final crossword."

His announcement resulted in murmuring and a shaking of heads.

"Let's be realistic and face facts," Hector Longstreet insisted. "None of us can go on forever, and I certainly can't. Air Commodore, I charge you with ensuring that this puzzle is published at the right time. And what is the right time? Take a look at 1-across."

The elderly schoolmaster rose slowly to his feet. He was too proud to ask Limberg to assist him once more, but she was next to him from the moment she heard his chair scraping the cement floor of the small conference room. The others snapped to attention. Were it not for the fact that British soldiers do not salute unless they are wearing their regimental headdress, all of them would have demonstrated their now limitless respect in that way.

"I bid you farewell. May all we meet again at a better time in a better place."

Each of them came up to him, shook his hand and wished him well. Then he turned to the door and slowly limped out on Limberg's arm.

The eight men sat down again and looked at one another, silently marveling at the transformation that impending death had wrought. Then Pankhurst picked up the envelope. It was unsealed. He took out the crossword.

"Let me see now. The clue for 1-across reads as follows: **I notice purveyor arranged my dying wish (7,2,6)**. I believe that the word **arranged** tells me that it's an anagram, an arrangement of the letters of **I notice purveyor**. The answer consists of three words: they are respectively seven, two, and six letters in length."

Just for once, none of them shouted out the answer, VICTORY IN EUROPE. Instead, they all sat in silence, staring down at the table directly in front of them, embarrassed that their colleagues might notice the tears rolling down their cheeks.

AFTERWORD

This book is a work of fiction. The characters are all figments of our imagination; none of them are based on real people. Where we have given characters the names of historical figures, such as General Dwight D. Eisenhower, Admiral Wilhelm Canaris, Captain Albrecht Soltmann, Lieutenant Norbert Hammermann, Prince Ludwig von Hesse-Darmstadt, and General Walter Schellenberg, the statements we have attributed to them are ours. Dr. Melinda Gascombe and Cameron Ramstad are fictitious, as are the Croydon Gang, Colonel Donndorf, and Air Commodore Pankhurst and the members of his team.

The newspapers that play a role in this story, including *The Daily Recorder* and *The Sunday Intelligencer*, are equally fictitious, as are their cruciverbalists, including Hector Longstreet, Vanessa Limberg, Bridget Hawkesbury, and Admiral Sir Philip Henderson-Peacock, GCB, OM, GCVO.

On the other hand, Edward Mathers ("Torquemada") was indeed the inventor of the cryptic crossword, and he was succeeded at *The*

Observer by Derrick Macnutt ("Ximenes"). One of the authors was overheard admitting that he misspent his youth by devoting most of his free time trying to solve the Ximenes puzzle that appeared every Sunday in *The Observer.*

Stragham College and its staff and students, the MI5 safe house, and the house at Kingston-upon-Thames do not exist. Broadmoor is still a high-security psychiatric hospital, but since 2007 houses only male patients. Civilian Internment Camp Ilag VIII was real, but other than P. G. Wodehouse, the prisoners there are our creation.

Saint-Auban-sûr-Lot does not exist, nor does Lower Stragham or Upper Stragham. However, the other cities, towns, and villages in this story are real, including Tost; Minto, North Dakota; Kingston-upon-Thames; Temple Ewell; and Sainte-Anne-la-Palud. In fact, the idea for this story came to the authors while they were enjoying a superlative lunch in the restaurant of the Hôtel de la Plage at Sainte-Anne-la-Palud. In 2016, the *commune* of Saint-André-Treize-Voies in the Vendée department was merged into the new *commune* of Montréverd.

Operation AMAZON is fictional. However, all other military operations mentioned in this book, including Operation OVERLORD, Operation BODYGUARD, Operation BERNHARD, Operation FORTITUDE, and Operation MINCEMEAT, were real. For the sake of simplicity, we have described only the key points of each. For example, Operation FORTITUDE NORTH was the Allied deceptive invasion of Norway. It was aimed at Stavanger (on the

Boknafjord) and also at Narvik, but we decided to keep Narvik out of the story to avoid complicating matters unduly.

An outstanding source as to what really happened during Operation MINCEMEAT is the book *Operation Mincemeat* by Ben MacIntyre. MI5 made use of carrier pigeons in World War II, but decidedly not in the way we have described in *Crossword Traitor*. For information as to what actually occurred, the reader should consult *Double Cross: The True Story of the D-Day Spies*, also by Ben MacIntyre.

After the war, German intelligence records revealed that about 115 agents had been sent to Britain, and that all but one of them were caught.[1] One *Abwehr* agent managed to evade detection, but he shot himself in a Cambridge air raid shelter after he ran out of money and food. Several of the captured German spies agreed to become double agents to save their lives. However, agent PICKFORD and his subagents are a figment of our imagination.

The 2007 Oscar-winning Austrian film, *Die Fälscher (The Counterfeiters)*, is loosely based on the biography of Adolf Burger, a Jewish Slovak book printer ordered to take part in Operation BERNHARD in the Sachsenhausen concentration camp. The film led to a number of articles comparing SS-Major Bernhard Krüger with Oskar Schindler. However, a

---

[1] en.wikipedia.org/wiki/MI5

2007 interview by Anthony Horowitz in *The Daily Mail* includes the following exchange:[2]

> *I ask Burger if the real Major Krüger was in some ways his saviour, a little like Oskar Schindler.*
>
> *"He was a murderer just like everyone else," he replies. "He had six people shot just because they were sick. He couldn't send them to hospital in case they said something about the operation, so he killed them."*

In fact, the reason that the counterfeiters managed to survive the Holocaust was that, after the evacuation of Sachsenhausen, the SS ordered them to be murdered at the Ebensee concentration camp. But only one truck was available and it broke down during the third trip, so they marched the last group of forgers to Ebensee. While they were en route, a large number of prisoners at Ebensee revolted. The guards of the first two groups of counterfeiters ran away; the forgers then hid themselves among the other prisoners at Ebensee. The SS order was to liquidate all the counterfeiters together and their lives were saved because of the delayed arrival of the third group.[3]

The role played by Major General Desmond Mangham as a young officer at Loch Fyne in convincing the Germans that the Allies could not

---

[2] www.dailymail.co.uk/home/moslive/article-483118/The-Fuhrers-forgers.html

[3] en.wikipedia.org/wiki/Operation_Bernhard

mount a sea-born invasion before September 1944 is described in his obituary in the *Telegraph*.[4]

A reader of an early version of this book queried our use of the Hebrew word *posul*, pointing out that in Modern Hebrew the word is pronounced *pasul* (with the accent on the last syllable). However, the overwhelming majority of the Jews of Eastern Europe at the time of the Holocaust used the Ashkenazi pronunciation, hence *posul* (stress on the first syllable).

Air Commodore Archibald Pankhurst was some six years ahead of his time when he declared, "As Sigmund Freud put it, sometimes a cigar is just a cigar."[5] The earliest instance of this quotation is apparently footnote 9 on page 139 of an article entitled "The Place of Action in Personality Change" by Allen Wheelis, in the May 1950 issue (Volume 13, Number 2) of the journal *Psychiatry*.[6]

Regarding the "Haversack Ruse," current research indicates that, contrary to popular belief, Richard Meinertzhagen did not plan the deception, let alone carry it out. For example, Brian Garfield, author of *The Meinertzhagen Mystery*, states that the idea was that of Lieutenant-Colonel J. D. Belgrave and that the soldier who rode up to the Turkish lines was Arthur Neate, as stated in *Crossword Traitor*.

In Chapter Thirty, Air Marshal Pankhurst said, "At twilight, the Australian Fourth Light Horse Brigade staged a four-mile charge, the last and the

---

[4] www.telegraph.co.uk/news/obituaries/11299656/Major-General-Desmond-Mangham-obituary.html.
[5] quoteinvestigator.com/2011/08/12/just-a-cigar
[6] books.google.com.au/books?id=nX85AAAAMAAJ&q=cigar

greatest cavalry charge in history." It has been claimed, wrongly, that light horsemen aren't cavalrymen, and therefore this was not a cavalry charge. Pankhurst, however, was fully aware that "light horse" is a synonym for "light cavalry," so his use of the phrase *cavalry charge* was quite correct.[7]

Finally, for information on purchasing eighteen-year old Lochervan whisky, "the crowning glory of the whisky maker's art," please see the Afterword of *Double Two* by Steve Schach and Sharon Stein.

---

[7] en.wikipedia.org/wiki/Light_cavalry

ACKNOWLEDGEMENTS

We warmly thank Howard Aksen, Kathy Bloomer, Joe Kensell, and Johan Koeslag for taking the time to read early drafts of the manuscript and for their constructive suggestions.

We are delighted that David Astle ("DA"), the cruciverbalist whom we admire so much, has written a thought-provoking yet amusing Preface; we are most appreciative. From now on we're going to keep an eye open for clue voodoo as we wrestle with his invariably challenging weekly crossword puzzle.

Fine art photographer Raphael Shevelev created the double portrait that appears on page 347. After seeing the work, photographic historian Dr. Anne Hammond wrote, "This is extraordinary. I don't know of any other photographer who has been able to merge two portraits into a double portrait ... I think of the composite photograph ... as combining and averaging the unique markers of personality, whereas you have preserved them and lovingly linked them ..." We thank Raphael for allowing us to reproduce his masterpiece in this book.

Our developmental editor, Michael Mann, read the manuscript as meticulously as always; we thank him for his helpful comments and criticisms. Once again it has been a delight to work with our publisher, Jennifer Chesak, of Wandering in the Words Press. And for the eighth time, we thank her for designing a striking cover.

SHARON STEIN

Sharon Stein is a pediatric radiologist. Born in Cape Town, South Africa, Sharon was a professor of radiology at Vanderbilt Children's Hospital in Nashville, Tennessee and an examiner for the American Board of Radiology. She is a former president of the Southern Pediatric Radiology Society. In 2009, Sharon moved to Sydney, Australia with her husband, Steve Schach, to be with their grandchildren. She is an accomplished cook and baker who loves to share her recipes and techniques. This is her fourth thriller co-written with Steve Schach; Wandering in the Words Press published the first, *Coopers Island*, in October 2013.

STEVE SCHACH

Steve Schach, a native of Cape Town, South Africa, moved to Sydney, Australia, in 2009, after twenty-six years as a professor at Vanderbilt University in Nashville, Tennessee. Before he began writing thrillers, Steve wrote thirteen best-selling software engineering textbooks, which are used in universities all over the world. Down Under, Steve intended to become a full-time grandfather, and limit his intellectual activities to solving cryptic crossword puzzles and avidly watching Sesame Street with his grandchildren. However, the urge to write proved to be far too strong to overcome. Wandering in the Words Press has previously published seven of his thrillers, most recently *The Book Buyer* in July 2017, co-authored by Sharon Stein.

© 2018 Raphael Shevelev, FRPS

Sharon Stein & Steve Schach

www.ingramcontent.com/pod-product-compliance
Lightning Source LLC
Chambersburg PA
CBHW070156260626
47160CB00002B/361